D1302225

Every Bride
HAS HER DAY

Center Point
Large Print

Also by Janice Thompson and available from
Center Point Large Print:

A Bouquet of Love

The Brides with Style Novels
Every Bride Needs a Groom
Every Girl Gets Confused

**This Large Print Book carries the
Seal of Approval of N.A.V.H.**

Brides *with* Style • 3

Every Bride
HAS HER DAY

Janice Thompson

CENTER POINT LARGE PRINT
THORNDIKE, MAINE

Scripture quotations are from the Holy Bible,
New International Version®. NIV®. Copyright © 1973,
1978, 1984, 2011 by Biblica, Inc.™ Used by permission of
Zondervan. All rights reserved worldwide.
www.zondervan.com

This book is a work of fiction. Names, characters, places,
and incidents are the product of the author's imagination
or are used fictitiously. Any resemblance to actual events,
locales, or persons, living or dead, is coincidental.

The text of this Large Print edition is unabridged.
In other aspects, this book may vary from the original edition.
Printed in the United States of America on permanent paper.
Set in 16-point Times New Roman type.

ISBN: 978-1-68324-068-6

Library of Congress Cataloging-in-Publication Data

Names: Thompson, Janice A., author.
Title: Every bride has her day / Janice Thompson.
Description: Center Point Large Print edition. | Thorndike, Maine :
Center Point Large Print, 2016.
Identifiers: LCCN 2016018558 | ISBN 9781683240686
     (hardcover : alk. paper)
Subjects: LCSH: Brides—Fiction. | Weddings—Fiction. | Interpersonal
relations—Fiction. | Large type books. | GSAFD: Love stories. |
Christian fiction.
Classification: LCC PS3620.H6824 E935 2016b | DDC 813/.6—dc23
LC record available at https://lccn.loc.gov/2016018558

To Michella and Josh:
your outdoor wedding served as a great
inspiration for this book and proved,
once and for all, that every bride
deserves her perfect day.

Every Bride
HAS HER DAY

1
Happy Girl

I believe in pink. I believe that laughing is the best calorie burner. I believe in kissing, kissing a lot. I believe in being strong when everything seems to be going wrong.

Audrey Hepburn

You. Are. An. Engaged. Woman." I spoke to my reflection in the mirror on the Monday morning after the love of my life popped the question. "Engaged!"

A little giggle followed as I thought back on the moment when my sweetie had slipped that gorgeous, perfect-for-me ring on my finger. The flawless princess-cut diamond was almost as amazing as the fella who'd given it to me. Almost. Then again, Brady James was in a class of his own. Comparing him to anything—even something as precious as a diamond—just felt wrong. What I'd ever done to deserve such a guy, I could not say, but he was mine all the same.

Mine.

Engaged!

I needed to get busy planning a wedding. Oh,

but right now I just wanted to dance down the hallway to the kitchen, eat breakfast with Aunt Alva, then head off to work at Cosmopolitan Bridal, where I would see my fiancé in person. A few sweet kisses would start my workday off right.

I did a happy little Texas two-step all the way from my bedroom to the Formica table in the kitchen, where I greeted my elderly great-aunt with a kiss on the cheek. "G'morning, Auntie!" I sang, my words coming out like a Disney musical in the making. "How are *you* today?"

"Well, aren't we happy this morning, Katie Sue." Aunt Alva's soft wrinkles seemed even more pronounced than usual as her lips curled up in a smile. "Love is in the air, I see."

"Indeed, it is!" I trilled, my melodic words filling the tiny kitchen. "Birds are singing, flowers are blooming, and all's right with the world! I'm engaged!"

"Love does make you feel young, doesn't it?" She attempted to stand, but her arthritis slowed things down a bit. "Never mind getting up. I guess you'll just have to fix your own plate. I'm so worn out from taking care of Lori-Lou's kids all week I can hardly move."

"No doubt."

"Feels good to be home, even if it's just for the weekend. And nice to cook in my own kitchen again. I made pancakes, honey. I know how much you love them and figured they'd hit the spot."

"Yum!" I turned my attention to my aunt, noticing how weary she looked. "And don't fret, Auntie. I'll fix my own."

"Before long you'll be fixing breakfast for two." A look of concern clouded her face. "In your own house. On the other side of town. Far away from me. Not that I'm complaining about you and Brady getting hitched. I'm just worried about living on my own again after having someone as sweet as you share my home."

I slipped my arms around her shoulders and leaned in close. "Think about it, Aunt Alva. I'm not the only one with a beau. I think we both know that Eduardo is planning to pop the question soon, and his house is near Brady's. We'll be neighbors."

Auntie brightened at this notion. "I do hope he'll hurry up. I'm eighty-plus years old. I don't have time to dawdle." She tried again to stand, this time managing the feat. "But if I move into that ridiculously large house of his, you'll probably have to send in a search party to find me. At least here I know the way to the bathroom." She toddled off down the hallway as if to prove her point.

As I filled my plate with food, I thought about all of the changes in our lives of late. Moving from Fairfield to Dallas. Meeting Brady. Landing a dream job at his mother's bridal salon. Moving in with my aunt. Falling head over heels for the greatest guy in the world. Had I really only been away from my hometown of Fairfield less than a year? Seemed like forever. Oh, but what a joy to start my life over again in a place with endless possibilities!

My happily-ever-after attitude continued to propel me as I drove to work later that morning. I entered Cosmopolitan Bridal, my home away from home, and was greeted by my co-worker Twiggy, who let out a deafening squeal the moment she clapped those overly made-up eyes of hers on me. "Katie! I still can't believe you're engaged! I mean, I *know* you are. I was there. I saw it firsthand. But it seems like a dream. Ooh, speaking of dreams, let me see your ring again."

I extended my left hand to show off the diamond, and she gasped. "Wowza! Is it heavy? Have you set a date? Are you guys getting married at your church here in Dallas or back home in Fairfield? Where are you going on your honeymoon? Don't go on a cruise. I've heard terrible stories about those tiny cabins. Not good for honeymooning. Have you chosen your bridesmaids?" A hopeful look sparked in her eyes at that last question.

Before I could say, "We haven't had time to think about all of that," the store manager approached. "So, Brady finally popped the question." Madge gave me a motherly look as she crossed her arms. "It's about stinkin' time. I've been laying on some pretty thick hints over the past few weeks, but he didn't seem to be taking them. I was starting to think Brady James planned to stay single the rest of his life, just like that stubborn agent of his." A hint of pain clouded Madge's eyes. "Some fellas are confirmed bachelors, I guess."

"I was just waiting for the perfect moment, Madge." Brady's voice sounded from behind me. I turned, finding it difficult to stop smiling as I gazed into my handsome fiancé's face. "And I'm pretty sure Stan isn't a confirmed bachelor. Time will prove that."

Madge rolled her eyes. "Whatever. And who was talking about Stan anyway? What does your agent have to do with this conversation?"

"You brought him up," I reminded her.

"Maybe that's a discussion for another day." Brady gave me a knowing look.

"Enough about confirmed bachelors. We have a wedding shower to plan!" Twiggy seemed delighted at this possibility. "What themes do you like, Katie?"

"Themes?" I gave a little shrug. "No idea. What do you mean?"

"Oh, bridal showers these days are all themed. Tiffany. Shabby chic. Chevron. Everything's built on the theme. So what's it going to be? We've got to start planning."

"In Fairfield all of the bridal showers are just alike. We meet at the Baptist church, drink punch, eat cake, and open presents. There's always a toaster. And a blender. And my grandmother always puts together a basket of cleaning products, though I've never understood why you would give cleaning products as a gift. I guess she's just trying to send some sort of message to the bride to keep a clean house?"

"Humph. Maybe that's how they do it in a small town, but it's not going to happen on my watch." Twiggy waggled her finger in the air. "We can do a sure sight better than that."

"We sure can." My boss, Nadia, sashayed next to Brady. "My boy deserves a top-notch wedding. And his fans will expect it to be grand. What about the Gaylord, honey? You've loved that place since you were a kid."

"It's a great hotel, Mom." Brady pursed his lips, and I tried to read his thoughts. "But this is really more about making the bride happy. You know?"

"Katie will be happy as long as you're happy." Nadia stared at me so intently that I felt beads of sweat pop out on my neck. "Right, honey?"

Before I could say, "But I've never even been inside the Gaylord," Nadia headed off to her office, muttering something about how she would pull a few strings to get us the grand ballroom for a midsummer wedding. Lovely.

Twiggy clasped her hands together in obvious

glee. "Ooh, the Gaylord! Perfection! I'm going to throw you the bridal shower of the century. It's totally going to be Texas-themed, cowboys and horses and the whole works. Perfect, since you guys got engaged at the stockyards. And I know the other girls will help me. Dahlia loves to design things. Hibiscus too. Crystal's probably a little too busy planning her own wedding right now to get very involved, but I could ask Jane." Her nose wrinkled. "No, on second thought, I doubt Jane would be terribly interested."

"I think it's a little early to be worrying about all of that," I said.

"Oh, it's never too early. Now, the first order of business is to look for ideas for the actual wedding, not just the shower. Fresh. New. Hip. Cool. Nothing too overdone." Twiggy swept her hair back with her hand. "We want something fashion-forward, not something from a magazine. By the time that magazine goes to print, the trend is already passing. We want something original, something perfect for Katie."

"Well, I'm a small-town girl, so—"

"Everything has to jive with the theme for the wedding. And if you're getting married at the Gaylord, then the whole cowboy-meets-cowgirl, riding-off-into-the-sunset thing will be perfect."

"Are you saying my wedding has to be themed too?" I slapped my palm against my forehead. "Really? Can't we just call it 'typical wedding theme' and leave it at that? I've been planning my big day since I was a girl, and I don't remember any theme at all."

"*Typical* wedding theme?" Twiggy stared at me as if I'd lost my mind. "I guess some girls still do that. But don't you worry, Katie. I'll start a wedding board for you on Pinterest, and I'll pin all sorts of ideas to share with you."

"Wait." I shook my head. "You're coming up with ideas for the shower or the actual wedding? Because I really want to do that my—"

"Both! It's going to be great." She sauntered down the hallway toward the design studio with Madge on her heels. I could hear them talking about my wedding as they disappeared from view.

Brady slipped his arms around my waist. "You don't have to listen to a word they say. They're just trying to be helpful, in their own intrusive way."

"It's not that, Brady." I leaned my head against his shoulder and sighed. "I'm just so embarrassingly small-town that I don't know much about how to do things in a big way. And if that's really what you want, what you expect, then . . ."

"All I expect is for you to be there, ready to take my hand in yours. Other than that, I couldn't care less. Just tell the planning committee that you want to go simple."

"Right. Is there such a thing as simple chic? Something that doesn't involve pictures from the internet? Or big hotels? Or cowboys and horses?"

"Yep. But you'd better tell them quickly. I have a feeling Mama's already mapping out the reception hall, and I'm guessing Twiggy is back in the studio by now, involving Dahlia and Hibiscus."

I shook my head and pinched my eyes shut. Maybe I should let them enjoy the moment. And perhaps I should look at whatever plans they came up with. They might just surprise me with something that felt right, after all. Just because we always did things the simple way in my small town didn't mean I wasn't open to change.

"I've already got my dress, anyway." I offered Brady a delighted smile. "Thanks to you."

"No, thanks to *you* and that prize-winning essay you wrote."

"Yes, the essay." I pursed my lips as I remembered the emotions I'd felt as I'd penned the winning essay. Felt like a lifetime ago. "But I guess my point is this: the dress is a Loretta Lynn style, which is simple. Country. Sweet."

"I like simple. Country. Sweet."

"Which explains why you fell for me, I suppose." I gave him a kiss on the cheek. "But I'm trying to say that the theme of our wedding could be just that. Simple. Country. Sweet."

"Yep." His word came out with a slow Texas drawl. Brady then tipped his imaginary hat, gave me a wink, and headed off to his office. I decided

I'd better get to my office as well. In spite of my enthusiasm for the wedding, there was still work to be done. Cosmopolitan Bridal wasn't paying me to plan my wedding, they were paying me to do marketing and PR for the store.

Several minutes later, as I was comfortably seated at my desk, my phone rang. I answered on the second ring. "Cosmopolitan Bridal, home of the Loretta Lynn gown. How can I help you?"

"You can help me by taking a break from your work and talking to me about your wedding." I recognized my mother's voice. "Pop and I are so excited about your big day. I'm sorry we couldn't stick around and help you plan it, but you know how he is. He wanted to get back on the road again, headed west. But we'll be there when you need us to help get things ready for the wedding, honey. I promise."

"Oh, no problem. I've hardly had time to think about it since Brady popped the question. It's been a whirlwind weekend, for sure."

"I hope you don't mind, but I took it upon myself to see when the church is available. I figured you'd want to do an early summer wedding, though that wouldn't give you much time, this being February and all. If that's too short notice, then late summer would be nice too."

"Actually, we—"

"I called the church, and they've got VBS taking place the second week of June, so you can't use

18

the fellowship hall that weekend. And there's the annual Peach Festival. You'll have to work around that. But I understand every weekend in July is open. Of course, it's hot as blue blazes in July and the AC isn't great in the fellowship hall, but maybe we could bring in a couple of window units? Those are loud, though. Might be kind of hard to celebrate with all that racket. What do you think?"

"I think Brady and I haven't even talked about dates yet. Plus we attend a great church here in Dallas, Mama. And just so you know, Brady's mom has her heart set on—"

"Dallas?" She spoke the word as if it brought her great pain. "Please tell me you're not thinking about getting married in Dallas. The people you love live in Fairfield."

"Half of them." I sighed. "The other half—the people I see every day at work—live here. And the girls at the bridal shop are already very invested, trust me. They're making plans as we speak."

"You're letting total strangers plan your wedding?" Mama sounded flabbergasted at this idea.

"They're not strangers, they're good friends. And they're not planning the wedding for me. They're just working on ideas. On Pinterest."

"Pinterest?" Mama groaned. "You don't need the internet to plan a lovely home-grown wedding, honey. And you certainly don't need to tie the knot in the big city. Dallas is just so far away from home." Her voice grew tense. "Don't you want the people you grew up with to attend your wedding?"

"Mama, Dallas is an hour away from Fairfield, not halfway across the country. If people really care about me, they would probably travel here. Not that I'm asking them to—at least not yet. Please don't fret. I'm sure Brady will agree that getting married in Fairfield is the best plan. And I'm pretty sure Queenie would kill me if I didn't get married at the Baptist church where I grew up."

"Maybe not. Queenie's a Presbyterian now. Did you forget?" Mama's voice held that crisp edge of disapproval she'd become known for.

The phone grew warm against my ear, so I shifted it to the other one. "I know she is, but her heart is still at the Baptist church."

"That's what getting hitched to a man of the cloth will do to you, I guess. You marry him and the next thing you know, everything's changing." Mama sniffled. "Kind of like what's happening to you, now that you're engaged."

"Brady's not a man of the cloth, Mama. He's a basketball player." Even as I spoke the words, I wished I could take them back. With his post-surgery knee still bothering him, my sweetie's professional basketball career was taking a backseat to helping out at the bridal shop. "He's not a Presbyterian either," I added. "We both attend a community church now."

Mama released an exaggerated groan. "I guess that proves my point. Everything's changing. The signs are all there. I've been trying to ignore them, but it's getting harder every day. You've left home for good."

"Left home?" I did my best not to laugh out loud. "Where are you calling me from, Mama?"

A short pause followed before she finally said, "We're headed to the Texas Panhandle, Palo Duro Canyon area. We plan to see that wonderful outdoor musical I've heard so much about."

"Yep. And where will you be next week?"

"Ruidoso, New Mexico."

"After that?"

"I believe we're headed to Colorado. Or maybe Arizona. You know how your father is, Katie. He's got the wanderlust."

"And wherever he wanders, you happily follow."

"He's my husband."

"Exactly." I did my best to punctuate the word.

There was a lengthy pause on my mother's end. "I suppose, when you say it like that . . ." Her voice trailed off.

"I'm just saying that when two people become one, they start carving their own path. Doing their own thing."

"Could you carve your path a little closer to Fairfield? At least for the wedding day?"

"I'm sure we'll get married in Fairfield, as I said. And I'll be calling the church myself to talk to Joni about setting a date."

"Joni's not at the Baptist church anymore, honey. Remember? Now that she's dating your ex-fiancé, she's changed churches too."

"Casey was never my fiancé, Mama, but thanks for the reminder about Joni switching churches. I guess I'll have to call Bessie May then. She's still Baptist, isn't she?"

"Yes, but stop avoiding the obvious. You and Casey were very nearly engaged once upon a time, before he started dating Joni. And I suppose it could be argued that he's the one responsible for nudging you off to Dallas. I still haven't quite forgiven him for that, you know."

"It's time you did. He and Joni are happily matched, and so are Brady and me. It will all work out in the end. So you and Pop enjoy yourself in New Mex—"

"The Texas Panhandle."

"The Texas Panhandle. And don't take any wooden nickels."

"I've never understood that expression." My mother laughed. "But if I've heard your father use it once, I've heard him use it a thousand times. 'Don't take any wooden nickels, Marie.'" She laughed a little louder. "Every time old man

Harrison would come into the hardware store, your father would say it loud enough for everyone in the place to hear."

"I remember."

"I . . ." She seemed to drift away for a moment. "I miss our days at the hardware store. Do you, Katie Sue?"

"Mama, you and Pop just passed off the store to Jasper and Crystal a few months back. And from what Jasper tells me, Pop is still trying to manage things, even from the RV."

"It's not technically an RV, honey. It's a fifth wheel."

"You get my point. You haven't lost ties with the hardware store, and I don't see that happening . . . ever. It'll always be a part of us, as will the wooden nickel phrase."

"Okay, okay." Mama disappeared for a minute, then returned, breathless. "Hate to run, honey, but your father is about to drive us off the road and into a canyon. I have to help him with the GPS."

"Dumb thing gets it wrong every time!" my father hollered.

"Pretty sure he's talking about the GPS, not me," Mama said. "But I can't be sure."

"Be safe and have fun, Mama. And don't worry about a thing. I will get married in Fairfield and you will be in the center of the plans, I promise. I won't leave you out."

"Thank you, honey." My mother ended the call.

I put the phone down and laid my head on my desk, my thoughts in a whirl.

"Things are that bad already?" Brady's voice roused me from my ponderings. I sat up straight and released an exaggerated sigh as I saw him standing in the open doorway.

In that moment, as I focused on him, I was reminded of the very first time I'd ever walked into Cosmopolitan Bridal and looked his way. That first day I'd felt sure I was looking at Adonis. The solid build. The height. The broad shoulders. The five o'clock shadow. The swatch of wavy dark hair that fell across his forehead. The compelling, magnetic smile. The mesmerizing blue eyes. These things had worked their magic on me then, just as they did in this very moment.

"Katie?" Those beautiful blue eyes now reflected his concern. "Have I lost you?"

"Hmm? Oh, no. Just more people trying to plan our big day. That's all."

"I see." He moved toward my desk, favoring his injured knee. "Well then, let's just run off and elope. What do you think of that idea?"

"I think they would all kill us. We'd be murdered in our sleep."

"But at least we'd be in each other's arms."

"True, that." Still, I couldn't help but fret. Wedding planning wasn't supposed to be stressful, was it? I mean, all of the bridal magazines made it look like so much fun. Our engagement was just one day old and we were already talking about running off to elope? What would the next few months hold?

I rose and took a few steps in Brady's direction. He slipped his arms around me and I nestled against him, all of my woes about the wedding slipping away. There, in that safe place, there were no cares, no anxieties.

Until Madge popped her head in the door and hollered, "I've got it, you two! Let's do a Hawaiian-themed wedding, luau and all! I'll bring the roasted pig!"

The groan I gave was pretty loud, but it was drowned out by the sound of Brady's laughter. "Now *there's* an idea," he whispered in my ear, his breath sending tingles all the way down my spine. "We'll elope . . . in Hawaii!"

Funny. That idea sounded better to me than all of the others put together.

2

Valentine

The beauty of a woman must be seen from
in her eyes, because that is the doorway to
her heart, the place where love resides.

Audrey Hepburn

I thought about Brady's "Let's run away to
Hawaii and elope" proposition all day. In fact,
the idea so captivated me that I actually dreamed
about it that night. In my dream the two of us ran
across the beach, toes in the warm sand, turquoise
waves lapping at our heels. My gorgeous Loretta
Lynn–inspired wedding gown floated around
my ankles in the salty Hawaiian air, and Brady's
bronzed skin glistened underneath a bright,
happy sky. We ran hand in hand at the water's
edge, embracing our new life together.

Then the dream morphed. Still at the beach, we
realized we weren't alone. Behind us, running
en masse, were all of our relatives and friends.
They shouted at us, angry that we'd left them out
of the plans for our big day. On and on we ran,
past the roasted pig, beyond the hula dancers,
through the palm trees, onto a steep, rocky path.

The dream continued to twist and turn, finally

ending at a volcano. With the accusations of our families and friends ringing in our ears, we raced to the rim. With no place else to go, Brady and I stared at the boiling lava below, unable to move forward or backward.

I awoke drenched in sweat. Okay then. Maybe we wouldn't run off to Hawaii and elope after all. Surely he'd just been kidding, anyway.

After I convinced myself the whole thing had just been a bad dream, I yawned and stretched, then got out of bed and walked down the hallway to the kitchen. This morning I'd have to fix my own breakfast. Aunt Alva was at my cousin Lori-Lou's house, tending to her children while Lori-Lou was on bed rest, awaiting the birth of her fourth child, a girl.

Without my aunt in the house, I decided on a quick breakfast—coffee and a bagel with peanut butter. She would've fussed at me, though. To Aunt Alva, morning wasn't morning without eggs, bacon, toast, or pancakes. The bagel tasted pretty bland in comparison.

I sat at the Formica table and watched the sunlight stream in through the kitchen window, past the curtains with the little roosters on them. Strange how cozy I felt sitting here. I spent a few minutes viewing the Bible app on my phone. I had to laugh when I read the verse of the day from Philippians, the fourth chapter: "I know what it is to be in need, and I know what it is to have plenty. I have learned the secret of being content in any and every situation, whether well fed or hungry, whether living in plenty or in want."

I traced my finger along the words, and a thoughtful smile tugged at the corners of my lips. No matter where I lived—Dallas or Fairfield—or what I ate for breakfast—eggs or bagels—I could not deny the obvious: I'd learned to be content.

Mostly.

I could almost imagine what Aunt Alva would say in response to that one. "What's *not* to be content about, girl? You're in the state of Texas, after all, the state of contentment."

Yes, I was in the state of Texas, all right. In Aunt Alva's home. Satisfied.

No, more than satisfied, really. I'd learned to love it here. I couldn't quite put into words why I'd fallen head over heels for my aunt Alva's little house. The seventies décor did nothing for my imagination, so it couldn't be that. And the ever-present aroma of her rose-scented perfume didn't exactly send me over the moon. Still, the house had a familiarity to it. The layout, the colors, the furnishings, the growing teacup collection that filled shelves and shelves . . . all of these things reminded me of home.

Home.

Fairfield.

Okay, so I did get a little misty every time I thought about my hometown.

For now, I'd settled my heart on staying with Aunt Alva. Doing so had, in its own weird way, kept me rooted. Grounded. Soon, however, I would leave her sweet, simple home. I would walk away from the Formica breakfast table and the Herculon sofa and would become mistress of the house in Brady's uptown condo.

A little shiver ran down my spine. Mama had once warned me that city dwellers had snakes in their kitchens. They came in through the plumbing, she said. And what was it Pop had said about neighbors living on top of one another? Ugh. Other than sharing a two-story house with my parents and brothers, I'd never had anyone living above me. Or below me. What would it be like to trade my simple, old-fashioned living environment for a fancy condominium on the fifteenth floor of one of Dallas's most luxurious high-rises?

And being married to Brady meant entering a whole new world. His life as a pro ball player—er, former pro ball player—meant that people recognized him. We'd never be able to go anywhere without the click of cameras. I let my imagination get the better of me as I thought that through. A few minutes later, however, I calmed down. We'd already been dating for months and hadn't run into too many problems with his fans. Besides, these days he spent more time in the bridal shop and less talking about basketball.

I finished off the rest of my bagel and walked down the narrow hallway toward my bedroom, pausing only to look at the pictures on the wall. I had to give it to Aunt Alva. She'd arranged the family photos in a rather creative fashion, squeezing approximately a hundred of them onto one wall. Clearly the woman loved her family. I couldn't help but think she was proving that at this very moment by caring for Lori-Lou in her hour of need.

I'd just finished dressing for work when my cell phone rang. I smiled when I saw my aunt's name on the screen. I answered right away with a feeling of great joy rising up. "Hey, I was just thinking about you."

"Same here. Good morning, sunshine." Aunt Alva's chipper voice rang out from the other end of the phone. "Miss me?"

"Terribly. How's it going over at Lori-Lou's place?"

"The doctor says it won't be long now. Maybe just another week or two before we see that darling baby girl." Alva chuckled. "I'm making an assumption she'll be darling, anyway. If she's anything like her older sisters, she might also be a little rotten."

"Right?" I laughed. "I know how those kids are, trust me. I stayed with them once upon a time."

"They're a handful, but I love 'em."

"Me too. I owe Lori-Lou a visit. I feel terrible

that I haven't been around much, but things at the bridal shop have been so busy. We've got a new line coming out—the Audrey Hepburn. Gorgeous."

"Yes, Eduardo told me. And it's true that things are pretty chaotic here, what with the kids being so rambunctious. Joshie's into everything and Mariela's going through some sort of emotional spell. But I'm handling things as well as could be expected. Eduardo brought dinner last night. You wouldn't believe the trouble he went to for the kids—set up a card table in the middle of the living room, put a fancy cloth on it, and even served them like a waiter. He spoke in French to Gilly. She laughed all evening long. The whole thing was priceless. I'd like to say I got some good photos, but you know how I am with that phone of mine. I can't remember how to use the camera thingy to save my life."

"I can picture it now, even without the photographs." In my mind's eye I could see Eduardo—with his televangelist hair—playing the role of French waiter, taking care of the children's every need. "He's a great man, Alva. Truly."

"Yes." She sighed. "He is. I don't know what I ever did to deserve such an amazing fellow. Just good, clean living, I suppose." She followed this statement with a snort. "Anyway, that's not why I called, to talk about Eduardo. I have something specific in mind."

"Oh?" This caught my attention.

"Yes. The kids are still snoozing and Lori-Lou is in the shower, so I thought this would be the perfect time to talk to you about your wedding."

"Sure, as long as you don't tell me I have to get married at the Gaylord and ride off into the sunset at the end."

"Um, no. Now, let's talk bridesmaids." The passion in my aunt's voice intensified. "I'm assuming Lori-Lou will be your maid of honor, since she's your BFF and your cousin. Though I suppose that will all depend on when you have the wedding, since she's about to have a baby and all."

"Yes." I chewed on my lip as I thought about that. Lori-Lou would soon have an infant. Not that Brady and I had set a date for our wedding yet, but we'd need to keep this in mind, should we plan to include my cousin in the lineup. "I think I've always known that she would be, even though life has separated us at times." I glanced at the clock and noticed the time. Just ten minutes until I needed to leave for work. Might as well put on makeup while talking to my aunt.

"And you have a plethora of girlfriends to choose from at the bridal salon," she continued. "Twiggy, Crystal, Dahlia, Hibiscus, and Jane. They'll all look lovely in bridesmaid dresses, I'm sure." For whatever reason her voice lost a bit of its animation.

I opened my makeup bag and reached for the lipstick, then glanced at my reflection in the mirror above the dressing table. "Yes, but I doubt I'd pick all of them. I'm not as close to Hibiscus and Jane as the others, you know." I swiped the lipstick on and then smacked my lips together.

"Right. So, Lori-Lou, Crystal, Twiggy, and Dahlia. That's four."

I considered that before responding. "Four sounds like a reasonable number." I closed the lipstick and put it back in the makeup bag. "Most of my friends from high school have moved on and we've lost touch, so I guess that makes sense." I fumbled around for the blush, which I finally located. I'd just started to color my cheeks when her words caught me off guard.

"Four, then?" My aunt paused as if questioning my decision. "Your heart is set on four, not more?"

I suddenly got her meaning. "Aunt Alva, are you asking if you can be a bridesmaid in my wedding?"

A nervous giggle sounded on her end. "I'm not asking, necessarily. It would be rude to come out and ask. But if you did ask, I wouldn't say no." She paused. "Not that I would match the other bridesmaids in figure or function, but I could do my best to fit in. I've been thinking about getting a gym membership. Maybe I could fit into a dress by then. I'd work double time trying, anyway."

I dabbed the blush on my right cheek, then gave it a scrutinizing look. Hmm. A little heavy-handed. With the back of my hand I swiped some of it off. "Auntie, there's no need to change yourself on my account."

I'd no sooner spoken those words than she let out a squeal. "So I'm in? I'm one of the bridesmaids? Oh, thank you, honey! You realize I've never been one, right?"

"Um, you were just in Queenie's wedding a few months ago."

"Well, yes. I was the maid of honor. But I've never been part of a group of bridesmaids before. It seems like a lot of fun, being one of the girls."

One of the girls.

I pondered her words. She was nearly four times older than most of the girls in my circle, but that didn't matter. Aunt Alva had the youngest personality of anyone I knew.

Before I could think another thing about it, my cell phone rang. I sighed when I saw my grandmother's name on the screen. I said, "Can you hold, Aunt Alva? It's Queenie calling," then took the call. "Queenie?"

"Just calling to make sure you remembered about this coming Saturday."

"This coming Saturday?" I shoved the makeup bag aside and took a seat on the edge of the bed, convinced I'd never make it to work on time.

"You're coming back to Fairfield, right? We're

putting together a final plan for Crystal and Jasper's big day, remember? And I'm sure everyone in town'll want to see that ring of yours. Have you and Brady set a date yet?"

"Actually, we're talking about—"

"I don't know if you've heard, but the Methodist church is getting a plumbing overhaul in July, so if you're planning to hold your reception there, you might want to rethink it."

"Oh, we're not going to do the reception there. I've had a lot of different ideas, but I really don't think—"

"So you're staying at the Baptist church for the whole thing, ceremony and reception? I applaud your decision to have the ceremony there, but if you're wanting a dance floor at your reception, the Baptist church is out. They don't allow dancing, remember?"

"I never said—"

"The charismatics might have you. I could ask. But I'm pretty sure they have some sort of rule that you have to be a church member to use the building. I never quite understood that one. I would think they'd be happy to have the rental fee, regardless of your membership."

"Actually, we have something altogether different in mind, Queenie."

"Please don't tell me you're getting married in Dallas. I don't think my heart could take it. Remember that episode I had last year? You guys had to call for the paramedics? I feel sure my poor heart couldn't handle the news that you're getting married anyplace but home."

"I didn't say—"

"Because Twiggy told Beau that you're thinking about getting married at the Gaylord. And even though I did think the whole cowboy/horse theme was interesting, I must tell you it would drive a stake through my heart if you went that route. You know how strongly we all feel about you getting married here in Fairfield."

"Twiggy shouldn't have said that, Queenie. I never agreed to getting married at the—"

"I'm not saying the Gaylord isn't nice, but it's not home. And you know what they say: 'There's no place like home for a wedding.'"

"I'm not sure that's exactly how the saying goes, but I get your point. And I love the idea of getting married in Fairfield, as I've said." A million times.

"We have horses here too," she said, "if you have your heart set on that cowboy theme. Though, frankly, that doesn't sound much like you."

"It's not." I rose and paced the bedroom, ready to get on with my day. "Queenie, I'm sorry to tell you this, but Alva's holding on the other line. Would it be okay if I called you back this evening after work?"

"No need to call back. Just don't forget to come

on Saturday. I'm serving brunch at my place—10:30. Bring Alva. Unless Lori-Lou goes into labor between now and then. But please ask her not to, okay? We've got a wedding to plan. Two if we count yours."

"Okay, I'll tell Lori-Lou to hold off on having the baby. No problem." *But if you don't mind, I'll plan my own wedding, thank you very much.*

"Good girl. Gotta run."

A click ended the call. I tried to go back to Alva, but she must've disconnected the call. No problem. I needed to get on the road to work, anyway.

I thought about my wedding as I drove. Surely people understood that every bride had the right to plan her own special day. Right? Why, then, didn't I have the courage to remind folks that I wanted to be in charge? I would start today. No longer would people boss me around.

By the time I arrived at Cosmopolitan Bridal, the shop was opening for the day. I'd never been this late before. Hopefully my boss—and future mother-in-law—wouldn't give me what for.

My concerns melted away the minute I walked in the bridal shop and saw Nadia's disarming smile. "Katie, such good news!" She clasped her hands together at her chest. "I called in a favor with a friend who works at the Gaylord. No promises—keep your fingers crossed—but I think the chances of getting the grand ballroom are pretty high, depending on the date. You and Brady need to decide quickly, okay?"

"Actually, we need to talk, Nadia." My purse strap slid off my shoulder and I caught it with my right hand. "The more I think about it, the more convinced I am that we should get married in—"

"June? I know most brides opt for June, so the hotel is completely booked. I think they've got some openings in the fall, though."

"I really need to talk to you about something, Nadia. I—"

"I have something to tell you too, but I was waiting till Brady got here so that you'd both be together."

"I'm here, Mom." His voice sounded from behind the counter at the front of the store.

She gestured for him to join us and reached out her hands to both of us. "The timing couldn't be better. It simply couldn't."

"Timing . . . for what?" Brady asked.

"I'm home from Paris—for good!" Her voice resonated with glee. "The internship isn't up yet, but I've made such good progress, my mentor opted to let me finish the last three months by Skype. Isn't that the best news ever? I don't have to go back!"

"That's awesome, Mom." Brady glanced my way as if expecting me to chime in.

"You know what this means, right?" Her eyes shimmered with tears as she squeezed his hand.

"I'll be here to help plan your big day. Oh, I'm so excited. Not every mother gets to help her only son plan for the day of his life."

She hadn't mentioned the bride, had she? Hmm.

I cleared my throat. "Glad you'll be back, Nadia. It'll be so much fun to have your help." *Once I tell you that I cannot possibly get married at the Gaylord.*

Of course, I still had to talk things through with Brady.

She slipped her arm through mine. "I want to be a blessing, honey. I know everyone in the wedding biz. In Dallas, I mean. And I'd be willing to bet I can get you two a great rate on a tropical honey-moon. Where would you like to go?"

"Haven't really thought about it," I said. "I just don't want to go to Cozumel and end up with a sunburn like Mama came back with."

With a wave of her hand, Nadia appeared to dismiss that idea. "Cozumel isn't even close to what I had in mind. I was thinking Bali!"

"Bali?" I swallowed hard. Where the heck was that, anyway?

Brady shook his head, a look of concern in his eyes. "Mom, one of my teammates went to Bali for his honeymoon and dropped 10K a night on his room alone."

"Yes, but I'll bet it was over the water, right?"

"Well, yes . . ."

"I have connections." Her eyes sparkled. "I'll

get you the trip of a lifetime. Promise you'll let me help with this? I want to help with everything. Planning the wedding will make coming home even more special."

Wait. Did she say "planning the wedding" . . . as in, planning the *whole* wedding?

Someone needed to stop this woman before she took over the whole show. Next thing you know, she'd be designing my wedding dress.

Oh, wait. She already had.

Hmm.

I had a hard time focusing on my work as I headed to my office. Strangely, I found Twiggy seated at my desk, using my computer.

"Oh, I hope you don't mind, but I wanted to create a Pinterest account for you. You don't already have one, do you?"

"No, I don't really have much time to spend on the internet. I'm too busy."

"A girl is never too busy to plan her wedding. Come and look at what I've done." She gestured for me to join her at my computer and then pointed at the screen. "See this folder right here? It's filled with pictures of cakes. Cakes, cakes, and more cakes."

"Ah." I glanced at the clock, startled by the time. I needed to get a promotional piece to the local paper before noon. Ack. My gaze shifted back to the computer, where I stared at some of the oddest-looking cakes I'd ever seen. They looked very . . . Texan. Made me proud of my state, for sure, but they weren't what I'd consider for my wedding.

"And this folder right here . . ." She clicked a couple of buttons, then pointed at the screen again. "Décor. Centerpieces. Tablecloths. Since we're going with a 'riding off into the sunset' theme, I thought you might like to see some samples."

"Wait . . . we? Riding off into the sunset?"

"And what do you think of these bridesmaid dresses?" A few more clicks and she landed on a page filled with country-western–themed gowns. "I like the feel of these. I mean, I don't want to tell you what to do—and I know you haven't technically asked me to even be a bridesmaid yet—but I'm sure that's just a technicality." On and on she went, planning my wedding for me. I finally gave up and sat in the chair on the opposite side of the desk while she rambled on about my big day. Only when Madge popped her head in the door did she pause for breath.

"Twiggy?" Madge's eyes narrowed. "Did you forget we have a shop to run? We're swamped with customers, and I can't wait on them all myself."

"Oops." Twiggy's cheeks flushed pink. "I'm just so excited about the wedding."

"You're getting married?" Madge let out a squeal. "Really? Beau proposed?"

"No, no." Twiggy rose and shook her head.

41

"I'm helping Katie plan *her* wedding. Not mine." The heightened color in her cheeks subsided.

"Don't you think Katie should do that herself?" Madge put her hands on her hips. "She's a big girl. I'm pretty sure she told me once upon a time that she's been planning for her big day since she was a kid."

"I was just helping, that's all." With a huff, Twiggy walked across the room and out the door.

"Don't let them do this to you, Katie." Madge gave me a motherly look. "It's your day, not theirs."

I agreed with her. Oh yes, I agreed. But voicing my ideas was getting harder every day. "I just don't know how to say no to people. It's a problem. I need a twelve-step program: Suckers Anonymous."

"I happen to have their phone number in my purse." She winked. "Now, get busy on that ad for the *Observer*. They need it by noon."

"I know, I know."

She'd just turned to walk out of the room when I realized something. "Oh no!" I clamped my hand over my mouth. "I just thought of something."

"What is it?" Madge rushed my way, her eyes widening. "Something happen I need to know about?"

"No, nothing like that. I just realized my wedding gown is in the cedar closet at Queenie's house."

"Cedar closet?"

"Yes. I need to get it out of there!" I paced the room, my anxieties growing. "Fast! It's going to smell like cedar."

"Wait. Are you and Brady eloping or something?" Madge asked. "'Cause if you are, Nadia's totally going to kill you, and I might just help her."

"No. It's nothing like that. I just don't want my dress to smell."

"You should've thought of that when you put it in the cedar closet, goofy." Madge laughed. "But there's no rush if you guys haven't set a date. It'll air out, and you can always take it to be dry-cleaned if you're worried."

"I just didn't think I'd be wearing it anytime soon. That's why I took it to Queenie's in the first place. Back then I totally thought I'd be single for, well, ages."

"Join the crowd. I certainly know what it means to think you won't get married for a while." Madge sighed. "Anyway, back to the dress. Just call your grandmother and ask her to hang it in a regular closet or something."

"She's out of town. They're visiting Paul's great-grandchildren in San Antonio. They won't be back for a few days."

"I'm sure it can wait till then. Don't fret, Katie. All will end well, I'm sure. And I promise, I won't let you walk down the aisle smelling like cedar chips."

"Thank you. That would be so embarrassing."

"Speaking of embarrassing . . ." She pointed to my face. "For some reason, you've only got blush on one cheek. Some kind of strange new fashion statement?"

I sighed and reached for my purse. After touching up my blush, I spent the next hour and a half doing what I loved: writing. I put together a lovely, descriptive ad about our upcoming sale and then emailed it to the editor at the newspaper. I'd just pressed the send button when Brady tapped on my open door.

"Busy?" He leaned against the doorjamb, his tall frame filling the space. I found myself captivated once again by his solid build—the strong shoulders, the muscular midsection. Then my gaze traveled to his legs and I was reminded of his recent knee surgery. No wonder he was leaning against the doorjamb. The poor guy's knee was probably killing him again.

Focus, Katie. Focus.

"I was busy, but I'm done now." I turned off the computer and leaned back in my chair.

"Everything okay? You seem a little . . . down." He shifted his weight, favoring his left leg.

I tried to add a bit of cheer to my voice as I responded, "I'm great. Everything's great."

"Faker." He laughed. "So, what's up . . . really?"

If I released the sigh that threatened to escape, he would suspect I'd been struggling with the

44

changes going on in my life. I did my best to sound upbeat. "Oh, just spent the morning sitting at Aunt Alva's Formica table wondering what life will be like when I move to your place. And don't even get me started on the people trying to run my life right now."

"Wait, slow down. You're wishing I had a Formica table at my condo? What does that have to do with people bossing you around?"

"Nothing. I don't know. Nothing makes sense right now."

"What are you really saying?"

"I don't know, Brady. I'm just scared, I think. So much is happening so fast. And I feel like such a weakling. I can't say no to people. That's the main thing. I have ideas in my head for how I want the wedding to be. I'd love to talk those through with you. But everyone else is trying to confuse me. And I can't say no. I can't."

"Sure you can." With a wave of his hand, he appeared to dismiss any concerns.

"No, I can't. Try me."

He paused a moment and appeared to be thinking, then gave me a pointed look. "Would you like to go out to lunch?"

"Sure." I nodded.

"How about Mexican food?"

"Yum. Sounds great." I sighed. "See what I mean?"

"But you really *do* love Mexican food."

"Yeah, but that's the problem. Every time I hear a great idea, it sounds, well, great. And when I'm the bride—which I am—not every great-sounding idea is really all that great. I mean, they all sound great, but they're not really great for you and me. I think the problem is there are *way* too many great ideas out there . . . only, none of them leave me feeling . . . great."

"I'm biting my tongue to keep from using the word *great*." Brady chuckled.

"Um, you just used it."

"Couldn't help myself." He paused and appeared to be thinking. "Hey, you know what you need? One of those idea boxes."

"What's that?"

"You know, a box. People can drop their ideas in completely anonymously. That way you can give each person opportunity to share but you won't have the pressure of saying yes or no. I'm going to build one and put it on your door. People will have the satisfaction of knowing they gave you their input, but you can take the box out back and burn it when no one's looking."

"What I need is a dose of courage. And some time to clear my head. Can we really go to lunch, Brady—just the two of us?"

"For Mexican food?"

"Sure. Whatever. But mostly to talk things through. We need to make a plan. Together. And then we have to stick with it. Otherwise we're gonna be inundated and confused."

"I'm already confused. But if it's all the same to you, I'd rather have Chinese food."

"Fine." I rose and grabbed my purse.

Brady took several steps toward me and swept me into his arms. "I was just testing you, to see how you'd respond."

I couldn't help the little groan that escaped as I realized I'd been had. Again. "Guess I failed the test."

"It's okay." He planted a kiss in my hair, then another. And another. "I grade on a curve."

Thank goodness someone did. The way things were going around here, I'd be the first bride in the history of the world to get a big fat F in wedding planning.

Not that I wanted to think about that right now. Nope. Right now I just wanted to eat some Mexican food.

Or Chinese.

Or . . . whatever.

3
This One's for the Girls

I love people who make me laugh. I honestly think it's the thing I like most, to laugh. It cures a multitude of ills. It's probably the most important thing in a person.

Audrey Hepburn

The following Saturday Aunt Alva and I made the drive to Fairfield. Though Brady and I hadn't come to any solid conclusions about our own wedding, I needed to help my future sister-in-law with hers. Unlike all of my friends and family members, I wouldn't try to overwhelm her with ideas.

As we buzzed down 287 through the town of Waxahachie, Aunt Alva fussed with her makeup, her attempts at eye shadow a little iffy from the passenger seat. She ended up with a bright streak of blue running underneath her left eye.

"I must confess, I'm getting terribly confused." Alva closed the mirror on the visor.

"About makeup?"

"No." She shoved her makeup bag down to the floor. "About all of these weddings. Crystal and

Jasper. You and Brady. It's all running together in my mind. If I ever get engaged, I'm going to run away and get married on a beach. By myself."

"Hopefully with your groom." I giggled. "But if it makes you feel any better, I'm feeling a little confused too. I don't know what I'll do when you and Eduardo get engaged."

"And Dahlia and Dewey." My aunt gave me a knowing look. "It's just a matter of time."

"And Beau and Twiggy. You know he's just biding his time until he becomes Stan's business partner at the agency, and that's going to happen soon. I feel sure of it."

"So many weddings, so little time. And again I say, if I end up engaged—"

"You will." I gave her a wink.

"If I get engaged, I'm running away from home. Or getting married on a random Tuesday when no one expects it. Either way, it'll be something simple, not a big event that people have to spend months planning for."

"As if Eduardo is capable of doing anything the simple way." I couldn't help but laugh at that.

"It's true." She sighed. "He is the most creative man I've ever met. No doubt he has some sort of plan up his sleeve. I just wish he'd pop the question so we can feel like we fit in with all of the other engaged folks."

I bit my tongue to keep from saying more. Brady had shared the news just yesterday:

Eduardo was definitely planning to pop the question, in his own time and way. How wonderful to think that Alva would finally, after all these years, have her happily ever after.

To avoid mentioning all of this, I changed the topic to the weather. We made small talk all the way to Fairfield, where I stopped by the hardware store to pick up Crystal. Something about being back in my hometown made me feel so comfortable, so at ease. And when I walked inside the store, my sense of family pride really kicked in. I let out a little whistle as I took in the work my brother had done on the store's interior—new paint, new layout, new . . . everything.

From behind the register, my brother gave me a wave. "Welcome to Fisher's Hardware, home of the two-dollar toilet snake." He chuckled.

I gestured to the shop as I walked toward him. "Jasper, it's fantastic. I'm overwhelmed. Great job."

"Isn't it just *luv*-lee?" Crystal appeared from the back room, several boxes of water filters in hand. "I'm tickled pink!"

"Yes, it's lovely," I responded. "You've both done such a great job. Jasper, Pop would be very proud if he could see all of this."

"Thanks." My brother squared his shoulders, and I could see the look of pride in his eyes as he led the way from shelf to shelf, showing off his work. If I hadn't picked up on the enthusiasm from Jasper, I would've noticed it in Crystal's eyes for sure.

My future sister-in-law pointed to the new "lighting" corner of the store, which boasted several gorgeous fixtures hanging from above. "Isn't it just the *bay*-est?" she crooned. "This fella of mine is handy with a *hay*-a-mer, and he's a great salesman to boot. Now, if we can just get him to agree to *way*-er a tuxedo at our *wed*-din', I'll be a happy *gur*-ul."

"Of course he's wearing a tux at your wedding." I slapped my brother on the arm. "He's just teasing you if he says anything otherwise. Right, Jasper?"

My brother squirmed. "Can't I just get married in my Sunday suit? I wore it to Queenie's wedding."

"Yes, you wore it to Queenie's weddin' because you weren't the groom." Crystal spoke in a motherly voice. "*This* time you're the groom . . . and you're wearin' a tuxedo. I can't be-*lieve* you're not playin' along for my sake. We've only got a few weeks, you know. The weddin's in May, honey. *May*."

"Okay, okay. I'll drive over to Teague and see about getting a tuxedo." My brother rolled his eyes. "If that's what it takes to make my bride happy."

"Over my dead body." I crossed my arms and stared him down. "You'll come to Cosmopolitan Bridal and let us fit you in the best tuxedo we've got."

"Oh, amen, honey. Preach it." Crystal gave me an admiring look. "Now you're talkin'."

Jasper did not look convinced. He raked his fingers through his messy hair and then tugged at the collar of his plaid shirt. "But Katie, I don't want to spend a lot of money on a—"

I waved my hand to dismiss his concerns. "Don't you worry about the cost, Jasper. You just come in and let Eduardo fit you in a tuxedo that will make your bride's head swim. It won't cost you much at all, I promise."

"All right, but I'm not sure I want her head to swim. It's already going to be the hottest May we've ever had. Have you been watching the weather reports? That fella on the weather channel says we're gonna have a heat wave like no other."

"A little ol' heat wave never bothered me none." Crystal giggled. "I'm used to it, bein' a Southern girl and all. Besides, I'll be a glistening bride on our weddin' day. A little perspiration never hurt anyone."

"That's what she tells me every time she wants me to rearrange another section of the store." Jasper laughed and gestured to the aisle on our right. "But I've gotta give it to her, it's worth the sweat."

"And our weddin' will be too." She reached over and gave him a kiss on the cheek. "Speakin' of which, we'd better get on the road to Queenie's place. Thanks for swingin' by to pick me up, Katie." She glanced through the window at Aunt Alva still seated in the front passenger seat of my car. "My goodness, I do hope she's asleep and nothin' more."

"Oh yes. She dozed off somewhere around Corsicana. I didn't have the heart to wake her. She needs her rest."

"I'm going to as well, if this weddin' plannin' gets too complicated." She reached for my hand. "I'm glad you're going to be with me."

"Yes, we need someone to run interference." Jasper turned to rearrange a couple of lightbulb packages on the shelf.

"Interference? What do you mean?"

My brother turned back to face me, and I could see the concern in his eyes. "At the brunch today—if Queenie or Bessie May or any of the others get too bossy, help Crystal reel 'em back in. Promise?"

I sighed. "I can only promise to try."

"I'm just saying." Jasper gave us both a knowing look. "You know how those WOP-pers are. They're going to try to arrange everything for Crystal, and I want to make sure someone's looking out for her best interests."

I did my best not to groan as he mentioned the WOP-pers, Fairfield's Women of Prayer group. They might be prayer warriors, but they also tended to be on the nosy, buttinsky side. Hopefully they wouldn't try to pull my future sister-in-law into their web.

Crystal's brow furrowed. "Oh, honey, put your mind at ease! I might be a gentle, sweet Southern girl, but I *know* how to get my way. I'm the *bride,* after all. They can make all the suggestions they want, but our plans are set. No one's changin' a thing."

I gave her an admiring look. "Where do I get that kind of moxie?"

Crystal put her hand on my arm. "I don't know what moxie is, Katie Sue. But if you're askin' how I plan to work up the courage to tell those ladies they're needing to back down, I'll just say it, plain 'n' simple. I've already had some practice with Ophelia. Would you believe she said my *Gone with the Wind* weddin' theme was ri-*dic*-ulous? Clearly the woman was *not* born and raised in the South. She has infiltrated from northern ranks."

I bit back a laugh. "Well, I know that everyone has their own ideas of how things should be done. Trust me, Brady and I are hearing from everyone about our own wedding."

"Promise me something, Katie Sue." Crystal took my hands. "Your day is yours. Don't let anyone steal it from you. If you want to walk down the aisle on pogo sticks, you do it. If you want to set up chairs on the moon, go for it. If you want to hold a picnic on the courthouse lawn, do it, girl!"

A picnic on the courthouse lawn.

Those words jumped out at me and rooted themselves in my imagination. Now, that might be a fun place to hold a reception. We could put in a large dance floor on the lawn, couldn't we? And lovely summery centerpieces for the tables. Hmm.

I thought about our conversation all the way to the car. As we got settled inside, I adjusted the rearview mirror and caught a glimpse of my future sister-in-law touching up her cotton-candy-pink lipstick. She looked so at ease, not at all worried about fending off the ladies at today's brunch.

My heart suddenly felt overwhelmed with pride. "Thank you for giving me courage, Crystal. I'm so proud of you for sticking to your guns and doing things your way. I hope to learn some things from you today."

"There's nuthin' to learn, honey." She gave me a wink and slipped her lipstick tube back in her purse. "I'll just tell you what the good witch told Dorothy before she left Oz: 'You've always had the power to go back to Kansas.'"

Alva stirred in her seat, and one eye opened a slit. "We're going to Kansas? I thought we were headed to Queenie's house."

"No, we're not—" I didn't bother finishing

because she fell fast asleep again. I slipped the car into reverse and looked around to make sure the road was clear. Seconds later we were on our way. I drove past the courthouse, my thoughts still wrapped tightly around Crystal's comment about the courthouse lawn. Maybe . . . just maybe.

In the backseat, Crystal carried on about how much she'd grown to love living in Fairfield, how it felt like home. I knew those feelings well, having been raised here. But something else hit me too—this precious young woman wasn't just my future sister-in-law. She was much more. When she paused for breath, I shared my thoughts on that matter.

"You've turned out to be one of my best friends, Crystal."

A quick glance in the rearview mirror showed her response. Crystal's eyes flooded with tears. "I'm *so* glad, and I feel just the same, Katie! Isn't it funny how life works out? You visited the bridal shop in Dallas, where we met. I moved to your hometown, you moved to Dallas . . . and we've still remained the best of friends."

"Just goes to show you, friendship has nothing to do with miles."

"True. But I do love it when you come back to Fairfield, even for a few days. It's always fun to have you home again."

Have you home again.

Those words stuck with me as I drove to Queenie's house. No matter how long I lived in the Dallas area, Fairfield would still be home to me. Not that I wanted to give up my job and move back. It wasn't that. But I still loved the quaint feel of being in this wonderful, loving place.

Maybe that's why I loved Aunt Alva's house in Dallas so much. The layout, the colors, the style—it all reminded me of home.

Speaking of places that made me feel at home, we arrived at Queenie's house at 10:30 on the dot. I knew she'd scold me for being late—she always felt that one should arrive at any engagement at least ten minutes ahead of time—but I didn't have time to worry about that right now.

Just as we arrived, Alva awoke. She startled to attention, and all the more as she realized Crystal had joined us. "I was having the loveliest dream ever." She yawned and stretched. "Mmm. Just wonderful. Eduardo and I were on our honeymoon in sunny Southern California. We were treated like movie stars everywhere we went. I think it might've had something to do with the fact that I was dressed like Glinda the Good Witch. You know that lovely pink dress she wore? I looked amazing in it . . . so young."

"Sounds dreamy, all right." Crystal laughed.

"It just felt so wonderful to be treated like

a princess." My aunt giggled. "Maybe that's a secret desire, one I never realized until now."

"Every girl wants to be treated like a princess." I turned off the car and pressed the keys into my purse.

We got out of the car and I followed on Alva's heels with Crystal at my side. Alva headed inside, saying something about needing to use the bathroom. Just before we got to the door, I felt led to share something with Crystal privately.

"I just want you to know that as my bestie, you've earned the right to be my right-hand gal when it comes to wedding planning—if you want that job, I mean. I know Joni will officially coordinate."

"I just love Joni. She's the *bay*-est! I couldn't have asked for a better roommate, and she's been such a wonderful helper with our weddin' plans!"

"Yes, she's great. And Lori-Lou will want to chime in, though we all know she's far too busy with the kids to do much. But I'll need a confidante, a true friend to bounce ideas off of, and I think you'd be perfect, especially since you're going through the same thing right now. What do you think?"

"What do I think? What do I think?" Crystal threw her arms around my neck. "I think I always wanted a sister but never had one. I think I'll love every minute of helpin' you, and vice versa.

Promise me you'll slap me silly if I ever come across as too forceful, though."

"I can't imagine you being forceful, Crystal. You're sweet as sugar."

Queenie waved from the front door. "What's all this hugging? Did someone die?"

"No, Queenie. I'm just telling Crystal that she's sweet as sugar. She is, you know."

"Ooh, speaking of sugar . . ." My grandmother's eyes narrowed. "Better tell you this before you go inside, just to give you a heads-up. You know the shop next door to the hardware store, the one that used to be a boutique?"

"Sure. I bought my favorite black dress in that shop. Still haven't had a chance to wear it."

Queenie gestured for us to come into the house. "They closed down a few weeks back. I don't know if you noticed or not, but the place has been vacant for a while now."

"Wow. That's sad." I followed my grandmother into the house. "I hope it's not a sign of things to come in Fairfield."

"Oh, no. It's not. In fact, that space has just been rented, and you'll never guess by whom."

"Wait, let me guess." I paused to think and then snapped my fingers. "I've got it. Joni? She's starting a wedding planning service?"

"That's a clever idea. I'll have to suggest it next time a building comes available. But no."

"Who then?"

"Ophelia. She's opening up a bakery, specializing in cakes, of course. But she's asked a couple of the other ladies to help her. Bessie May, for instance. They'll be working together, side by side, in a commercial kitchen! Your wedding cake will be made in an official bakery."

"Wow. Aren't they, well, a little old to be starting a new business?"

"Don't let them hear you say that. They'll throttle you. According to Prissy, when you're passionate about something, age is irrelevant."

"Which may explain why Mr. Peabody, the local mortician, is still going strong in his eighties," I said. "I guess he's passionate about embalming."

"Everyone has to be passionate about *sumthin'*," Crystal added. "For me, it's arrangin' the store to look nice. And helping with the window displays."

I offered her a warm smile. "Just one more thing we have in common. That's my favorite part of working at the bridal salon."

"Do you suppose we're really sisters, separated at birth?" Crystal asked. "We have *so* much in common." She headed toward the kitchen to join the other ladies.

Queenie rattled on about the changes coming to Fairfield, but she'd lost me back at her comments about the new bakery. I had a feeling the ladies weren't here today just to help Crystal plan her reception. I knew in my gut they were going to try to overwhelm her with their plans, their ideas.

And I for one would stand in the gap to make sure that wouldn't happen. I'd just gathered the courage to say something in advance to Queenie—just to give her a heads-up—when she took me by the arm and whispered, "I have something to tell you. Top. Secret."

A thousand what-ifs ran through my mind. I held my breath, waiting for whatever news was about to come my way. But with my heart pounding so hard in my ears, I doubted I'd be able to hear anything Queenie had to say.

Seconds later, however, her words came through loud and clear. "Joni Milford and Casey Lawson are married."

4

My Baby Loves Me

When you have nobody you can make a
cup of tea for, when nobody needs you,
that's when I think life is over.

Audrey Hepburn

W hat?" I stared at my grandmother, wondering
if I'd heard correctly.

"Yep. They tied the knot a week and a half
ago. She's sitting at my kitchen table right now,
wedding ring on her finger, sharing details about
their honeymoon in Grand Cayman."

I leaned against the wall and tried to make
sense of what she'd said. "But, I just talked to
Joni a couple of weeks ago. She didn't mention a
thing about being married. I mean, I know they've
been a couple for a little while now, but Joni
Milford would definitely tell me if—"

"She's Joni Lawson now. They're most assuredly
married. They up and got hitched without so
much as inviting one person, even Casey's mama,
which has her in a snit, as you can imagine. Every
parent wants to see their child's wedding day."

"You're serious? They're actually *married?*"

"Yes. But with Joni being a wedding planner

and all, you'd think she'd want a wedding of her own. Just doesn't make a lick of sense, does it?"

"No. No, it doesn't." In fact, many things about this story made no sense. Just a few months ago Joni appeared to be interested in Levi Nash. And Casey . . . Hmm. I didn't want to speculate about what Casey might've been thinking. And what was up with Crystal not telling me? She and Joni were roomies, after all.

"We have a bigger problem than the two of them running off and getting married, honey. Would you believe there are still folks in this town who think Casey broke your heart by marrying Joni? They don't seem to remember that you moved away months ago and are dating Brady James. These poor ladies are stuck in the past."

"Probably because they're so used to seeing Casey and me out and about around town—at the Dairy Queen and at ball games and such. We were a duo for over seven years, and in a small-town environment. But maybe someone should remind these busybodies that I'm not just dating Brady James, I'm going to marry him. This coming summer. In Fairfield."

"Yes, that's true. Anyway, several know-it-alls—a few of whom are sitting at my breakfast table right now—have labeled Joni as 'the other woman.' So you might want to set the record straight when you go inside. In a nice, vague sort of way."

"But today is all about Crystal," I reminded her. "I doubt I'll have time to squelch any gossip while we're busy putting plans in motion for her big day. And how in the world could I possibly be vague about something so . . . so . . . dumb?"

My grandmother pursed her lips. "I suppose you're right. Maybe folks'll see you and Joni together and notice that you're speaking to one another. Then they won't see her as the other woman."

I sighed. "Queenie, anyone who's been paying attention already knows that Joni and I are friends. We co-planned your shower, remember? We get along great. Nothing will change that, not even her marriage to Casey Lawson."

"That's sweet of you, honey. So, you're not the tiniest bit jealous that they flew off to the Cayman Islands to get married? That's what has poor Casey's mother in such a state. She's always wanted to go to the Caymans, ever since she got a brochure in the mail from one of those cruise lines. She considers it a silent jab from her son to get married in a place she's always wanted to go. Without inviting her, I mean."

"Who knows why people do the things they do, Queenie. I guess Casey and Joni have a perfect right to get married wherever they like and invite whomever they like. Or not invite them."

"Promise me you and Brady won't follow their lead, Katie Sue." My grandmother sniffled. "I'd just die—and I do mean that literally—if you and Brady up and eloped. I don't think my heart could take it."

Wow. Did she really think I would do that? No way. I'd dreamed of my wedding day all my life. I'd talked about it incessantly, poring over bridal magazines until it drove my family nuts. How could she think I'd skip out on the big day?

"You know me better than that, Queenie. I'm so excited about getting married in front of the people I love, I could never do that—to them or myself. So rest easy."

"All right, all right."

I followed behind my grandmother into her kitchen, where I found Bessie May, Ophelia, Prissy, Joni, and Crystal seated at the breakfast table, nibbling on breakfast sweets.

"I told you not to touch those till I got back." My grandmother clucked her tongue. "Honestly, you ladies are like children sometimes."

"I just couldn't help myself, Queenie." Crystal giggled and held up a yummy-looking breakfast treat. "These muffins are so good. You'll have to give me your recipe."

The flattering words seemed to melt Queenie. They certainly stopped her from scolding.

I set my purse down on the living room sofa, and before I could say "Good morning," Ophelia appeared at my side. She patted my arm and leaned in to whisper, "My thoughts and prayers are with you, honey. Stiff upper lip now, you hear? You just look that hussy in the eye and show her you're the better woman. Don't let what she and Casey have done devastate you. Life will go on."

"But Ophelia, I'm *not* devastated."

"Just keep saying that, sweetie, and before long you'll start believing it."

"But I'm really not. I—oh, never mind." Why dig this hole even deeper?

"Attagirl." She winked. "Just keep telling yourself that."

"And I'll tell my fiancé while I'm at it," I muttered.

Ophelia didn't hear me, which was probably for the best. She returned to the breakfast table, where she grabbed an empty plate and started filling it.

"What was all that about?" Alva asked as she passed through the living room after leaving the bathroom.

"Don't. Even. Ask."

"Alrighty then." She gave me a kiss on the cheek and trotted off toward the kitchen.

I joined the ladies, pausing first to give Joni a big hug and a cheerful "Congratulations."

Out of the corner of her eye, Ophelia watched me. She gave me a nod and a thumbs-up and mouthed, "Attagirl!"

I forced a smile and reached for a plate. How I'd

landed in this room filled with women my grand-mother's age, I could not say. The WOP-pers had their fingers in every pie in Fairfield, that much was sure and certain.

I loaded my plate with quiche, muffins, and bacon. Lots and lots of bacon. When we'd eaten our fill, Joni—who'd spent the better part of the meal answering inappropriate questions about her tropical honeymoon—turned the attention to the bride-to-be.

"Enough about me, all right, ladies?" Joni's cheeks flushed pinker than the silk flowers in the vase on the center of the table. "We've all come together today to honor Crystal and to set a plan in motion for her shower and her big day. Now, I've already talked to her in advance, and we have everything planned, from the *Gone with the Wind* wedding and shower theme to the Southern foods at the reception. We just need folks to help us bring her plan to fruition."

"I just don't understand this whole *Gone with the Wind* theme," Ophelia grumbled as she reached for another muffin. "Never heard of such a thing." The lines on her upper lip became more evident as she pursed her lips together.

"Just play along, Ophelia," Alva said. "You were young once. You got to plan your big day."

"No I didn't." Ophelia's brow wrinkled and she broke off a piece of her muffin. "And if you'd ever met my mother-in-law, you'd know that.

She took the reins away from me and planned the whole thing. All I did was show up and marry her son."

Ouch.

"All the more reason to let Crystal have her big day," I said. "*Gone with the Wind* it is, folks."

"I suppose I can use that whole Southern thing to craft a lovely wedding cake." Ophelia popped the muffin piece into her mouth. "There is that."

Joni cleared her throat and shot a glance at Crystal, who stared out the window. Uh-oh. I felt a conflict coming.

"To be honest, Ophelia . . ." Joni gave her a pensive look. "Crystal was thinking of going a different direction with the cake."

Ophelia paled. She swallowed her food, then turned to face Crystal, who suddenly looked as if she wanted to bolt. "Now, honey, don't tell me you're going to fall for the schemes of that Betty Kay Collier down at that highfalutin cupcakery place in Teague. Just because she can bake a cupcake doesn't mean she can put together a full four-tiered wedding cake like I can. Promise me you'll let me make your cake, even if the new bakery's not open yet. You know I've got the goods."

"Ooh, but cupcakes can be arranged in such a darlin' display! And Betty Kay does the most de-*lec*-table flavors." Crystal's face lit up.

"Lemon chiffon with raspberry, mocha turtle, Italian cream cake . . . yummy!"

"Lemon chiffon sounds great." Alva nodded. "I can see why you'd be tempted."

"Jasper and I drove over to Teague a few days ago and spent a good hour or two just samplin' the wares." Crystal's eyes sparkled with obvious delight. "*So* tasty. Jasper agreed. They were to *die* for."

"Die. Hmm." Ophelia's penciled-on eyebrows elevated slightly. "I did hear a rumor that Mildred Watson had a stomach issue after eating Betty Kay's cupcakes. Had to be hospitalized."

"Mildred Watson has had stomach issues for as long as I can remember." Queenie shook her head. "Could we get back to talking about the wedding, please and thank you?"

Ophelia still had a determined look on her face. "I watch those cupcake shows on TV. I know they're popular right now, but it's just a phase. Who wants a cupcake when they can have a whole wedding cake? I challenge you to rethink this decision, Crystal."

"I for one love a good cupcake," Alva said. "They're small and handy, kind of like these muffins. Only, without all the bran inside." She rubbed her stomach. "Don't think the wedding guests need the added oomph."

This somehow morphed into an argument about the cupcake controversy—who knew cupcakes were controversial?—and before long Crystal was teary-eyed and Ophelia was red-faced.

As I had anticipated, this lovely brunch at Queenie's wasn't just a "How can we help Crystal with her wedding?" gathering. The ladies were declaring full-out war if they didn't get their way. I sat in stunned silence, shoveling pastries in my mouth, as I listened to idea after idea, most of them completely unsuited for a *Gone with the Wind* wedding.

Poor Crystal. Poor, poor Crystal.

And poor me! If she had this tough of a time pulling off a wedding in Fairfield, I could only imagine what my big day would look like.

I pondered this dilemma while eating another muffin.

Joni, perhaps in an attempt to change the direction of the conversation, cleared her throat. "Enough about the cake. Let's talk about the food."

"What's to talk about? That's what Sam's is for." Bessie May nibbled on a piece of bacon. "Sam's caters all the big weddings round here. Everyone knows that."

"But what if I don't *want* Sam's to cater?" Crystal's words came out as a hoarse whisper.

All of the ladies turned—almost in slow motion—to look at her. I could tell from the dropped jaws that her question had stopped them in their tracks.

"But honey, you *have* to let Sam's cater." The piece of bacon slipped through Bessie May's fingers and landed on the table. "That's just how it's *done* in Fairfield."

The women bored a hole through Crystal with their stares. I sent up a silent prayer that she would remain courageous in the heat of the battle.

"I know that's how it's been done in the past, but what if I want somethin' *dif*-ferent?" Crystal's words sounded strained at best.

"Oh, I see where you're going with this!" Queenie clapped her hands together and grinned. "You're suggesting the WOP-pers band together and cook for the big day? Because I think that might be doable, as long as the recipes are workable."

The conversation shifted to recipes, but I could tell from the expression on Crystal's face that the ladies had once again missed the point.

"No, I'm not saying that either." Crystal looked exasperated. "Jasper and I went to the yummiest little café in Corsicana. They have the best Southern foods ever. I talked to the owner and she's very excited about the possibility of catering our big day. And she's so reasonable too."

"I don't believe it." Bessie May paled. "I really don't believe it. You're planning to just do this whole thing your way, even if it flies in the face of how things should be done? Is that it?"

At this point, Joni rose and picked up her plate.

She gripped it so tight I thought she just might break it. "Now look, ladies. Just because things have always been done a certain way doesn't mean it's the only way." She set the plate on the kitchen counter. "I mean, Casey and I eloped. We didn't get married the usual way. But it was right for us."

"You put a *knife* in your poor mother-in-law's heart." Ophelia wagged a finger in Joni's face. "She may *never* recover. If this is your version of doing what's right, then you have a lot to learn, girlie."

Poor Joni. Her face shifted from its usual color to pink to bright, bright red. Rooster red, actually. No, barn red. Yikes. I'd never seen her this angry before.

Yep. Looked like our good-natured wedding planner was about to blow, and I'd be a firsthand witness.

"Oh dear." Alva's eyes widened. She grabbed another muffin and took a big bite, then leaned back in her chair. "Oh, oh dear."

Just as quickly, Joni's eyes fluttered shut, and I could see her mouth the words, "One, two, three, four, five," and so on, all the way to twenty. When she reached twenty, her eyes popped open, and she gave Ophelia a strained smile and said, "Well now, where were we again? Oh yes. We were talking about how Crystal is getting married and is going to have a Southern ceremony that will be the most brilliant event anyone's ever attended. Cake's taken care of." She sat back down at the kitchen table and put a check mark on her paper. "Food's covered." Another check mark. "Now, let's talk décor. Bessie May, I understand you have quite a few items at the historical society that date back to the Civil War era. Would you perhaps be willing to loan some of your lovely things to Crystal for her big day?"

This seemed to get Bessie May calmed down. Interested, even.

Out of the corner of my eye I watched as Crystal breathed a sigh of relief.

Until Prissy interrupted. "Now, Crystal, I hear what you're saying about the food and cake and such, but you really must let me make your punch. I make the punch for all of the weddings in Fairfield."

She made the punch, all right. At my grandmother's wedding, she'd tossed in a few extra ingredients—like prune juice.

Never. Again.

Crystal turned to face her with a confident smile, unforgettable warmth in her eyes. "Well, to be honest, Prissy, we're talking about having peach tea instead of a traditional punch. And the caterer is providin' it. Isn't that just *luv*-lee?"

"Humph." Prissy took a swig from her coffee cup and leaned back in her chair.

"Mmm. I love peach tea." Alva wiped the

crumbs off her fingers with a napkin. "Perfect choice, and very Southern. Fits the theme!"

"Exactly!" Crystal gave a little shrug. "And that's the idea."

We somehow made it through the rest of the meeting, though I had a feeling it might be a while before Ophelia recovered. Queenie seemed to take it all in stride, even stepping in a time or two to calm the waters, but the real pro—the real champ—was Crystal. She somehow managed to keep on course. She got her way without coming across as bossy or rude. Truly, a stellar performance by a bona fide Southern belle.

Looked like I had a lot to learn from her.

5
She's a Butterfly

Living is like tearing through a museum. Not until later do you really start absorbing what you saw, thinking about it, looking it up in a book, and remembering—because you can't take it in all at once.

Audrey Hepburn

When we wrapped up the meeting, the ladies all headed off their separate ways. Joni lingered, but she still looked a bit shell-shocked from the whole thing. I joined her at the table to offer both my condolences and my congratulations. I started the conversation with a quiet, "You okay over there?"

She glanced my way, eyes wide. "Wow. Just . . . wow."

"Tell me about it." Crystal joined us, taking a seat to my right. "That was gruelin', if I do say so myself."

"The whole thing kind of reminded me of a church board meeting." Queenie plopped down in a chair. "And I've never been a fan of board meetings. Too many folks trying to get their way. Pure selfishness."

I reached over and patted Crystal's hand. "Well, I for one am very proud of you, Crystal. Not just proud—astounded. In your own sweet way you managed to get what you wanted while still including the women. I need to learn from you, oh wise one."

She laughed. "Oh, Katie, it wasn't easy, but this day means everything to me. It's mine. And yours is yours. I'm not strong or demanding, but this is my weddin'. My *wed*-din'!"

"And you deserve to have whatever you want, for your big day and beyond. Which reminds me, have you two decided where you're going on your honeymoon?"

"Home to Atlanta, of course." She clasped her hands together. "Oh, I can't wait to show off my hometown to Jasper. He's gonna love it there. I'm gonna take him to see Tara. The real one, I mean."

"You know that's a fictional location, right?" Joni asked. "It doesn't really exist."

"Neither does Scarlett O'Hara," I echoed.

Crystal giggled. "So they tell me. But she's as real as real can be to me. Anyway, there's a museum that pays homage to Tara and I just *luv* it there. Jasper will too. And a'course I want to show him the house where I grew up."

"Just promise you won't talk him into moving away," Queenie said. "I don't think my heart could take it if another one of my grandkids moved across the country." She fixed her gaze squarely on me.

"Queenie, really? I live in Dallas. It's an hour away, not halfway across the country."

"Might as well be when you're my age. I don't drive much these days, in case you haven't noticed."

"Isn't it nice, then, that I come home so often?" I put my hands on my hips. Honestly? Had she been talking to Mama about this? Were they both out to make me feel bad for living in Dallas?

"I can assure you, Jasper and I aren't going anywhere." Crystal offered Queenie a confident nod. "We want to stay put in Fairfield and run the store. Now that we have the Fisher family home, we want to raise our children there. It'll be so lovely, just like a story from a book." A little sigh followed her words.

This served to calm Queenie down, thank goodness.

"Have a wonderful time in Atlanta, honey," my grandmother said. "Glad you're able to show Jasper the town you love."

"I can't wait," Crystal said. "But we have to get married first."

"Speaking of weddings . . ." I turned my attention to Joni. "Tell me about your big day. I want to hear every detail! And you"—I pointed my finger at Crystal—"have some 'splainin' to do, young lady. Why didn't you tell me you'd lost your roommate when we were talking about Joni earlier?"

"Didn't figure it was my place. And I didn't fib, honey. I just said I couldn't have asked for a better roommate." Crystal giggled. "Now, Joni, fill her in on your big day."

"I can still hardly believe it myself." Joni sighed and a faraway look came over her. "We flew down to Grand Cayman—George Town—and got married on the beach. The water was the most beautiful shade of turquoise you've ever seen, and the sand was so white. And Casey looked so adorable. I wore a really soft, flowy sundress, one I bought in a little shop down there. I felt like a princess."

"Aww!" Crystal and I sighed in unison.

Joni's eyes sparkled. "Such a crazy, impulsive way to tie the knot, but I'm not sorry we did it. When you know something's right, you just go for it."

"I understand completely. I feel like my whole relationship with Brady was ordained from the very beginning."

"It's been a whirlwind," Joni said. "We're still living in my parents' house while they're away doing missions work."

"And I still have a room there." Crystal laughed. "Awkward."

"Well, it's not for long," Joni reminded her. "Anyway, I'm still working as a wedding planner, only now I'm working out of my home. It's been good, because I'm not limited to just the Baptist church. You know? I've been thinking of putting together a list of potential vendors too—everything from photographers to videographers."

"A real wedding planning service, then." I nodded. "Next thing you know, you'll be talking about opening a wedding facility."

"Well, it's funny you should say that. My parents' property is huge—sixty-three acres of prime ranch land. And they've got that amazing old barn out there. I've often thought about converting it."

"Sounds dreamy. Maybe you should tell Twiggy. I have a feeling she wants to have a good old-fashioned Texas wedding. Ranch land would be perfect."

"Ooh, maybe she and Beau can be my first customers. If he proposes, I mean."

"He'll propose," Crystal, Queenie, and I said in unison.

At that point the conversation shifted. Before long we were all smiles. Until Joni asked me how my own wedding plans were going.

"Chaotic," I admitted. "Things are a little awkward with my future mother-in-law, who also happens to be my boss."

"You're kidding." Joni took a sip from her tea glass and settled back in her chair. "Why?"

"Because she got a little heavy-handed with her

ideas for the wedding. I just feel like I'm walking on eggshells when I'm around her now. I don't know what to say when she starts dumping all of her ideas on me about the Gaylord Hotel."

"Ooh, great place." Crystal sighed. "Oops. Sorry, Katie. *Not* saying you should get married there. I'm not."

"It's okay. It *is* a great place. And she has a point. Everyone has a point."

"Tell me about it." Crystal rolled her eyes.

"I'd say I'm tempted to run away from my job and come home to Fairfield, but today's drama put an end to that idea." A nervous laugh escaped as I voiced my thoughts.

"You're not really thinking of coming back, are you?" Crystal looked intrigued by this notion. "I mean, Brady wants to live in Dallas, right?"

"Oh, I didn't mean I'd really do it. I just thought about it for a minute. Then the minute passed and reality set in. I love my life in Dallas. It's different, but I love it. If you don't count the part where my future mother-in-law suddenly wants to play puppeteer."

"I'm so sorry." Crystal nodded. If anyone understood my dilemma, she did.

Joni offered to drive Crystal back to the hardware store, which left me alone with my thoughts. I decided to sneak into my guest bedroom and give Brady a call. I put the phone on speaker so I could look through a bridal magazine I'd brought with me.

Brady's voice came on the line. "Hey, you. How did the get-together go? Crystal and Jasper's wedding all planned out?"

"Don't ask. Let's just say my heart goes out to Crystal, and to me too. Those ladies are something else."

"How so?" he asked.

"I'll fill you in when I get back. One thing's sure and certain: they're not going to make it easy on us. Just about the time I think I've got a workable plan in my head, I begin to imagine what the WOP-pers will say about it." I didn't mean to sigh, but there it was. "I have so many fun ideas . . . but I'm sure they'll all come under debate."

"Ah."

"Mostly I'm just worried about your mom. I don't want to hurt her feelings, but I want to get married here, in Fairfield. Is that so wrong?" I couldn't quite finish my thoughts.

"Of course not, and she knows that I want you to be happy."

"So, you just want to get married at my church to make me happy? That's it? If you got to choose, you wouldn't go that route?"

"How in the world did you get all of that out of what I just said?" Brady groaned, and I could almost picture him slapping himself on the forehead. "I feel like I can't win for losing here."

"Now you know what I feel like." I plopped down on the bed and leaned back on the pillows. "I'm doomed."

"You're not doomed. You're just overwhelmed."

I shook my head. As if he could see that. "No, I'm doomed. Doomed if I do and doomed if I don't."

"I don't think that's exactly how the expression goes, Katie."

"I know, but you get the point. If we get married there, my parents will flip. If we get married in Fairfield, your mom and all of my bridesmaids will flip."

"Which leads me back to my earlier idea of eloping in Hawaii."

"It would be great, but we would regret it later. Ask me how I know."

"How do you know?"

"Because Joni and Casey just did that."

"What?" This seemed to stop him cold. "They did what?"

"Flew to the Cayman Islands and eloped. They just got back. And you'd think they'd committed murder, based on how mad everyone is about it, so trust me, we can't elope."

"Well, all right."

"I want the people I love gathered around me. I just don't want them armed with shotguns, ready to take each other down because they're mad over our decision one way or the other."

"I'm having a hard time picturing my mother with a shotgun." Brady laughed.

"You know what I mean. We don't want to start off our life together with our families hating each other. Can you imagine?"

"And again I say, we need to do what works for us, not them."

A little knock on the door sounded and Alva walked in. "Yoo-hoo. Do you mind if I come in a minute? Queenie wants me to grab a couple of the old photos from that drawer there." She pointed to the oak dresser.

"Sure." I gave her a nod and she walked across the room.

Brady's voice sounded from the speakerphone. "You're the bride. Do what you like."

"As if." I paused as my emotions kicked in. "I want to come up with my own plans, but I can't seem to think straight. Have you ever been so overwhelmed, so confused, that nothing made sense?"

"Oh yes," Alva said. "More times than I can count." She rooted through the drawer, making a lot of racket.

"One time in the middle of a game against the Rockets," Brady said, "we were in the fourth quarter and the coach asked me to run a long shot from the outside. Didn't make a lick of sense to me. I thought for sure he would've asked for something more straightforward. Why a long shot? But it turned out he was right. I ran that ball all the way to the opposite end of the court, just outside the arc, then aimed, fired, and landed a three-point shot. We won the game."

"Really? You're comparing this situation to a basketball game?" I groaned.

"Hey, it ended well. Did you hear the part about the three-point shot?"

"I'm sorry, what were we talking about?" Alva turned my way, arms loaded down with photo albums. "You scored a three-point shot, Katie Sue?"

"No, I was just saying that I'm confused, Aunt Alva."

"About basketball?" Alva nearly dropped one of the books. "I didn't know you ever played the game, honey. Was this in high school? Of course, I didn't really know you back then, which might explain why I never knew." She held tight to the albums. "Though, I'm a little surprised, to be honest. You're rather petite for basketball."

"No." I slapped myself on the head.

"No, you're not petite? I'd say you're only five feet three at best. That's petite in my book."

"I'm not saying I'm not petite. I was just telling Brady that I'm overwhelmed and confused. That's all."

"Brady?" She looked around the room as if

expecting him to materialize. "Brady's with us?"

"I'm with you, Alva." His voice came through the phone's speaker again. "I'm right here."

She looked around again, then shook her head. "Boy, you think you're confused, Katie Sue . . . imagine being me. One minute I think I'm living with my niece who works at a bridal salon, the next I find out she's a basketball player. And her fiancé is invisible."

At this point, Brady busted out laughing.

"Sure. Go ahead and laugh," I said. "This is all very funny."

"I'm not laughing at you, honey." My aunt patted me on the knee. "If the team was counting on me to make a three-point shot, I'd be overwhelmed too."

"There's no way to redeem this, is there?" I sighed.

"We could start over," Brady said, "but I'm not sure it would have a different outcome, if you catch my meaning."

I caught his meaning, all right.

"I'm just telling you to keep your eye on the basket," Auntie said. "You won't land the shot if you lose your focus. Don't let anyone pull you off course."

"Okay, okay."

We somehow managed to get the conversation back under control, but I couldn't stop thinking about the basketball analogy. Really? "Keep your eye on the basket"? Was that the best I could get, some silly sports analogy?

I headed back out to look through photo albums with my grandmother and my aunt, who couldn't quite seem to figure out why there were no photos of me playing basketball. I did my best to smooth that one over.

Pap-Paul arrived home from his fishing trip midafternoon and greeted us with an open, friendly smile. "How'd the meeting go?" he asked.

Queenie's abrupt "Don't ask" left him shaking his head.

An early dinner at Sam's was followed by an evening of playing Skip-Bo with my aunt, my grandmother, and Pap-Paul. Those sweet moments almost made up for the craziness of the morning.

About midway into the game, my grandmother gazed at me with tenderness and tears in her eyes.

"You okay?" I asked.

"Just thinking . . . about the things we can control and the things we can't."

"Oh?" I put my cards down to focus on her.

"Attitudes?" Queenie shuffled the cards in her hand. "Totally controllable. Making plans for your own wedding? Controllable . . . if you have courage."

"What aren't you saying, Queenie?" Alva asked. "Are you beating around the bush on purpose?"

"I'm saying that life already presents enough

situations where you lose control. So you need to hang on to the reins when you have the opportunity. Don't give them away to anyone." She put the cards down on the table. "Take this situation with my knee. I couldn't control the fact that it started giving out on me. I can't control the fact that I'm getting older, losing some mobility. I mean, I can do everything in my power to slow that down, but I can't stop it. There are simply things in this life that we can't control. But, that said, there are plenty of things we can. So when I see someone handing off the reins to others unnecessarily, I want to say, 'Don't do it! This isn't one of those uncontrollable situations.'"

"Handing off the reins." I sighed. "Okay, I get it."

My grandmother swiped at her eyes with the back of her hand. "When I got sick last year—when I had that episode with my heart—I had to admit that I'd lost control, at least for a while. And when the surgeon put in this titanium knee, I couldn't do much except trust that I'd eventually walk again."

"Like Brady, after his surgeries." A lump rose in my throat.

"Exactly. And let me tell you, there's nothing more frustrating than sitting and waiting for your situation to change. It's a helpless feeling, losing control." She looked at me so intently that I felt her emotions grab hold of me. "So promise me you won't give it up willingly. Unless God speaks directly to your heart, I mean. If he's telling you to do this or that, then do it. But don't bow to the whims of people just because you're afraid of what they'll think. Before long you'll lose control completely, and then the person you'll be most upset with is yourself."

"Wow, Queenie." I considered the wisdom of her words. "You've given me a lot to chew on."

"Speaking of something to chew on, are there any of those muffins left?" Alva pushed her chair back and stood. "All this talk about losing control is making me hungry."

I thought about my grandmother's words further as we continued the game. I couldn't help but think of Brady and what he'd been through over the past year. How awful it must've been to lose control—of his pro basketball career, his ability to walk, his income. Those two surgeries on his knee had done a number on him physically, but they'd also affected him mentally and emotionally. How good of Queenie to put this in perspective for me. I wouldn't let go of the reins. It would take courage, but I wouldn't let go.

Around nine o'clock Alva was ready to hit the hay. She headed off to the guest bedroom while my grandparents and I continued to chat.

Another hour went by before an idea hit. "Hey, would you guys like to see my wedding gown?"

Queenie looked perplexed by this. "I see it all the time in the cedar closet, honey."

"No, would you like to see it on me? In person, I mean. I know you saw a picture of it on the cover of *Texas Bride*. But I've been itching to try it on again."

"That would be lovely, Katie Sue." She shifted her position on the sofa and attempted to stand. From the expression of pain in her eyes, I could tell her joints were bothering her.

"Don't get up, Queenie. I think I can manage."

"Really? Won't you need me to zip it up?"

"I'll call you when I'm ready. It'll take a while."

And it did. I managed to get into the petticoat and then eased my way into the gown, which smelled a little cedar-ish. I'd have to take it out of this closet and return it to Aunt Alva's place before long.

Speaking of Alva, about the time I got the dress on, she walked down the hallway toward the bathroom.

"Ooh!" She clamped a hand over her mouth. "I missed your wedding?"

"No, Aunt Alva." I bit back a giggle. "Just trying on the dress to show Queenie and Pap-Paul."

"Well, I dozed off and was dreaming of weddings, so maybe I'm a bit confused. My bladder woke me up. Poor old lazy bladder." She put her hand on her tummy. "But you look lovely, honey."

"Could you zip me up?"

"Well, sure." She bounced up and down a bit to hold her bladder in check while she zipped my gown. Then she gave me the sweetest look. "You look terrific, honey. I'm sure a basketball uniform wouldn't even come close to this."

"Thanks, Alva. Now, don't let me keep you." I pointed to the bathroom and she headed toward it, a spring in her step.

I made my way down the hall, practicing my bridal walk. What would it be like, I wondered, to walk the aisle on my father's arm, headed straight toward Brady? I could hardly wait!

When I arrived in the living room, I found Queenie half asleep on the sofa. Pap-Paul had gone missing.

"Queenie?" I said, and she stirred and slowly came awake.

When she laid eyes on me, Queenie let out a squeal. "Oh, honey. Oh . . . oh . . ." Her tone elevated, and she angled her head toward the kitchen. "Paul, get in here and look at this gorgeous granddaughter of mine in her wedding dress!"

Seconds later Pap-Paul stood in the open doorway with a teacup in his hand, giving me an admiring look. "Wow, Katie. You look . . ." He shook his head and his eyes brimmed with affectionate tears. "You look . . ."

"Like the cover of a magazine?" I said and laughed.

"Well, that too, but I was going to say you look like every groom's dream bride and every daddy's little girl all grown up."

Quite flattering, coming from a man who'd only been my grandfather for a matter of months. I had to give it to him, he really knew how to make a bride-to-be feel good about herself.

I walked over to the mirror above the mantel and stared at my reflection. I couldn't fully see the dress, what with the mirror being so high and all, but I saw enough to make my heart want to burst into song. Queenie pushed herself to a standing position and walked over to me. She stopped just beside me and we stood side by side, looking into the mirror.

"Remember when you used to hate your freckles?" Queenie spoke to my reflection. "I'll never forget that time I caught you with a jar of pickle juice. You were rubbing it on your face."

"Queenie! I was hoping you'd forget all about that."

"Forget? My house reeked of pickles for hours." Her gentle laugh rippled through the air.

"Pickle juice?" Pap-Paul asked from the other

side of the room. "Must be some beauty treatment I've never heard of."

"Not really." I laughed. "The crazy part was, I had the wrong kind of juice. It was supposed to be lemon juice. Don't ask how I got them mixed up. Just young and foolish, I guess. Desperate to get rid of those freckles."

"Why?" Queenie asked as she turned to face me. She brushed my loose hair off my shoulder. "I never understood why you wanted to change yourself. Those freckles are an asset, girl. Trust me. They're not just adorable, they're what make you . . . you."

"Aw, thank you." I turned back to look in the mirror and tried to imagine the freckles as assets.

"Do you know what girls would give to have your gorgeous blonde hair?" Queenie ran her fingers through my messy locks. "And naturally blonde to boot."

"Thanks." I pivoted on my heels to face both of my grandparents. "You two sure know how to make me forget about my woes and focus on the good."

"There's plenty to focus on," my grandfather said. "Look for it. It's there."

"I'm trying." I felt my shoulders slump as I thought about all of the decisions yet to be made. Suddenly I felt weary.

Queenie reached over and put her knobby index finger under my chin, then lifted it, putting the two of us eye to eye. "I know you're inundated with advice right now, Katie Sue, and I don't want to add to your dilemma. Just a word of advice, if you please."

"Of course." I ran my fingers along the skirt's fabric, loving the way it felt.

"Planning a wedding is a little bit like looking in the mirror. The reflection looking back at you is yours. Don't change it to make other people happy. Just be yourself. When it comes to planning your big day, I don't want a repeat of what happened this morning. I'll make it plain to the WOP-pers that times are changing. Just because we've always done things one way doesn't mean it's the only way. I for one am glad Crystal spoke up."

"Oh, Queenie!" I threw my arms around her neck. "Thank you so much."

"You're welcome," she said. "Now, that's not to say you should get married in Dallas. Don't let those folks at the bridal shop talk you into that, okay?"

"Okay. I'll get married right here. And it will be a day everyone will remember for years to come."

"That's sweet, honey," she said. "But more than anything, I want you to make sure it's a day the bride and groom will remember for years to come. Promise?"

"I promise." I gave her a tender kiss on the cheek. Suddenly I couldn't wait to talk to Brady, to put together a solid plan.

6

Cry on the Shoulder of the Road

Let's face it, a nice creamy chocolate cake does a lot for a lot of people; it does for me.
Audrey Hepburn

Alva and I spent Saturday night at Queenie's place. The following morning we attended the early service at the Baptist church. I would've preferred the second, more contemporary service, with Levi Nash and Joni leading worship, but I knew my aunt wouldn't be as pleased. Not that I really minded.

This church still captivated me. The size of the sanctuary might not be as impressive as other churches in the area, nor were the stained-glass windows as elaborate as the ones the Methodists boasted. The pews were chipped and worn, especially on the armrests, and the sanctuary walls needed a fresh coat of paint. But no one could deny the feelings that swept over me as I entered these hallowed halls. Perhaps it had more to do with the many Sundays I'd spent here in worship, singing alongside people I loved. Listening to messages that pricked my heart. Marching up the aisle toward the pastor to declare my faith publicly. I hoped those memories would never fade.

Once the early service finished, I stopped off at the ladies' room before heading out. As I walked the hallway beyond the classrooms, I couldn't help but reminisce. These were the same rooms where I'd been taught the names of the twelve disciples and where I'd memorized the books of the Bible. The rooms where I'd learned to pray aloud and share my faith with others. Beyond the classrooms, I passed the fellowship hall. If I closed my eyes right now, I could picture at least forty or fifty potluck dinners I'd attended in that room over the years. Okay, sixty or seventy, but who was counting? I'd eaten my first piece of pecan pie in that room. I'd also pleaded with Mama to let me attend my first boy-girl party in that room and had cried buckets of tears when she'd insisted I wasn't old enough.

Yes, this church certainly held pieces of my heart, and I could hardly wait to get married here. But first I had to get back home—Dallas—and come up with a plan for the big day.

Minutes after we left Fairfield, Alva dozed off, her snores sounding rather musical. As I pulled up to a stoplight, I glanced over at my aunt. Her petite frame didn't take up much space in the passenger seat. As she gently snored, I found myself captivated by her hands. Tissue-paper skin, wrinkled and soft, stretched across knobby joints, revealing exaggerated veins. My gaze shifted to her face. Alva's makeup had been applied with a loopy hand, leaving her cheeks a bit pinker than one would expect. And the eyeliner job proved a bit cockeyed too. What she lacked in makeup technique, however, my aunt more than made up for in personality.

Behind me, a car horn beeped and I realized my light had turned green. Better step on it. I needed to get back home and spend some time with Brady. Surely we could put together a plan, if we put our minds to it.

Plans. Hmm.

I spent several minutes in inner turmoil. Despite my grandmother's words the night before, I couldn't help but wonder if my wedding plans—should I ever come up with any solid ones—would come under fire by the WOP-pers, my parents, and/or my future mother-in-law. Why did wedding planning have to be so complicated?

I spent the next several minutes pondering my situation. Just about the time we reached Waxahachie, my aunt startled awake. "Ooh, potty break required! Pull over quickly, if you please."

"There's a Dairy Queen at the next exit, Aunt Alva."

She shifted her position and then grimaced. "I do love their ice cream. Might just have to get a cone." She yawned and looked my way. "You know, I had the funniest dream. It was about you. I dreamed you played basketball. Isn't that the silliest thing ever?"

"Definitely. I'm only five feet two, you know."

"That's what I told you in my dream." She giggled. "There was more to it than that, but I'll fill you in later. Right now I just need to hit the ladies' room. Pull off quickly, please and thank you."

We stopped at Dairy Queen, where Alva visited the ladies' room, and then we both chowed down on Oreo Blizzards. I couldn't help but think of my ex-boyfriend as I swallowed spoonful after spoonful of the yummy stuff. As a teenager, I'd just known Casey and I would get married in our local church. It would be a simple, sweet ceremony with a traditional but lovely reception in the fellowship hall. That's how everyone in Fairfield did it . . . mostly, anyway. Only, now Casey was married to Joni and Crystal was having a *Gone with the Wind* wedding and my future mother-in-law wanted me to get married in Dallas and Twiggy wanted a full-out Texas cowboy–themed cake.

Life had been much simpler when I was a teenager. I wouldn't mind riding off into the sunset with Brady right about now, just to avoid all of the drama.

Oh, but when I thought of my precious fiancé, when I pondered our life together, I realized that all of the ups and downs of planning for our big day would be worth it in the end.

"Keep your eye on the basket." As I spoke the words aloud, they sank deep into my heart. In that moment, clear as day, I saw Brady at the end of the court, arms outstretched. I pictured myself running straight into those arms, our happily ever after a slam dunk.

"Still thinking about your basketball days, Katie?" Alva looked my way as she swallowed the last of her Blizzard.

"I guess you could say that." I wiped my hands on a napkin and tossed my cup in the trash can to my right. "Thinking about life in Fairfield. And I've been giving a lot of thought to Jasper this weekend too."

"What about him? He play basketball too?"

"Well, yes, but I'm not thinking of anything sports related. Just thinking about the fact that he'll be married. Soon. At our home church. It's just so ironic. We always thought he'd move away from home to someplace like Houston, but he's stayed put in Fairfield. And my parents, who were always such homebodies, are off gallivanting around the country in their RV."

"Technically it's a fifth wheel, not an RV."

"I know, I know. I guess my point is, life doesn't always turn out like you think."

"Right. It doesn't." My aunt licked the remaining ice cream off her spoon and then waggled it in my direction. "Sometimes it turns out better."

"True, that." I took her empty cup and spoon

and tossed them in the trash. "Ready to get back on the road?"

"Ready as I'll ever be. Can't wait to get back home for a long nap."

No doubt she'd be snoozing within five minutes of being in the car, but I didn't mention that. I led the way back to my vehicle and climbed inside, only to discover a call coming through. I startled when Lori-Lou's husband came on the line.

"Katie, where are you?" Josh sounded anxious. "You didn't answer my texts."

"On my way back from Fairfield. I didn't realize I'd missed any text messages. What's up?"

"Izzy is coming."

For a second I thought I'd heard wrong. "W-what? Is this a joke?"

"No, I'm not kidding. The baby's on her way—today. Right now. Lori-Lou's at four centimeters and this is our fourth baby, so it won't take long, I'm sure. I started texting you at eleven, when we left the house for the hospital. When I didn't hear back, I just kept trying."

"Oh. My. Goodness!" I turned the key in the ignition and looked around to make sure I was clear to back out, then eased back onto the highway. "I'm so sorry! I never heard the texts come through. Please forgive me. What should I do? Can I come up there?"

"Yes, please. I'm going to need help with the other kids. Do you think Brady might come too?"

"I'm not with Brady, but Alva's right here. We'll come together."

"I'm . . . where am I?" Alva stirred and then promptly fell back asleep.

Josh disappeared for a minute and I could hear him fussing at one of the kids. When he returned, his words sounded rushed. "Okay. We can use all the help we can get, so rally the troops to help with the kids, if you can. Maybe you could call Brady to meet you here?"

"I can."

I phoned him the minute I hung up with Josh. He agreed to head up to the hospital right away.

"Stay calm, Katie."

"I will. I'm just mad at myself for missing his texts. My cousin went into labor without me."

"Nothing would be any different if you'd been there."

Those words sounded ridiculous to my ears. "Of course it would have! Josh is there alone with their three kids, and you know how they are."

"I'm guessing he's not alone. Surely Lori-Lou's mom is there. And her dad."

"Maybe. I forgot to ask. They live in Arkansas, so it's more likely they're not in the Dallas area yet. Probably on the road. Like me." I glanced at the clock. "Lori-Lou was at four centimeters and this is baby number four."

"I have no idea what that means, but don't take

off driving faster just because you're anxious. Promise?"

"Okay, okay." I glanced down at the speedometer. Yikes. Seventy-six in a seventy. I should ease up a bit. Better to get there alive than to cause an accident along the way.

We ended the call and I prayed for my cousin as I drove. All of my wedding planning woes now paled in comparison to what was taking place in her life.

I arrived at the hospital an hour later and dropped Aunt Alva off at the door. A couple of minutes later I found a parking spot, texted Brady, and then sprinted toward the door. By the time I got there, he was standing next to Alva, who still looked a bit groggy and confused.

I gave my sweetie a quick hug, and we all raced inside and followed the signs to the maternity floor. We located Eduardo in the labor and delivery waiting room with Lori-Lou's three rambunctious children playing at his feet.

"Lori-Lou's parents aren't here yet?" I asked.

Eduardo shook his head. "No. I think they're still about an hour away. Hope they make it in time. Just got here myself."

"It was so good of you to come." Alva plopped down in the chair next to him. "I can always count on you."

Eduardo leaned over and gave my aunt a kiss on the cheek. "Mmm. You smell like roses."

Stains of scarlet appeared on her soft, wrinkly cheeks, making them more youthful in appearance.

"Any word on Lori-Lou?" I asked. "How is she?"

"Seven and a half centimeters. Baby's coming soon. Josh said to send you and Alva back as soon as you arrived. They're in room 331—that way." He pointed through the double doors.

My nerves kicked in. "You're sure it's okay for me to go in there?"

Eduardo nodded. "Josh says she's an old pro at this, and she won't mind a little company. Those are his words, not mine, in case anyone's wondering."

"You guys okay to watch the kids?" I looked back and forth between Brady and Eduardo.

"Are you kidding?" Brady scooped up Gilly and began to tickle her until she squealed with glee. "We've got this."

By now Alva had already trotted off in the direction of the patients' rooms. I tagged along behind her, coming to a stop at room 331.

"Okay, this is it." I tugged at the collar of my sweater, suddenly feeling a little warm.

"Knock-knock!" Alva's cheery voice rang out as she tapped on the door.

From inside I heard panting. At least, it sounded like panting.

I peeked inside and saw my cousin seated on the bed with her husband standing next to her.

"Okay to come in?" I asked.

"Sure. C'mon in and—ow, ow, ow!" Lori-Lou's face turned red. After several seconds of panting with her eyes squeezed shut, she looked Josh's way. "How. Long. Was. That. One?"

"Forty-seven seconds. Sorry, honey."

My cousin released a long breath and her face returned to its normal color. "This little girl had better be well behaved once she arrives. She's putting me through more grief than all the others rolled into one."

That didn't sound good, especially when one considered how precocious her other three children were. I hoped this wasn't a sign of things to come.

"We just wanted to stick our heads in the door to say hello." I gave her a little wave. "We won't stay."

"Definitely not." Aunt Alva fanned herself and her face grew pale. After a few seconds she sputtered, "Well, have a nice delivery, you two," then turned on her heels and took off out the door.

"Chicken," Lori-Lou called out.

"You have to give it to her," I said. "She's fast on her feet. Not bad, considering her age."

Lori-Lou's glare seemed laser hot as she looked my way. "You'd. Better. Stay! I can't do this by myself!"

Okay then. She couldn't do this by herself. I took a couple of steps toward her, arriving at her bedside just in time for the blood pressure cuff to activate.

"This stupid thing!" She tugged at it and then started panting again as another contraction hit. Oh boy. I needed to escape from this room—and quick!

7

I Just Call You Mine

If I get married, I want to be very married.
Audrey Hepburn

I'd no sooner started planning my escape route than the nurse arrived. She took one look at my cousin's blood pressure results—173/96—and pushed me out the door, claiming Lori-Lou needed to calm down.

She didn't have to tell me twice. I left in a hurry, promising my cousin that I'd pray for a safe and healthy delivery. As Alva and I made our way back to the waiting room, anxiety kicked in.

"Do you think she's going to be okay, Auntie?"

"Sure." With a wave of her hand, Aunt Alva appeared to dismiss my concerns. "She's done this a time or two."

"Yeah. I'm sure you're right." Only, I wasn't so sure, to be honest. Fear gripped my heart as I thought about my cousin's elevated blood pressure.

We headed down the hall and I did my best to calm my stomach. I'd always hated the smell of hospitals. We arrived back in the waiting room to find the kids playing tag and the two guys engrossed in a conversation about basketball.

Go figure. Gilly asked to play on Alva's phone and she handed it to her, no questions asked.

"You sure that's safe?" I asked.

"Yeah." Alva took a seat next to Eduardo once again. "Josh showed me how to download some of those app things the kids like. You'd be surprised at how many minutes of peace I can get in a day just by passing off my phone."

"But what if she calls Australia or something?"

"Hmm." My aunt appeared to consider that. "Hadn't thought of that, to be honest. If she does, I guess it'd be cheaper than reimbursing the hospital for any furniture they might break by running around the waiting room like animals."

"Good point." I settled into a chair next to Brady, my thoughts in a whirl.

I'd just started to say, "Pray for Lori-Lou and the baby," when Brady's cell phone rang. He glanced at the screen and then rose and took the call. With all of the chaos from the kids, I couldn't quite tell who he was talking to, but from the look on his face, it involved me. Sure enough, a few minutes later he ended the call, shoved the phone in his pocket, and headed my way.

"Well, she did it."

"Who? Did what?"

"Mom." Brady took a seat. "She contacted a travel agent to talk about booking our honeymoon. To Bali. She wanted to know if we'd settled on a date."

"Did you tell her we're still talking about that?"

"Yep. Just told her late summer."

"Ooh, Bali!" My aunt let out a squeal. "Just like in that song from South Pacific!" She started to sing "Bali Hai" in a rather off-key voice. Eduardo joined her, his pitch near perfect. At the end of the song, they received applause from others in the waiting area.

This proved to be the perfect distraction. I turned my full attention to Brady, my voice lowered to a whisper. "Are you serious?"

"Yep," he responded in low tones. "I hope you're okay with the tropics, because we're going to have ten days in a luxury suite over the water. I can't even imagine what that'll cost her. Probably ten or twelve wedding dresses. Or more."

"Wow. Just . . . wow."

I had to wonder about the cost too. But I wondered something else as well. Now that she'd made this decision, did we owe her? Would I end up paying in ways other than financial? Did this solidify my attachment to her plans for my wedding? Ugh.

"I know what you're thinking." Brady reached for my hand and gave it a squeeze. "And the answer is no."

"Really?"

"You aren't stuck with her ideas for the wedding just because she's doing this for us. That's not how it works."

"Wow, you're good."

"Well, it's a logical conclusion to draw. She does something amazing for us and we feel like there are strings attached."

"But there aren't. Right?"

"Right." He paused. "I think. I mean, I know. She's my mom. She wouldn't do that. I really believe she wants to bless us, no matter where we end up having our wedding."

"That's great, Brady, because Bali sounds amazing. I looked it up online and couldn't believe it. I've never seen anything more beautiful in my life." In that moment reality hit. Soon we would be together, just the two of us, in the tropics. On our honeymoon. Alone. Away from the chaos. Away from the customers at the store. Away from people trying to tell us what to do and when to do it. Away from—

"She's at ten centimeters and pushing!" Josh's excited cry pulled me from my ponderings. I looked up to see him standing next to my aunt, his eyes wide.

"Well, for the love of all that's holy, what are you doing out here in the lobby?" Alva asked. "Get in there to your wife."

Josh nodded. "I am, but since her mom's not here yet, she's asking for Katie."

"K-K-Katie?" I managed.

"That's you, honey." Alva gave me a little wink. "Now, get in there and help her birth this baby."

Oh. Help.

Josh gestured for me to join him. "The nurse says it's okay. But we have to hurry."

"M-m-me?" I'd never witnessed a birth before and wasn't sure this was the day to start. Still, how could I say no?

To my right, Alva startled as her phone rang. She glanced at it, then back up at me. "Queenie. Probably checking in to see how Lori-Lou is doing. You go on back there, Katie, and text me if you can, so I can keep her updated."

"O-okay."

As I took a few steps away, Alva took the call from my grandmother. Unfortunately the volume was turned up so high on my aunt's phone that everyone in the place could hear their conversation. Typical.

I did my best to keep up with Josh as he sprinted down the hallway toward Lori-Lou's room, then followed his lead as he used the hand sanitizer before entering. We pressed our way inside, and my eyes grew wide as I saw Lori-Lou, feet in stirrups, already pushing. Turned out she didn't just want me there for social purposes.

"You . . . pray!" She pointed at me and then started huffing and puffing again.

"Her blood pressure is still up," the nurse explained. "Way too high, in spite of the medications I've given her by IV. I've called the doctor but she's running behind. I might have to deliver this baby myself."

"Aye-aye-aye. I'll pray!" And I did just that, the last traces of my resistance vanishing as I entered a world I'd never known until this very moment.

I prayed for exactly two minutes and thirteen seconds, which was how long it took the doctor to arrive. Then I prayed another forty-seven seconds, which was exactly how long it took baby Isabel to make her entrance into the world. She arrived with high-pitched wails, ten fingers, ten toes, and a face pink as a strawberry and as wrinkled as Aunt Alva's.

Having never seen a newborn before—at least not one just minutes old—I hardly knew what to make of the little scrunched-up features. I wanted to say, "Sweetest thing ever!" but could only manage, "Whoa, she's small!"

The doctor continued to work on Lori-Lou, whose gaze was now permanently fixed on the baby in the incubator. A teary-eyed Josh and I watched as the nurses cleaned Izzy up. At this point, she started to look a lot more like I would've imagined a newborn to look. Not so slippery, anyway.

"Take pictures, Katie." Lori-Lou pointed to her phone on the bedside table. "Please?"

"Of course." I fidgeted with her phone to find the camera app, then snapped at least a dozen photos of Izzy as she received her first bath. Then a few more as the nurse measured her head and her height. I got a really cute one as the nurse diapered her for the first time and a great one as Izzy was swaddled in a pink and white receiving blanket.

The best picture, by far, was the one of the contented newborn curled up in Lori-Lou's arms. Josh took a seat on the bed, and the nurse turned down the lights in the room to give them some privacy. I couldn't help myself. I had to snag a photo of the three of them all looking so blissful. So . . . content.

I know what it is to be in need, and I know what it is to have plenty. I have learned the secret of being content in any and every situation, whether well fed or hungry, whether living in plenty or in want.

The words to the familiar Scripture wove their way through my memory once again. In that moment, as the babe quieted in my cousin's arms, I forgot about the chaos of Lori-Lou's life with the older kids. All negative memories disappeared.

The only thing that remained? The picturesque image of the precious new life in front of me and the realization that perhaps, someday, the one holding a newborn baby in her arms . . . might just be me.

8
Wrong Again

You can tell more about a person by what
he says about others than you can by what
others say about him.

                              Audrey Hepburn

The next couple of days were spent going
back and forth to the hospital. I could read the
weariness in Lori-Lou's eyes whenever I visited.
The fact that she'd developed an infection didn't
help. It did buy her an extra day in the hospital
on IV antibiotics, though, and she desperately
needed the peace and quiet. Not that hospitals
were really peaceful. Or quiet. I'd never seen so
many people coming and going from one room
before.

Aunt Alva looked pretty peaked too. She needed
a break from the kids, no doubt. Eduardo did
his best to help out, but his ever-growing workload at the shop wouldn't allow him to do much.

Nadia, God bless her, gave me a couple of days
off to help my cousin and Aunt Alva deal with
the chaos of bringing a new baby home. By
Tuesday night, I'd worn myself to a frazzle, fixing
meals for the kids, picking up toys, and changing

112

dirty diapers. By Wednesday morning, exhaustion had firmly rooted itself in every joint, every muscle of my body. Still, I had no choice. I had to go back to work. I had promotional pieces to write, ads to place, calls to make.

After two cups of coffee, a breakfast sandwich from a drive-through, and a couple of vitamin tablets, I finally made it to Cosmopolitan Bridal. Madge took one look at me and sent me straight to my office, probably to keep me from frightening the others. A short time later our morning customers started arriving, but I did my best to stay put at my desk, working on promotional materials for the new Audrey Hepburn line. Around ten o'clock, though, I had to cry uncle. I dropped my head down onto the desk and dozed off. How long I slept, I could not say, but Madge's voice roused me from my slumber.

"Hey, sleepyhead. Yes, you, Katie Sue Fisher." I lifted my head and dried the dribble of drool from my lip.

"Hmm?"

"Earth to Katie. Come in, Katie. Can you hear me?"

"I hear you." A yawn followed. "But it sounds like 'Wa-wa-wa-wa-wa.'" I rubbed my ears to see if I could get the echo to go away. No such luck. I gave up and dropped my head back down on the desk, mumbling, "Postpartum blues are real."

"Wait, are you saying *you've* got them?" Madge sounded concerned. "Because if you are . . ." Her words trailed off.

"No." I lifted my head and glared at her. "*Lori-Lou* has them. She's home from the hospital, and she's done nothing but cry. None of us can figure out why. Poor Aunt Alva has done everything in her power to cheer her up, but every word she speaks only seems to make things worse. Josh finally sent us home last night because Lori-Lou was a mess."

"Wow. How long will it take to get over this?"

"Eighteen years? Until the baby graduates from high school? I don't know. I really don't. I've never been a mother. But I've had just about all the drama and emotion I can possibly take." I dropped my head down onto the desk again and muttered, "Calgon, take me away!"

"Well, don't go too far away," Madge said, her voice now carrying a familiar stern, motherly tone. "That new bride from Houston is set to arrive in fifteen minutes. You're the one who arranged her meeting with Nadia, right? Bridget Pennington? She called a little while ago and said she could hardly wait to meet you. So pack your postpartum hormones away and put on your smiley face for her, okay? Up 'n' at 'em, sunshine!"

"O-okay." I lifted my head, albeit slightly, and tried to nod. "Just let me sleep for twelve minutes, okay? That'll give me three minutes to freshen up before she walks in."

"Whatever. Just don't be late." Madge turned and walked away, closing my door behind her. If I dozed off, I couldn't remember it. I just remember hearing the buzzer on my office phone and Madge's cheerful, "Katie, you're needed up front!" over the store's intercom.

I sat up, rubbed my eyes, and straightened to relieve the aches in my neck and shoulders. Then I staggered to my office door, things still not coming into complete focus. I somehow made it out into the hall, my eyes still sticky from sleep. I swiped at them with the back of my hand, but my vision didn't seem to improve much. Still, I needed to keep plowing forward. The new customer wouldn't wait forever.

Before I reached the register, I stumbled into Twiggy. Literally. She looked at me, eyes wide in obvious horror, and clamped a hand over her mouth.

"Um, Katie?"

"Yeah?" I yawned.

She pointed me toward the full-length mirror. I gasped when I saw my hair standing on end. I worked like the dickens to smooth it out, then turned my attention to my face.

"What's up with the mascara on your cheeks?" Twiggy asked. "Trying to make a fashion statement?"

"I rubbed my eyes. They were bothering me. I guess I rubbed off my mascara in the process. I don't know."

She handed me a tissue. I leaned into the mirror to get a closer look and then started scrubbing at the mascara spots. Before long the spots under my eyes looked more like heavy bruises. Lovely. I looked like I'd just come out of the boxing ring.

"Do you need to borrow some lipstick?" she asked. "Maybe darkening your lips will balance the other colors out. I hope."

"If you have some handy." I yawned again.

"I have Pollyanna Pink. It's my favorite."

A couple of minutes later I made my way to the front of the store, doing my best to put the concerns about my appearance out of my mind.

Until Madge saw me. She gave me a wide-eyed stare. I didn't have a chance to check my appearance again because our customer—aka the bride from Houston—greeted me with a squeal.

"Are you Katie?"

"I am." I extended my hand. "Please forgive my appearance, I dozed off for a few minutes. You see, I . . ." I couldn't remember what to say next. In fact, I couldn't even remember my own name. "I . . . I . . ." I slapped myself on the forehead, ready to admit defeat.

"It's a postpartum thing." Madge patted me on the back. "We're hoping it'll pass soon."

"Oh, I had *no* idea you were a new mommy!" The young woman clasped her hands together. "I can't wait to start having babies. But first I have to get married."

"Wait . . . who's having babies?" Twiggy looked back and forth between the customer and me, clearly confused.

I couldn't put two words together to explain. I tried. I really tried. "No, I'm not . . . I mean, I never said I . . ." Another yawn escaped.

"Poor thing." Our bride from Houston offered a sympathetic smile. "I know just what you're going through. My best friend had a baby a few months ago. She hasn't slept since. I hardly recognize her anymore. But the baby's adorable. He's a boy, by the way."

"Ah. Well, this one's a girl. Izzy. Short for Isabel." I rubbed at my eyes with the back of my hand and for the first time found myself coherent enough to take in the gorgeous young woman standing before me. I'd picked up on her Southern drawl already. She and Crystal could have a Southern drawl duel. But what really stood out to me was the young woman's physical appearance. She was breathtaking, from her tall, slender physique to her expensive shoes and Gucci handbag. Wow. All of that stuff must've cost a pretty penny.

Her high-end clothes caught my eye—I'd have to be blind not to notice them, actually—but what really snagged my attention was her hair. Long, dark curls fell within inches of her slender waist. She'd pinned the top of her hair up with the tiniest bit of a poof—not eighties style, but a fashionable woman of the twenty-first century.

I could almost read Madge's mind. *I know this type. Daddy's got deep pockets. We're going to make a pretty penny off this gal.* She gave me a little nudge with her elbow. Not that making a sale was my job. I would leave that to Twiggy, who stood next to me with an inviting smile on her face.

Brady joined us a couple of minutes later, and the young woman glanced his way and waved as if she knew him. *Did* she know him? I looked up at Brady's face and saw no hint of recognition there. Still, she continued to stare at him. Her face lit into the most delightful smile, revealing perfectly placed dimples. Really? Could this girl get any more perfect?

"Brady? It's me, Bridget Pennington. Remember?"

"Pennington." He shook his head. "Sorry, it's not coming to me."

"My dad is Bradley Pennington from Pennington Oil and Gas. We lived down the street from you when we were kids, remember? On Wilson Street? Our parents were friends. We used to do everything together. Bingo night at the country club. Dinners on the lake. Our parents even took a vacation to Galveston together once. We ended up covered in tar because of an oil spill in the Gulf."

"Bridget Pennington." He nodded. "I think I remember now." Brady's lips curled up. "Seems like you looked a little different back then. Did you used to have shorter hair?"

"Yes. My mother cut it in a little bob when I was a kid. She couldn't keep up with it because I was always into something. I was the kid with the scraped knees and broken arms from climbing in trees. My parents thought they'd never drive the tomboy out of me, but they gave it the old college try."

"It's all coming back to me now." A warm smile lit his face. "Do you still live on Wilson Street?"

She shook her head. "Not even close. Daddy moved his business to Houston about ten years ago. He bought the penthouse at Williams Tower in the Galleria area. He's done very well for himself. Houston's the place to be for oil and gas, and I'm in the thick of it now myself. I guess you could say I'm his right-hand gal."

Brady gave her a thoughtful look. "Good for him. And good for you."

"Yes." She gave a little shrug. "Hard to picture me dressed in business attire every day, right? I couldn't even get my socks to match when I was a kid. And my stinky tennis shoes have been replaced with heels." She waggled her ankle, and

Brady's gaze traveled downward to the expensive pumps.

"Nice shoes."

Watch it, buddy. No point in examining the woman's ankles just because you two used to climb trees as kids.

"So, you're in the oil and gas business now." The admiration in Brady's expression was more than evident as he spoke. "Who would've guessed the little tomboy would end up in a penthouse suite."

"All those years of climbing trees got me over my fear of heights." Bridget's laugh was contagious. "I'm second in command to Daddy, if you must know."

"I see. I understand how that feels," Brady said. "Working for my mom isn't always easy either."

Bridget released a sigh. "Daddy puts a lot of demands on me." She grew silent for a moment, and I thought I saw a hint of pain in her eyes. Just as quickly she snapped back to attention. "Anyway, I didn't drive all the way to Dallas to talk about all of that. I'm here for a dress. And that's the funny thing. I was looking through a bridal magazine awhile back—one with the cutest Loretta Lynn–style gown on the cover. When I saw the designer's name was Nadia James, I couldn't believe it. I just knew it had to be the same Ms. Nadia who used to sew those cute little

Halloween costumes for all the neighborhood kids. Remember that one year when you wanted to go as a robot? I think I still have a picture of that in my scrapbook. Priceless."

Brady groaned. "Did you have to remind me?"

"Right?" Bridget laughed. "Well, I've followed your career, so I knew all about . . ." Her gaze drifted down to his knee. "Anyway, I'm sorry about your injury. But it didn't take me long to put two and two together and figure out you were working here with your mom."

Brady slipped his arm over my shoulders. "Well, since you brought up the magazine cover, I'd like you to meet the cover model, right here in the flesh. Bridget Pennington, meet Katie Fisher!"

I rubbed at my eyes once again and bit back another yawn. My face grew hot. Though I had appeared on the cover of *Texas Bride* magazine wearing the gorgeous Loretta Lynn gown, no one had ever called me a cover model before. I wasn't sure I liked the description.

"Wait . . . Katie? *You're* the girl in that magnificent dress?" Bridget let out a squeal and grabbed my hand. "Well, congratulations on winning the contest!" She paused and little creases formed between her eyes. "Sorry, just trying to figure out the timing of all of this. If you just had a new baby, then when . . . how . . . ?" The beautiful young woman shrugged. "Sorry, not trying to get into your business. I guess that photo shoot must've taken place quite a while before the baby was born?"

"New baby?" Brady scratched his head. "I'm completely lost."

I cleared my throat and tried to figure out how to proceed. "Okay, I'll get to the baby part in a minute, but let me start by saying that we weren't engaged when I won the dress."

"But we remedied that in a hurry." Brady took hold of my left hand and lifted it to show off my diamond ring.

"So, you got the dress first and the ring after? And when did the baby come?" She grimaced. "Sorry! I guess I'm getting too personal, but inquiring minds want to know."

"Yes, inquiring minds want to know." Twiggy crossed her arms at her chest and gave me a "How are you going to get yourself out of this one?" look.

"I'm really confused." Brady raked his hands through his hair.

"We're talking about baby Izzy," I explained.

"I'd love to see pictures, if you have any." Bridget clasped her hands together. "I just love baby pictures."

"I don't have any handy," I said.

"I do. I have some on my phone." Brady pulled it out of his pocket. "She's cute as a button. Wait till you see her expressions. Never seen anything like it. Then again, I haven't been around babies before this one, so I'm on a definite learning curve." He flipped through photo after photo.

"Ooh, she's a doll!" Bridget looked at one picture after another. "Congratulations, you two! So excited for you. I had no idea, Brady. I can't believe I haven't read this in the papers or online. Usually the paparazzi won't let you get away with anything, especially something this big. How old is she?"

"I'm so confused." Brady looked my way, eyes widening. "I'm a father?"

Twiggy snorted and erupted in laughter.

"I'm sure it must seem like a dream." Bridget patted him on the back. "Probably every new dad asks himself that same thing. You'll get used to the idea, as soon as you've had some sleep, I mean. I've heard a lot about how tough the first few weeks can be."

Brady gave me another look. Oh boy.

Bridget turned her attention to me. "Where is your big day taking place, Katie?"

"We're still trying to figure all of that out." I lowered my voice in case Nadia happened to be nearby. "But it will be late summer. That's as far as we've gotten. You know what they say: 'The devil's in the details.'"

"Tell me about it." Her cheerful expression faded in a hurry.

"Well, speaking of weddings, didn't you drive

all the way up from Houston to try on gowns?" Madge, ever the businesswoman, jumped back into salesperson gear.

"Yes, that's right." The edges of Bridget's lips curled up in a smile. "When I called, Katie set up an appointment for me with Nadia. But I daresay I already know which gown I'm going to choose. I saw it in a magazine just a couple of weeks back."

"Nadia's in the studio. I'll go get her." I hurried down the hall, half relieved to get away from the dark-haired beauty and half frustrated as I recalled how Brady's eyes had sparkled when he recognized her. Oh, if only I could go back and start this day all over again!

9

Chances Are

As you grow older, you will discover that you have two hands, one for helping yourself, the other for helping others.

Audrey Hepburn

Brady followed on my heels. He tapped me on the shoulder just as I reached the studio. I turned to face him and saw the expression of shock and disbelief on his face. "What. Just. Happened. Back. There?"

I did my best not to groan. "A total misunderstanding, that's all. She saw me yawning and probably noticed my hair and makeup are a little messy, and—"

"A little?"

"Anyway, Madge said something about how no one has slept since the baby was born, and Bridget just took the ball and ran with it. I tried to explain but got cut off every time."

"I see. So, the baby is yours, and I'm the father, and we're just now planning our wedding after the birth of our child?"

"Something like that. And I don't know how to unravel this mess, at least not until I've had more sleep." I wanted to go back in my office, put my head on my desk, and doze off.

On the other hand, maybe I was sleeping now. Yes, this was all surely a crummy dream. I'd wake up soon and laugh about it. Only, first I had to rally the troops and then get back out to the bride-to-be. Through my stupor, I managed to do all of that.

Minutes later Nadia joined us. She took one look at Bridget and extended her arms. "I remember this little girl. The tomboy's all grown up!"

"She is, indeed." Bridget did a little twirl to show off her fully grown self.

"Is your mama coming in to watch you try on gowns?" Nadia looked toward the door as if expecting the woman to materialize. "We were such great friends back in the day."

Our bride-to-be's joy seemed to dampen right away, and she shook her head. "My mama passed away when I was ten." A pause followed before she added, "Colon cancer."

Nadia placed her hand on Bridget's arm. "I'm so sorry, honey. Truly. Your mother was always a lovely woman. Such a kind neighbor and friend. I'm very sorry to hear that she's passed away. That must've been so hard on you."

"Yes." An awkward silence rose. When Bridget finally spoke, the sadness in her voice was undeniable. "My father has done a fine job of raising me, but I'll be honest—he doesn't really understand girl things. Like this wedding, for instance." She released an exaggerated sigh. "Let's just say we don't always agree."

"Well, at least you can choose your own gown," Nadia said. "He's not here to give input, right?"

"Well, it's a little more complicated than that. He's already chosen a gown that he loves from your website."

"Which one?" Fine lines formed between Nadia's carefully made-up eyes.

"The Audrey Hepburn."

"Ooh, a lovely choice!" Twiggy looked delighted by this. "It's one of my favorite designs."

"Mine too," Nadia said. "But I sense you have something different in mind, Bridget?"

Bridget's nose wrinkled, and for the first time I noticed a light spattering of freckles there. "See, here's the thing: Daddy has his heart set on a high-end wedding. For me, I mean. Ceremony at our church, which is large and very ornate. Reception—if he gets his way—at the River Oaks Country Club, the most exclusive upper-crust facility in town with a long, rich history of catering to those who strive to impress."

Madge let out a whistle. "Sounds like quite a place."

"Oh, it is." Bridget sighed. "It's great. Perfect, in fact."

"You're hesitating?" Twiggy looked perplexed. "Because that all sounds lovely to me."

"Well, yes, I'm sure some people would be thrilled. Daddy's business associates, for instance. But the tomboy in me wants to go a different route. My fiancé's family has property in Magnolia, outside of Houston. Beautiful property. There's a gorgeous pond, a large barn . . . very rustic."

"O-okay?" Nadia seemed confused by the direction of the conversation.

"You want to get married outdoors, don't you?" I put my hands on my hips, suddenly ready to befriend this poor harassed bride. I understood her plight. Fully. "You want a country chic wedding."

"Yeah." She gave me a sheepish look. "Is that weird? I mean, to trade in the most exclusive place in town for a wedding in a field with a reception to follow in a barn? But I think it would be amazing. An evening wedding next to the lake. Guests seated on bales of hay covered in pretty pieces of fabric. A grape arbor to say our 'I dos' under." Her eyes took on a faraway look as she shared her vision for the perfect day.

"Gosh, when you describe it like that, it even sounds good to me." Madge shrugged. "And I'm not the outdoorsy type at all."

"Neither is my dad." Bridget leaned against a mannequin, nearly knocking it down. "And therein lies the problem. My fiancé, Evan, loves the idea. And his parents are more than happy to work on the barn to get it ready for the reception. Evan's dad is a rancher and a wonderful carpenter. He does the most amazing woodwork. I can picture it now."

"But your dad can't?" Twiggy asked. "Is that it?"

"I haven't told him yet. He'll flip. I know he will. He wants the best for me."

"Sounds like this is what you want, so isn't that the best for you?" Nadia asked. "I think this would be simple enough. Just tell him what you want. Don't let him boss you around."

Sure. Easy for my future mother-in-law who wanted me to get married at the Gaylord to say.

Bridget sighed. "Anyway, we should probably drop it. I know it's never going to happen. If Daddy ain't happy, ain't nobody happy."

"Well, that's a crying shame." Madge clucked her tongue. "And it flies in the face of what I believe. We always say, 'If the *bride* ain't happy, ain't nobody happy.' "

"Right." Bridget released a slow breath. "But I guess it's all silly. Getting married outdoors . . . who does that? I mean, who does it out in a field with a lake and bales of hay? I'm not a rancher's daughter, I'm a businessman's daughter. It's probably a dumb idea."

Before speaking a word in response to all of this, I thought about my own situation. I'd been so busy trying to make everyone else happy— Nadia, Mama, the girls at the bridal shop—that I hadn't really spent a lot of time thinking about my own happiness. When would someone ask, "What do you want, Katie?"

"It's your day." I spoke the words with fervor, probably as much for my own benefit as hers. "And you should do what feels right to you and your fiancé, no one else. I say you have the best country chic wedding ever, and make no apologies for it."

All of my co-workers nodded in agreement. Even Nadia, though she did give me a sideways glance.

Bridget didn't look convinced. "That's easier said than done, sadly."

"Well, start with the dress," I suggested. "Choose something that will work for a country chic wedding." I pointed to the Audrey Hepburn gown on a nearby mannequin. "I mean, it's gorgeous—"

"And it would be great for the country club set," Madge chimed in.

"But out in a field?" Nadia shook her head. "Never. Never ever."

"I'm not saying you shouldn't try it on," I clarified. "Just saying you should keep your options open. Find another dress that has the look and feel of a country wedding. Try it on for size and feel. Picture yourself standing in the field wearing that dress."

And that's exactly what Bridget Pennington did. She tried on the Audrey Hepburn, then the Grace

Kelly, then the Loretta Lynn, which she loved. She tried on dresses in ivory, white, and oyster— some flashy, others simple. Some with sweetheart necklines, others off-the-shoulder. Some with lace appliques, others with organza. Still, nothing felt just right, to her or to those of us helping.

At the end of the session, she and Nadia agreed to meet at a future date to design something perfect for the occasion. After she and her fiancé solidified their plans. I thanked my lucky stars that she hadn't congratulated Nadia on being a new grandmother. How would I have explained that one?

After Bridget left, I went back to my office and sent several emails. Brady headed off to a meeting with his agent just about the time I finished, so I drove back home, deep in thought. At the last minute I decided to stop by Lori-Lou's place, just to check in.

I found her in a puddle in the kitchen—not a literal puddle, like one caused from dirty dish-water, though I found plenty of that in the sink. This puddle was more the emotional kind. Seated at the breakfast table with the sleeping baby in her arms, she poured out her heart about her tough day. She lost me about halfway into a story about Gilly having a meltdown just before bedtime.

I got up and walked to the sink, where I began the lengthy process of loading the dishes into the dishwasher. Lori-Lou didn't even seem to notice. I did my best to listen to her woes, but my exhaustion made it difficult to focus. She finally drew me in with several tears choking her voice and a final lamentation: "Being a mother is so hard!" She put the sleeping baby in the little bassinet nearby and leaned over as if in agony. She wept aloud, rocking back and forth. When she finally dried her eyes, pain still flickered there.

Now what? I needed to say something—do something—but my mind went blank.

In that moment, in a stroke of brilliance, I decided to share what had happened to me at the bridal shop. Lori-Lou would get such a big kick out of the story, no doubt. I told her all about Bridget Pennington and how she'd misunderstood about the baby. How she'd thought I was the mother of a newborn. About how Brady and I never had the chance to clarify or to tell her the real story.

At the end of my exaggerated tale, Lori-Lou's brow wrinkled. "So, let me get this straight," she said. "That bride-to-be from Houston thinks you're the . . . Mother. Of. My. Baby?" She began to cry all over again. "That you're Izzy's mama?"

"Yes." I put another dish into the dishwasher and turned to face her. "Don't even get me started on how she came to that conclusion, but that's the long and short of it. She thinks Brady and I have a daughter. Together."

"Really?" My cousin stormed into the living room, leaving me high and dry in the kitchen. I wiped off my hands and followed her, concerned by her actions. She reached down to pick up a toy from the floor, her eyes welling with tears. *"Really?"*

"Of course, I tried to tell her the real story, but one thing led to another, and before I could get a word in edgewise—"

"You'd be a better mother than me." Lori-Lou choked the words out. "It's true. You would."

"W-what?"

She tossed a stuffed rabbit across the room toward the toy box, but it missed by a good three feet. "See what I mean? I stink at this."

"So you didn't hit the toy box. Who cares?"

"No, Katie." She turned in slow motion to face me head-on, a look of total anguish in her eyes. "I. Stink. At. Parenting."

"What? Are you kidding me? You—"

"I've lost control. I try . . . I really try . . . but no one listens to me. I tell the older kids to be quiet so the baby can sleep. Are they quiet? No, they're not. I sing to the baby to get her to calm down, but does she calm down? No, she doesn't. I tell Josh that I'm on the verge of a breakdown, and does he buy me double chocolate chunk ice cream like I ask for? No! He buys me mint chocolate chip. I. Can't. Stand. Mint. Chocolate. Chip."

"Hey, they were out of double chocolate chunk."

Josh's voice sounded from the doorway. "And just so you know, I tried again at the grocery store on Hollister and they don't have it either. It's not my fault, Lori-Lou. I'm doing the best I can."

"So am I." My cousin sobbed as she plopped down onto the sofa, which was still covered in unfolded laundry. "And it's not good enough."

Josh made his way through the pile of toys on the floor to the sofa, where he nudged the laundry aside and took a seat next to his wife. "Baby, it's okay."

"Don't say *baby*. Please don't ever say *baby* again!" She dissolved into a pool of tears and then ran from the room, all the way to her bedroom.

I put my hand over my mouth, horrified that I'd upset her so badly. After a few seconds I pulled my hand down and stared at Josh. "I. Am. So. Sorry!"

"What got her so stirred up?"

"It's my fault. I was telling her a funny story about how one of the customers at the store thought I was the one who just had a baby, and the next thing you know, Lori-Lou—"

"Has a meltdown." He raked his fingers through his hair. "Just like the one she had right before I left the house, and just like the one she had this afternoon when I told her that her parents had to leave to go back to Arkansas."

"I've never seen anything like this. It's scary."

"We saw glimpses after Joshie was born. Man,

I sure hope this season passes quickly. She had the postpartum thing with the others, but nothing like this. I'm worried enough that I've called her doctor."

"What did she say?"

"To give it time, but to keep a close eye on her. I just walk on eggshells all the time. I never know when something will set her off. That's why I'm so grateful you and Alva have been coming by so often. Thank you for that."

I couldn't help the little yawn that escaped. "You're welcome."

"This might not look like anyone's dream life"—he pointed to the messy room—"but it's our life and we love it. Except for the postpartum depression part."

I pondered my cousin's words as I drove home. She felt as if she'd lost control. She couldn't seem to get the train back on track. In some ways, I knew just how she felt. Hadn't I said the same thing? Hadn't the last couple weeks proven that I had no control at all over my own decisions? Hormones had nothing to do with it, of course, but just as I'd thought about my cousin, I couldn't get the train back on track.

Only, I had to. I had to regain control. I had to move forward. And somehow I had to keep on going, no matter how overwhelmed I felt. If Lori-Lou could do it with four children, surely I could do it with none.

10

Whatever You Say

I decided, very early on, just to accept life unconditionally; I never expected it to do anything special for me, yet I seemed to accomplish far more than I had ever hoped. Most of the time it just happened to me without my ever seeking it.

Audrey Hepburn

The next several days passed by without any major catastrophes. By the time the weekend arrived, I'd had a few good nights' sleep behind me and felt like a champ. I wasn't sure as much could be said about Lori-Lou, but time would tell.

On Sunday morning I invited Alva to church with me. She usually attended her own church—something a bit more liturgical than my contemporary community church—but these days her ability to drive was diminished.

She agreed to go with me, but as was often the case, she dozed off the minute she got into the passenger seat. I'd noticed more and more of this over the past few months and wondered if perhaps I should suggest a visit to the doctor, to make sure she was in good health.

As she slept, I listened to worship music on the radio and spent a few minutes in prayer. After such a crazy week, I certainly needed to center myself once again. Just about the time I exited the highway, my cell phone rang. I pushed the button on the dashboard and the call came through on my Bluetooth. I didn't recognize the phone number right away, and the woman's opening line totally threw me.

"Martina McBride."

"I'm sorry . . . what?" *And who is this?*

"Martina McBride. I love her music. And I love her whole style. Yes, my father envisions me at a highfalutin event wearing a high-end gown like the Audrey Hepburn—which is nice, don't get me wrong—but it's not my style."

Ah. Bridget Pennington.

"I love Martina McBride."

"Ooh, I love her too." In the seat to my right Aunt Alva yawned and stretched. "Always have."

I put my finger to my lips and pointed to the dashboard to try to clue my aunt in to the fact that Bridget could hear her.

"All I keep thinking is, 'What would Martina McBride do?'" Bridget sighed. "Would she have her reception at the River Oaks Country Club just to please her father's clients, or would she set up the prettiest wedding out in a field with bales of hay for seating and an exquisite backdrop that includes a beautiful pond?"

"Bales of hay for seating?" Alva's nose wrinkled. "Who wants to sit on a bale of hay?"

"Oh, we'll cover the bales with the prettiest fabrics you ever saw," Bridget said. "But that's not the point. The point is, I've made up my mind. Daddy doesn't get his way this time. I'm the bride and what I want matters most."

"Exactly." I secretly wondered if her daddy would agree to pay for the wedding-in-the-field, reception-in-the-barn event.

"Does Nadia have a Martina McBride gown in her line?" Bridget asked. "If not, do you suppose she'll make one for me?"

"To my knowledge she's never done a Martina McBride gown. I can't even imagine what that would look like, but I'm sure you could talk to her about it."

"I will. I saw Martina at the CMA awards a few years back in a simple gown, but gorgeous. Very classy, actually. It was off-the-shoulder on the right. No, the left. No, the right." Bridget laughed. "Actually, I don't remember which shoulder, but the dress flowed so beautifully down to the floor."

"Sounds easy enough. You should call the store tomorrow and talk to Nadia about this."

"I just wanted to run the idea by you first because I know how busy she is. I don't want to overwhelm her. You know?"

"If this dress is easier than the Audrey Hepburn, then she might be glad you're going this route."

"Right. That's what I was thinking. But I don't want my dress to be just like Martina's. I don't think hers had any lace, and I'd love a pretty overlay. The waist was what really caught my eye. Picture a sash—or a belt, whatever—made of gold fabric flowers with Austrian crystals in the center of each. And then picture a skirt that's floor-length in front with a train about five feet trailing in the back."

"That's a typical train for a wedding dress."

"Now that I think of it, I loved the fabric on the Audrey Hepburn gown. Maybe she could just use that lace and crepe for this design?"

"Maybe. But only she can answer that question. Just promise me one thing, Bridget—get the gown your heart wants, not what someone else wants for you. Promise?"

"I do!" She giggled. "I mean, I do promise. Yes. I will get what makes me happy. I know it will be a hurdle for my daddy to jump—I mean, what kind of father wants to sit on a bale of hay to watch his daughter get married?—but he'll come around. I know he will. Ooh, it's going to be great, Katie!"

"I agree." I pulled the car off the feeder road and into the parking lot of the church.

"Thank you. I wanted you to be the first to hear that I'm standing up for myself." She paused a moment. "Now, fill me in on the baby. How's she doing? Are you getting any sleep, or has that postpartum thing still got ahold of you? You've been on my mind all week."

"Postpartum thing?" Alva looked at me, eyes wide. "Huh?"

My pulse quickened as I saw the fear in my aunt's eyes. "The baby's great, Bridget, but there's something I need to tell you." To my right I noticed a police officer guiding traffic into the church's parking lot.

"Oh, I know. You wanted to tell me that you're sorry you looked so worn out the other day. It's okay. I understand. And just for the record, I'm dying to see more pictures of your baby, Katie. The ones Brady showed me were a little fuzzy. Have you had professional ones done yet?"

Aunt Alva stared at me, her jaw dropping. "What did that person say, Katie Sue?"

A flicker of apprehension coursed through me as I pondered what to say next. Unfortunately, I couldn't squeeze in a word just yet.

"I want to see pictures of the baby," Bridget repeated. "I'll bet she's blonde like you but is going to be tall like Brady."

Alva clamped a hand over her mouth, and I could read the panic in her wide eyes.

I couldn't avoid this any longer. "Bridget, there's something I need to tell you. That whole baby thing was just a huge misunderstanding."

"Having a child is never a misunderstanding, Katie. It might've been an accident, but she's a blessing—a living, breathing blessing. That's how you have to look at it. The same thing happened to a friend of mine once, and she and her boyfriend eventually got married and had two more kids. It all worked out in the end, and I know it will for you guys too."

"No, that's not what I meant. I'm just trying to tell you that Brady and I aren't really . . ." I got distracted by the officer trying to direct me.

"I'm sure you felt you weren't ready to be parents, but you are. I'm guessing you're better with children than you think. Am I right?"

"No, you're wrong. She's terrible with kids," Alva said. "*Terrible*. You should see her with Lori-Lou's brood. Boy howdy, Katie doesn't have a lot of patience. I keep thinking she'll get better with time, but that doesn't appear to be the case."

"I'm sorry . . . who's this?" Bridget asked.

"I'm Katie's aunt Alva, and I'm mighty mixed up right now. Who is this? Are you a new character on the radio program?"

Bridget laughed. "Well, I've been called a character a time or two, but not on the radio."

Alva shook her head. "I don't understand what you were saying about Brady and Katie having a baby."

"That's what I've been trying to say all along, Bridget," I interjected. "Brady and I don't have a baby. The person who has postpartum blues—the one you heard me talking about in the store the other day—is my cousin Lori-Lou."

"Well, for pity's sake." Bridget grew silent. "So, it really was a misunderstanding. That's what you were trying to tell me."

The officer waved me on, but I hesitated when Bridget didn't respond right away.

"I see," she said at last.

Only, I could tell that she did not.

"I'll tell you the whole story next time you come in, I promise." I waved at the officer, who seemed a bit perturbed that I hadn't moved forward yet. I tapped the accelerator and headed toward a parking spot. "I'm so relieved to finally tell you. Brady and I have no children. Maybe someday, but not now."

"I wondered how you could have posed for the magazine cover if you were expecting, but I didn't want to pry. Now I feel so ridiculous for making that assumption. Please forgive me."

"Nothing to forgive."

"Of course there is. I celebrated your good news in front of all your co-workers. Only, it wasn't your news. Gosh, I messed this one up."

"I'm just glad we've got it all straightened out now. You were wrong about something, and I straightened you out. That's what you have to do with your father."

She grew silent again. "You think?" she said after a moment.

"I know. If you don't straighten him out, you will lose total control, and I happen to know a thing or two about what that feels like. So be brave. When we hang up, call him. Tell him that you're having your wedding in a field. With bales of hay."

"I had an allergic reaction to hay once," Alva said. "As a girl. Broke out in a rash. Started sneezing. It was awful."

"Well, like I said, I'll cover them with fabric," Bridget reminded her. "No problem there. But just one more question for you, Katie, and then I'll quit. Did I misunderstand the part about you and Brady getting married too?"

As I pulled into the parking spot, I shot a quick glance at Aunt Alva, who looked stunned.

"No, you got that right," I said. "We're getting married. It just had nothing to do with a baby, that's all." I shifted the car into park.

"Whew! That's a relief. I didn't want to make any assumptions, but you had me nervous."

"Boy, if you think she's nervous, you oughta get inside my head for a minute." Aunt Alva whacked herself on the forehead with her palm. "Color me confused."

"I just got to church, Bridget, so I need to let you go. Feel free to call Nadia tomorrow, okay? And we'll talk soon."

"Yes. That'll be great. Thanks again for everything, Katie."

With a click the call ended. I turned the car off and leaned back against the seat, my heart in my throat. Oy vey.

"Katie Sue?" Alva's voice was tinged with nervous energy. "Is there something you want to tell me?"

"No. It was all a misunderstanding."

"Well, that's a relief, but I must say those radio programs are getting more and more ridiculous. Who in their right mind would ever believe that a woman would get married in a field and have her guests sit on bales of hay? Surely those soap opera writers could write something more believable than that."

I sighed. "Alva, it's the Bluetooth you were hearing."

"I'm hearing that crazy actress lady talking about having a wedding reception in a barn, and I'm just saying that a good writer could've come up with something more believable than that. Who celebrates their big day in a barn?"

"People do weddings differently these days, Auntie. Even Joni is thinking about converting a barn into a wedding facility. It's the trendy thing to do."

"Well, I'm clearly not trendy. And I'm awfully glad you and Brady are the traditional sort too. I'm looking forward to your wedding at the Baptist church, where I don't have to wipe pieces of hay from my ever-bloomin' backside when the ceremony's over. And thank you very much for not holding the reception in a barn, where the smell of manure might wreck the whole ambience."

"Actually, since you mentioned my reception . . ." I reached into my purse and pulled out a tube of lipstick. "I have been thinking about suggesting to Brady that we hold our reception outdoors, because we want to offer folks the option of dancing if they like. Not in a barn, but something completely different."

"Outdoors . . . in summer?"

I swiped on the lipstick and smacked my lips. "We haven't settled on a final date yet, though we've definitely narrowed it down to sometime in August. I'm thinking about suggesting the evening, Aunt Alva, because things cool down at night. If we held the wedding at six, we probably wouldn't even start the reception until seven. By then the temperature will be down."

"From a hundred down to ninety, maybe. Sounds about as loony as that whole wedding-in-a-field idea. Maybe you need a better writer too."

I felt my temper rise at once. "No, I don't." My voice started to quiver as my thoughts tumbled out. "I don't think anyone's been paying attention to what's going on. Everyone's been weighing in on our big day without giving any thought to what I want."

An awkward silence rose up between us, and I wanted to kick myself for lashing out at one of the few people who hadn't—until now, anyway—tried to tell me what to do.

"Auntie, I'm sorry," I squeaked out. "I just wish

I had the courage that Bridget and Crystal have, to stand up to all the people who are trying to tell me what to do. This is my big day, and every bride deserves her day. Her plan. Her dream."

"I'm so sorry, honey. You're right, of course." She reached over and put her hand on my arm. "Listen, I don't care if you want to get married on the softball field in Fairfield, I'll be there. What's important is that you and your honey get what you want."

"Thank you." I realized the tube of lipstick was still in my hand, so I shoved it back in my purse.

"Not that I'm engaged yet or anything, but Eduardo has already talked to me about our ceremony. He wants it to be unusual. Unique. Nothing traditional. And you know what?" She turned to me and I noticed the shimmer of tears in her eyes. "I love that man so much. If he said, 'Let's get married on the moon,' I'd figure out a way to do it. Getting the guests to and from might be a problem, but it'd be worth it, just to see the smile on his face. That's all that's important here, Katie Sue. If you're happy—if Brady's happy—then who cares what all the rest of us think?"

I'd just about gushed, "Thank you, Aunt Alva," when she added, "Even if we do melt into the pavement in the middle of August just so the two of you can be happy."

Oh well. Her heart was in the right place, anyway.

11

That's Me

For beautiful eyes, look for the good in others; for beautiful lips, speak only words of kindness; and for poise, walk with the knowledge that you are never alone.

Audrey Hepburn

We made our way through the crowded foyer of the church and into the sanctuary, where I settled into my usual spot in the eleventh row, with Aunt Alva to my right. Minutes later Brady joined us. He slipped into the spot to my left, gave my aunt a wave, and then planted a kiss on my cheek.

"How's your morning been?" he asked.

I'd just whispered, "Don't ask," when the opening worship song began. I rose and did my best to put some of the craziness of the week behind me.

The service was great, from the music to the sermon to the altar call at the end. The message on turning the other cheek really hit the spot. With all the opportunities to forgive folks who'd offended me lately, I was spinning in circles just from turning the other cheek. No wonder I felt dizzy.

Afterward, as Brady and I walked with Alva across the parking lot, I awaited her assessment of the morning.

"I'm sorry, Katie," she said as we drew near to my car. "I'm really trying to like this new church of yours, but I've just never been a fan of rock and roll."

"It's contemporary worship, Auntie."

"I've heard folks call it that. But with all the ringing in my ears, who could tell what it was? I hope you don't mind, but I don't feel up to going to Lori-Lou's for lunch today like we talked about. I'm worn out."

"Are you sure? I made lasagna last night. Just need to pop it in the oven when I get to her place. Lasagna is one of your favorites, right?"

"Right." She yawned. "But I need to take a little nap. I'm worn out from spending so much time with those kids. I don't have it in me to help out today. I'll just eat a sandwich and take a nap. Please give her my apologies."

"Of course."

Brady followed me home, and then we loaded up the lasagna, salad, and sodas into his truck to make the drive to Lori-Lou's place. As we drove, I expressed my concerns about, well, everything. It seemed like everyone in my world was falling apart. Hopefully this season would pass.

My first shimmer of hope came when Lori-Lou answered the door, fully dressed, hair combed, and a relaxed expression on her face. No tears, praise the Lord. Talk about restoring hope in a hurry!

We all gathered around the table to share the meal, and I silently thanked the Lord that Lori-Lou appeared to be recovering from the hormonal swings. After finishing our meal, we headed into the living room so the guys could watch a game on TV. Off in the distance, the older children played with puzzles.

I couldn't help but notice my cousin's post-baby physique as I took a seat on the sofa next to Brady. Her tummy had receded a bit, though not as much as I might've expected. Her feet—once huge—looked perfectly normal, and the swelling in her face had gone down. How the human body managed to pull off such fascinating post-pregnancy transformations, I could not say. Perhaps one day I'd find out firsthand. Not that Brady and I had any plans to have children right away.

Then again, we'd never really talked about it, had we? For all I knew, he wanted a whole basketball team, and the sooner, the better. Yikes. Maybe I'd better have a little chat with him about all of that.

For sure, I wasn't ready to go through labor. All of the panting—and the people running around the room talking about you as if you weren't even there—was difficult to comprehend. Maybe one day the idea would make more sense, but right now it just felt foreign to me.

"Did we lose you, Katie?" Lori-Lou passed the baby off to me, and I shifted my gaze down to that darling face, then back up at my cousin, who couldn't seem to stop grinning. "Thinking about what it'll be like for you one day?"

I studied the infant, lost in my thoughts, but didn't answer.

"Being a mother is the most wonderful thing in the world." She released a little sigh. "I can't describe it, but it's better than Disney and Six Flags all rolled into one."

Josh, Brady, and I stared at her in stunned silence. Clearly the postpartum blues had sailed away. Thank God. But had she really forgotten the pain of childbirth? Surely not.

Lori-Lou helped me wrap the baby in her receiving blanket and showed me how to tuck in the corner to hold it in place. "You're a natural at that, Katie Sue. Like I said the other day, you're going to make a great mommy."

No, what you said was, "You'd be a better mother than me," and then you had a complete meltdown.

"You think I'll do okay?" I traced my finger along the baby's porcelain cheek.

My cousin clasped her hands together. "I *know*. So let's get this show on the road already. Now that I've had the baby, it's time to start planning for your big day so you can have a few of your own."

To my right, Brady choked on a sip of his coffee.

Lori-Lou put her hand up. "*Not* that I plan to tell you what to do or when to do it. I've heard enough from Aunt Alva to know that everyone in Fairfield—and half the people at the bridal shop—are already trying to take the wedding reins away from you."

"Thank you for acknowledging that," I said. "Is it so awful to want to plan my own wedding without a bunch of committees chiming in?"

"Not awful at all," she said.

"I just feel like I can't please anyone. Everyone is tugging on me, right and left, and I'm going to end up hurting someone's feelings, no matter what I choose to do."

"You've seen plenty of brides go through this before. I know, because you've told me so many horror stories. They come into the bridal shop with their families in tow and end up in tears because they're not allowed to do what they really want. They're manipulated."

"Manipulated." I sighed. "Yep."

"Don't let it happen. You just stand up for yourself. Better yet, put it all on me. I'm your matron of honor, right? Tell them I've insisted on a wedding at your home church without all of the frills."

"Good idea," I said. "I'll pin it all on you."

"I'm going to make sure you get what you want. So tell me what that is. What *do* you guys really want—in your heart of hearts?"

Brady looked away from the TV long enough to chime in, "Whatever makes her happy."

"Okay then. What will make you happy, Katie?" Lori-Lou asked.

Brady turned his full attention to me. He slipped his arm over my shoulders and waited for my response.

"I want . . ." I gazed down into baby Izzy's face. "Sweet. Like, hometown sweet. Nothing gaudy. Not really country-western, though I know most of the people in town would expect that, being from Texas and all. More . . . old-fashioned. I like the idea of old love songs. Maybe take people back in time a little, but not in a theatrical sort of way. Just quaint."

"So, Fairfield at its finest," my cousin said.

"Yes. But not necessarily the same old, same old. I've always pictured myself getting married at the Baptist church."

"Brady?" Josh glanced his way. "You okay with that?"

"More than okay," Brady said with a firm nod. "And just so you know, I've already made that plain to my mother. She won't be bringing up the Gaylord anymore."

"Well, that's settled." Josh turned his attention back to the game. "See what happens when you put a guy in charge? We get things done in a fraction of the time."

"Puh-leeze." I rolled my eyes.

"I'm serious, though." Brady pulled me closer. "No more interference from my mom. We had 'the talk.' "

A wave of relief washed over me, and I leaned into him to whisper, "Thank you."

"You're welcome." He kissed the tip of my nose. "Anything for my bride-to-be."

"Okay, wedding at the church." Lori-Lou reached for her phone and started typing into it. "And the reception?"

"Not at the church," I said. "I picture it outdoors."

"In summer?" Lori-Lou asked.

"Maybe evening? Sunset?" A thoughtful look passed over Brady's face. "Might be pretty to watch the sun go down during the reception, and that would certainly make Twiggy happy."

"Why?" she asked.

"She's got this whole 'riding off into the sunset' picture in her mind. Don't even get me started on the rest."

Lori-Lou glanced down at her phone and then back up at me. "So, outdoor reception, but where?"

"I do have someplace in mind, actually. It's close to the church so that people don't have far to drive." I felt my excitement grow as I shared my thoughts. "What would you think if I said I wanted to hold the reception on the courthouse lawn? Kind of like a picnic on the grounds, only much nicer. No red and white checkered tablecloths—I'm talking really nice tables with pretty centerpieces. But outdoors. And I love the idea of being there at sunset, Brady. So romantic."

"That's me, romantic." He squeezed my hand. "I think we're getting somewhere. That courthouse lawn is perfect. Do you think the city will let us use it?"

"I don't see why not."

"The mayor won't give you any trouble," Lori-Lou said. "And the landscaping is gorgeous. We've had so many picnics out there over the years. Brings back so many sweet memories of growing up in Fairfield."

"That's kind of what I was thinking." I shrugged. "Sort of a cross between formal and informal, if that makes sense. I'd invite everyone in town—and they would show up, because they'd know they were all welcome. We could have elegant foods, but maybe served in a way that would make it easy to visit with others. Maybe . . . skewered? Shish kabobs? I've seen a zillion recipes that would work in a really nice setting. And I'd traipse around the courthouse lawn in my Loretta Lynn gown, chugging cups of lemonade and greeting everyone I saw. That's what I would do."

"Then why don't we do just that?" Brady asked.

"Which part?"

"All of it." His eyes sparkled, and I could read the joy in his expression. "Get married at your home church, have the reception on the courthouse lawn, and drink sweet lemonade while carrying the blender?"

"I don't recall mentioning a blender."

"You did. In a prior conversation. It stuck with me. People in Fairfield always give blenders. And toasters."

"And baskets of cleaning products. Did I forget to mention that?"

"Oh yes, Queenie always gives cleaning products," Lori-Lou said. "Because one can never have too many of those."

"See how easily this is coming together when you put a man in charge?" Josh looked up from the game once again, ignoring his wife's grunt. "Now all you need is a date."

"Right, a date." I sighed.

"It might be easier to tell you when we can't have the wedding," Brady said. "Turns out the church has a lot of summer events. I think the only weekend that will work for everyone is the second Saturday in August."

"All the more reason to hold the wedding later in the day with the reception at sunset," I said. "It won't be so hot then."

"Well now, it looks to me like you two have officially planned your wedding." Lori-Lou fidgeted with her phone. "I'm sending all of these notes to you by text so you don't forget."

"Oh, I won't forget. But thank you."

"You're welcome." My cousin leaned down and took Izzy from me. "We need to get you two hitched so you can start producing gorgeous babies like this little doll."

At this point, we lost her to the oohing and aahing. Not that I minded. It felt so good to see Lori-Lou acting more like herself again. A few minutes later I followed her into the master bedroom, where she changed the baby's diaper and put her into the bassinet.

"So, what does it feel like?" I asked as we gazed down at the sleeping babe. "To be that much in love with a baby you've only just met?"

"Hey, you're the writer, not me." Lori-Lou gazed at her baby girl with admiration and love flowing from every pore. "Not sure I could put it into words like you could."

"Me? A writer?" I laughed.

"Well, yeah, Katie. You write articles and ads for the store all the time. So you tell me how to put into words what love feels like."

I gazed into the adorable face of that innocent baby and reached down to trace her cheek with my finger. "It feels like . . . the best gift you've ever received. Only, it's not Christmas, so you weren't anticipating the gift. And it's not your birthday either. The gift arrived in a completely blissful and unexpected way, when you least expected it."

"Um, I was expecting Izzy for nine months, remember?"

"You asked me to describe what love felt like, not just the love for a child, but in general. When I think about love, I can't help but think about Brady." A few quiet moments of introspection followed my words.

"You're smiling." Lori-Lou chuckled.

"Yeah."

"You know, I remember a time when you thought you were in love with Casey Lawson."

"Ugh. Did you have to go there?"

"Point is, you now know the difference between the real deal and the not-so-real deal."

"Yeah. I guess it's like they always say, you don't know a counterfeit dollar bill until you've handled a real one. Brady's the real bill. Er, the real deal." I laughed out loud. "And you're right. I thought I was in love. There's a difference between thinking it and actually being in it, if that makes sense."

"Perfect sense. And trust me when I say that one day you'll be sitting where I am now, holding a beautiful little baby in your arms and realizing that loving your husband is more beautiful—and more complex—than you knew. It goes so far beyond feelings and into the commonplace, everyday stuff—the dirty dishes, the screaming kids, the icky diapers." Her eyes filled with tears. "I think that being a mom has taught me to understand God's love for us, his kids. Does that make sense?"

"Perfect sense." I leaned over and gave her a hug. "And just for the record, I think you're one of his favorites."

"You too," she said.

That evening Brady and I talked all the way back to my place. I could tell from the excitement in his voice that he loved the idea of the outdoor reception. And I had every reason to believe our friends and loved ones would too, once the idea settled in. As for Nadia, I couldn't be sure. No doubt she would smile and carry on as if it made no difference, but I wondered if she might secretly hold a grudge, feeling as if her son had somehow gotten a raw deal on his wedding day. Hopefully not.

One thing was sure and certain: Brady and I needed to share our plans with our friends and family members so that they would stop trying to interfere . . . and the sooner, the better.

12

There You Are

People, even more than things, have to be restored, renewed, revived, reclaimed, and redeemed; never throw out anyone.

Audrey Hepburn

Okay, so explain this to me one more time, Katie Sue." My mother's voice faded a bit as she fidgeted with her phone. Then her volume rose several decibels. "I've. Put. You. On. That. Speakerphone. Thingy. So. Your. Pop. Can. Hear. You."

Alrighty then. But why did she feel the need to overenunciate?

"Tell him what you said." Mama's volume leveled out. "Even the strange parts."

Don't sigh, Katie. Don't sigh.

I sighed.

"I said, Brady and I are going to get married indoors at the church on the evening of Saturday, August 13th, at six o'clock, with a reception to follow outdoors on the courthouse lawn."

"Well, that's different," my father said.

"At least she's not doing a *Gone with the Wind* theme like Crystal," Mama said. Her volume rose once again. "You're. Not. Are. You?"

"No. No theme to speak of, unless you call quaint and old-fashioned a theme. And that's what I wanted to talk to you guys about. I'm going to need some help with ideas for the picnic."

"Wait . . . picnic?" Pop asked. "Did I hear that right?"

"Yes, but not a traditional one. The reception will have a picnic feel. For example, we're thinking about offering a lemonade stand instead of punch."

"Excuse me?" Pop asked. "Couldn't quite make out that part."

"I think she said lemonade stand, Herb," Mama said.

"Well, if it's a warm day—and it will be—I think we need to do an old-fashioned lemonade stand with all different flavors people can add to their home-squeezed lemonade."

"Home-squeezed? I'm going to have to employ all of the WOP-pers to squeeze lemons. I think Prissy has a great lemonade recipe."

"Prissy? Hmm. Well, that's why I need your help . . . with the WOP-pers. You're hereby hired as intermediary, Mama."

"Oh, joy to the world." She groaned. "Okay, job accepted. I'm sure Crystal will help. She's such a sweet girl. But remember, honey, I'll have to do most of the planning from out of state. You okay with that?"

"Yep. But we'll see one another at Jasper and Crystal's wedding. And Joni asked when she should plan my bridal shower. I suggested the day after their wedding—a Sunday—because we'll all be together anyway."

"Everyone but Jasper and Crystal. I hear they're going to Atlanta for their honeymoon. So where are you guys going for your honeymoon, Katie Sue?" Mama asked. "Have you decided yet?"

I'd hesitated to tell her the expense Nadia had gone to for our honeymoon, but I couldn't put it off any longer. "We're going to Bali, Mama. It's in the—"

"Pacific!" Pop's voice grew more animated. "I know, honey. I've been researching it myself. Did you know that it can cost you up to ten grand a night to stay in some of those rooms?"

"I heard something like that. Anyway, we're going to Bali. But back to our reception. We want it to be fun and summery, sort of a cross between formal and informal. The lemonade stand will help. We'll have raspberries, blueberries, and peaches."

"Peach lemonade?" Mama asked.

"Of course. That's what I'm thinking, anyway. Someone can serve the lemonade next to the cake, which will be light and summery too. Nothing heavy or overly decorated."

"So, that shabby chic thing everyone's doing?"

"No, not that either. Just sweet. That's the word

I'm looking for here—sweet. To match the Loretta Lynn gown. To match my life, Mama. I've had a sweet life in a sweet town with sweet people gathered around me. I've been so blessed."

"Well, when you put it like that, I guess I can't argue about the outdoor reception. It's going to be perfect, honey. But don't tell your dad about the lemonade stand. He'll want to put on that old-fashioned ice-cream getup of his and serve it."

"I'm right here, ladies," my father said. "And I just heard every word of that, remember."

"Oh, right."

"Ooh, that's a cute idea, Mama. Ice cream. Maybe we can do an ice cream stand too. Near the cake, I mean. And what would you think about doing summer flavors in the cake? Strawberry. Lemon. White with raspberry filling? We can do a separate chocolate cake for the groom's cake, but the wedding cake can be light and summery. Great with ice cream. And raspberry lemonade. Yum."

"I think it's perfect. What kind of music will you have?"

"We've talked about doing a lot of older songs, from days gone by. Sweet stuff. Do you think Mr. Harrison is still in that band? You know, the one with the old-fashioned music? Brady suggested hiring a band to play throughout the whole reception. Doesn't that sound like fun?"

"Yes, but this isn't at all the way you've

described your wedding plans to me in the past," Mama said. "Everything was going to be very traditional—all of it in the church, including the reception. But I'm not arguing. I love these ideas."

"Thank you for understanding, Mama. Times change." I gave a little shrug. "People change."

"Just promise you won't have corn dogs. Remember what happened at the fair a couple of years back, when Gilly choked on a corn dog and scared us all half to death?"

"Of course."

"And no barbecue. It's so messy."

"We were thinking about easy foods that people can eat while they're visiting with others. I can tell you more about that later, but I've been looking up a ton of easy recipes. I was hoping the folks at Sam's could help with that."

"I'm sure they could do anything you need. It all sounds lovely. And I'm just so relieved you're getting married at home. What a blessing. How's Nadia taking the news?"

"She knows we're not getting married at the Gaylord, but she doesn't know any of the particulars about the wedding yet. I'm actually on my way to the store now. Brady and I are going to tell her together. In fact, we're going to tell everyone. We're going to gather the troops just before opening the store."

"Great idea. Now maybe they'll all leave you alone and let you make your own choices."

Pop snorted.

"Well, I have to go, Mama. Can't wait to see you at Jasper's wedding."

"I'll be happy to be back home in Fairfield, honey. It'll be nice to see everyone again."

We ended the call and I breathed a sigh of relief. After all of my fretting, Mama had taken the news in stride. Hopefully the others would too. Especially Nadia.

I arrived at the store before nine o'clock. Since we weren't due to open until ten, I knew that I had time to grab a cup of coffee and check my emails. As I walked past all of the wedding gowns and into the hallway just beyond, I saw Nadia come out of the studio door. She took one look at me and an easy smile played at the corners of her mouth. "Hey, you."

"Hey, yourself. Did you have a good weekend?"

"I did. Busy, but good. I just got off the phone with Bridget Pennington. Looks like she'll be coming back in tomorrow. She talked me through her ideas, and I've already started sketching."

"Really? What do you think, Nadia? Did you like the Martina McBride idea?"

"Oh, I loved it." Nadia's eyes sparkled with obvious delight. "I adored the simplicity of the design on Martina's CMA dress. It served as the perfect foundation. Want to see the sketches?"

"Yes!" I followed her into the studio and gasped when she pulled out the sketches. "It looks just like she described! I love that off-the-shoulder look, and the train is magnificent."

"I agree. She's getting married in July, so Dahlia and her team will have their hands full getting it made and fitted, but I'm sure it will be perfect for her outdoor event."

"Has she mentioned anything about her father?" I asked. "Did he ever come around?"

"She did say that he'd reconciled himself to her ideas, but I have a feeling there's still a bit of resistance there. I've been giving some thought to calling him myself. We used to be friends. Maybe I could come up with something to say to win him over. You know?" As she spoke the words, Nadia's brow wrinkled.

"Something wrong?" I asked.

"Katie, all of this reminds me that I owe you a huge apology."

"O-oh?"

"Yes. Not for anything work related. I wanted to say that I've had time to think about my, well . . . zealous behavior over the past few weeks. I owe you an apology for getting too heavy-handed with my suggestions. I was out of line." Her eyes brimmed with tears, which really threw me. "Please forgive me."

"Nadia, I do. Of course. You're just excited." I gave her a hug.

"I am, yes. What mother wouldn't be excited about her only child's wedding? But there's more to it than that, Katie. When Brady's father and I got married, we were poor as church mice. We had nothing. I never had the big wedding. Everything was so simple. It was sweet, but I always wished I could've done more. So I guess in some small way I've been trying to create the wedding that I wish I'd had myself. Does that make sense?"

"It does. And one of these days you'll have that wedding, Nadia. I know you will."

"Me?" She shook her head. "Honey, I'm married to my business. I pity any man who would take me on as a wife. I work seventy hours a week and I love it that way. I wouldn't change a thing."

"Well, when he does come along, he'll love that about you. And the two of you will have the best wedding the Gaylord has to offer. I'll be right there in the center of it all."

"Hopefully rocking a baby or two." She gave me a little wink.

"Oh, now you've got me tending to a houseful of children?" I chuckled. "We'll see how that goes."

"Well, one or two would be nice. Before I get too old to play with them, okay?" She gave me a hopeful look. Just as quickly she pinched her eyes shut. "There I go, telling you what to do. Again. Forgive me?"

This time I laughed out loud. "It's okay, Nadia. You love me. It's clear you do. And I love you too. I wouldn't expect anything less from the woman who's going to be grandmother to my children."

At that, she shivered. "Ooh, *grandmother*. Sounds so old. Do you think the children could call me Nonny? I'd be Nonny Nadia."

"Anything you like." I paused to think something through, then dared to voice the question on my heart. "Do you mind if I ask why you decided to talk to me about this? Did Brady ask you to apologize or something?"

"No." She looked stunned by this notion. "We did talk, and it didn't take me long to realize I'd overstepped my bounds. But my conversation with Bridget really drove the point home."

"Oh?"

"Yes. When I realized how traumatized she was over her wedding plans, when she told me that her father had tried to take control, I realized that I'd sort of treated you the same way. Not *exactly* the same way, maybe, and not to the same effect, but I know when I've gone too far. I want you guys to be free to choose what you want to do and where you want to do it."

"We already have. I don't know if Brady told you, but we've definitely set our plans in motion. Not just the where and when parts, but the rest too."

"He refused to give me details. Just told me I'd have to wait until 9:00 a.m. to hear with everyone else." She glanced at the clock on the desk. "And it's 9:00."

"So it is. I'd better get out there. He's probably waiting on me."

I found Brady at the register with all of our workers clustering around him. To his right, Alva and Eduardo had locked lips.

"Hey, no PDA, you two," Brady hollered.

"PDA?" Eduardo looked perplexed.

"Public displays of affection," everyone else said in unison.

"Well, pooh on that." Alva threw her arms around Eduardo's neck and gave him another big smooch. We all erupted in laughter.

"Okay, okay, enough kissing," Eduardo said as he untangled himself from my aunt's tight embrace. "This morning is all about Brady and Katie, not us."

"Ooh, wedding plans!" Twiggy rubbed her hands together. "I can't wait!"

"Yeah, are you guys gonna tell us, or what?" Hibiscus asked.

"Can you make it quick?" Dahlia glanced back toward the studio door. "I have a bride coming at ten straight up for a fitting, and I still have some work to do on her gown."

"It's okay if you need to leave before we're done," Brady said. "But Katie and I wanted to let you guys know that we've settled on a plan for our wedding."

"At the Gaylord?" Twiggy asked.

"No." Brady shook his head.

"Cowboy themed, like I suggested?" Twiggy tried.

"Not that either," my sweetie responded with a firm smile.

"Did you read all of my ideas that I left on your desk?" Hibiscus asked. "Because I had some good ones. Of course, I totally understand if you don't want to use my starlight idea. It might've been a little far-fetched. But what about my idea of the Parisian theme? Little Eiffel Towers on every table?"

"Puh-leeze." Madge rolled her eyes. "You'll be happy to know I offered no ideas, Katie. Did you notice? There was nothing from me."

"I noticed." I gave her a thank-you smile and then nodded. "While I appreciate all of your great ideas—really, there were some doozies—Brady and I have decided to do the following." I reached to take his hand and gave it a squeeze as I spoke to our friends and loved ones. "We're getting married on Saturday, August 13th, at 6:00 p.m. at my church in Fairfield. The reception afterward will be held outdoors on the courthouse lawn. It's going to be the sweetest thing you ever saw. Twiggy, you'll be happy to know it's going to take place at sunset."

"Well, that's good, anyway." Still, she didn't look convinced about the rest.

"Interesting," Dahlia said. "Very interesting."

From the looks on all the faces in front of me, I could tell they hadn't quite caught the vision. No problem. Give us just a few minutes to explain, and we'd win 'em over.

13

If You Don't Know Me by Now

I heard a definition once: Happiness is health and a short memory! I wish I'd invented it, because it is very true.

Audrey Hepburn

Okay, so you're getting married at the church and having the reception outdoors at sunset." Twiggy put her hands on her hips and stared at me, her brow wrinkled in obvious confusion. "Sounds sweet. But I still can't figure out your theme."

"I guess you could say we're creating our own," Brady explained.

"We'll call it 'quaint and old-fashioned.'" Joyous feelings swept over me, just thinking about it. "Picture lemonade stands, possibly an ice cream area with a variety of toppings—all of the things you might equate with a small-town social gathering from days gone by."

"Cotton candy?" Twiggy asked. "Checkered tablecloths?"

"Um, no." I directed my answer to Nadia, who looked concerned. "We're not going that far. It's going to be gorgeous. I want it to be summery but classy, if that makes sense. Beautiful round tables with soft-colored linen cloths and sweet centerpieces."

"It's going to be great," Brady said. "A step back in time. Oh, that reminds me, we're hiring a band to do the music. Old-timey music."

"Old-timey music?" Nadia looked perplexed.

"I've never heard of a wedding like this before." Twiggy's nose wrinkled. "But I guess if that's what you want, Katie."

"It's not just what she wants, it's what I want too." Brady slipped his arm over my shoulders in a show of support. "We loved the idea of the picnic because it brings people together. Just the idea of it makes people happy. People lay down their differences and gather around the table to celebrate."

"Oh, and speaking of the tables, we decided to use beautiful hand-painted picnic baskets for centerpieces. They'll be opened with gerbera daisies peeking out. Cute, right? And we'll string lights all over the place, so it will be well lit when the sun goes down."

"Well, I for one think it sounds amazing." Jane gave me an admiring look. "You won't hear any arguments from me, Katie. And I'll be the first to line up to help. I saw some great picnic baskets at a hobby store the other day. Reasonably priced too. And I happen to know someone who's great at painting." She nodded in Eduardo's direction.

"Ah, I do enjoy painting as a hobby. A picnic basket will make an unusual medium, but I could give it a try, if you show me a sample."

"And I know a wonderful florist," Dahlia added. "I'd be willing to bet she can get you a great deal on the daisies."

Eduardo grinned. "And if you're looking for old-timey costumes for the vendors—the person manning the lemonade stand and the ice cream area—I have some connections."

"Thank you all. And most of all, thanks for understanding. This is our big day and it's going to be perfect. The thing that will really be the icing on the cake will be having you all there."

"I wouldn't miss it for the world, Katie," Dahlia said. "It's going to be great."

"Now, tell us about the bridesmaids." Twiggy twisted her hands together as if anticipating my response. "And what they're wearing."

I chose my words carefully. "Well . . . Lori-Lou will be matron of honor and Alva will be maid of honor."

"Ooh, I love that idea." Madge sighed.

"But what if Alva and Eduardo get married between now and then?" Dahlia asked. "Then what?"

Every person in the room turned to Eduardo, who turned all shades of red. Alva cleared her throat and gave him an imploring look.

"Then I guess I'll have two matrons of honor, which would be fine with me. As for the bridesmaids, they will be Crystal, Dahlia, and Twiggy."

"Whew! I'm in!" Twiggy giggled.

I turned to the other girls in the room, hoping no feelings were hurt. "I'd like to ask Hi and Jane to serve at the reception, if they're willing."

"I'm willing," Jane said.

"Me too," Hibiscus echoed. "Sounds like so much fun."

"But you didn't answer the important question. What are we *wearing?*" Dahlia asked. "Colors and styles, I mean."

Spoken like a true fashion designer.

"If we're going with pastel daisies for the bridesmaid bouquets, the gowns will complement. Soft yellows and blues and pinks and—"

"Lavender?" Alva clasped her hands together. "Ooh, my favorite color ever!"

"Okay, lavender," I said. "But nothing bright or startling. Just pretty. Summery. And I'm not thinking floor-length. Since it's summer, why not pick gowns that are calf-length. Or knee-length, even."

"Merciful heavens, have you seen my knees?" Alva groaned. "They're as knobby and ugly as bedposts. Can we please say calf-length?"

"You're my maid of honor, Auntie. Your dress can be completely different from the others.

And even their gowns don't have to be the same style, as long as they all work together."

"So, something off the rack, or something we design?" Dahlia asked. "We need to know pretty soon if we're going to be making all the gowns from scratch."

I looked Nadia's way. "Actually, I've been thinking about the Ever-After line you designed in Paris. So simple and elegant. Those dresses could be done in soft pastels, couldn't they?"

"Of course. I have the most luscious crepes in all the colors you're talking about: mint green, baby blue, peach blossom, cotton-candy pink, lemon chiffon, linen . . ."

"And lavender?" Alva asked.

Nadia nodded. "Well, technically it's called African violet, but it's similar, yes."

"We'll use the same pastel flowers on the cake," I said. "Multi-tiered for sure, since we're expecting lots of people. Not too fussy in design. I know everyone these days is going with that messy look with the burlap ribbon, but that's not really what I'm thinking. I like traditional."

"But not fussy," Nadia interjected.

"Right. And flowers in those same pastel colors."

"All of this talk about mints, cotton candy, peaches, and lemons has me hungry." Alva rubbed her stomach. "Wish I hadn't skipped breakfast."

"I have breakfast tacos in the studio," Eduardo said. "If we want to move this party back there, I'm happy to share with everyone."

"Sounds great," Brady said. He whispered in my ear, "That went well," and I nodded.

Everyone headed down the hallway toward the studio, but I remained in the front of the store, breathing a huge sigh of relief. A couple of minutes into my "thank you, Lord" prayer, Nadia appeared beside me. She patted me on the arm.

"Katie, I just wanted to say that I hope you're not going with my design on the bridesmaid dresses just because, well, you know . . . because you feel pressured to do so."

"Not at all, Nadia." I gave her what I hoped would be a reassuring look. "You know more about bridal fashions than anyone I've ever known in my life. It just makes sense that I'd choose something from one of your lines. Besides, you already did my gown, and I want everything to have a similar feel."

"The dresses in the Ever-After line will be perfect with your wedding gown, Katie. They're soft and flowing and very much in keeping with that whole stylish but simple look. Nothing too froufrou."

"Right. I've never been a froufrou kind of girl. Well, except when I was little and ran around in Lori-Lou's ballet tutu."

"Lori-Lou took ballet class?"

"Oh yes. She was the pride and joy of Fairfield's ballet studio and the first in our family to go en pointe."

"Who would've guessed?"

"Yes. She traded in her pointe shoes for receiving blankets." I laughed. "I think she'll look so pretty in one of those pastel colors. I just love how muted the colors are."

"Me too. They're pearlized. Lovely."

"I'm thrilled that peach is an option, color-wise. You know I was Peach Queen my senior year in high school, right? Lori-Lou was too—a couple of years ahead of me, of course."

"We'll put Lori-Lou in peach then, if that's okay with you."

"It's perfect, Nadia. She's going to be tickled pink. Er, peach." I laughed again. "I guess we'll let the other girls decide which colors they like best."

We headed down the hallway and into the studio, where we found the others laughing and talking. And eating breakfast tacos. Aunt Alva and Eduardo giggled as they fed one another.

"I guess we'll need to talk about Alva's gown," I whispered to Nadia. "It'll have to be different from the others."

Nadia quirked a brow. "You know what's going to happen there, right?"

"Eduardo?"

Nadia nodded. "Yes. He'll want to design her gown. With your permission, I'll let him. He'll come up with something in keeping with the Ever-After line. I know he will."

"Perfect."

"Ooh, speaking of perfect, I just love your outdoor picnic theme." Twiggy's voice sounded from my left. "And as for worrying about what others think, why bother? If I were you, I'd just plow forward with my own plans and forget what everyone else thinks."

"You? The one who created a Pinterest account for me? The one who told me I should keep everything Texas-themed? You would just tell everyone that you didn't care what they thought?"

She sighed and plopped into a chair. "Okay, okay. I get it. I've been a little pushy. But if you want the truth—and I'm just being honest here—I guess I got excited about your wedding because I'm just so excited about planning my own. Eventually. If your brother proposes."

"He's going to propose."

Twiggy's eyes lit up. "Really? Soon? Does he have a ring? Don't answer that. Ooh, but you have to tell me! Should I be trying on dresses?"

I put my hand up. "Slow down, girl. I'm sure a proposal is coming soon. I don't have an exact date, but the good news is, when it comes, you'll have the Pinterest account ready and waiting."

"Guess I'd better change the name on the account to my own." She gave me a sheepish look. "You okay with that?"

"Very okay, because Brady and I have our own plans. But they don't look anything like all of those pictures you've been pinning. Sorry to disappoint."

"Don't be. You have your wedding and I'll have mine."

"Who's having a wedding in here?" Madge asked as she took a couple of steps in our direction. "Twiggy? You gettin' hitched too?"

"Not anytime soon, I guess." Twiggy bit her lip. "Beau's career as a sports agent is really taking off. I mean, *really* taking off. He's flying to Phoenix this weekend and then he's going to Houston. His client list is really growing, thanks to Stan."

"Well, that's good . . . right?"

"Right." But Twiggy didn't sound confident. "I think he's just waiting to propose because he wants to make sure his career is solid."

This started a whole new round of conversations about careers. Not that I really minded. At least this time all of the attention was on someone else, not me.

In the middle of the chaos, Eduardo approached me. He took my hand in his and kissed it. "Congratulations, Katie. I'm so thrilled for you both."

"Thank you, Eduardo." I gave him a hug. "It's going to be wonderful. I can't wait."

"I would like to do something for you," he

178

said. "I know you're probably having a bridal shower in your hometown, but I wanted to offer my home for a party here as well. An engagement party, maybe? Or a shower for your local friends who don't care to travel to Fairfield? At any rate, *mi casa es su casa*."

"Eduardo, that's a lovely gesture. Very generous."

"We're family, sweet girl, and that's what family members do. They care for one another." He headed back over to my aunt, whose face melted into a buttery smile the moment he slipped his arm over her shoulders.

As I watched the two of them together, I had a suspicion it wouldn't be long until we really were family. Glancing around the room at so many of the people I loved, I had to conclude— we were already one big happy family, and I wouldn't trade them for anything in the world.

14
How I Feel

The most important thing is to enjoy your life—to be happy—it's all that matters.
Audrey Hepburn

After letting the others know about our plans, I somehow managed to get my wedding planning train back on track. The next several weeks were spent putting all of my ideas in motion. The girls seemed delighted with the pastel dresses they chose—Dahlia especially. I couldn't help but think that she would look gorgeous in her soft pink dress. And Lori-Lou, who now had her hormones in alignment, was tickled to hear she'd be wearing peach.

We weren't the only ones making plans. Bridget Pennington came and went from the shop, her Martina McBride dress looking more and more like the gown she'd dreamed of. We laughed and talked with every visit, and even commiserated about the woes of wedding planning. Most of all, we swapped stories about crazy friends and family members and their nutty attempts to derail us. We made a pact to forge ahead no matter how crazy things got.

The planning buzzed along until the second week in May, when Alva and I headed back to Fairfield for Crystal and Jasper's wedding festivities. I couldn't wait to spend time with Crystal and with my parents, who'd made it back to town in their fifth wheel, which—from what Mama told me—they'd parked in Queenie's driveway.

We arrived in Fairfield on Friday at noon. With the rehearsal, the bachelorette party, and so many other fun things to attend to, I needed to get my act together. First things first, however—finding a place to park at my grandmother's house. I'd never seen so many vehicles in one place before. Looked like the whole family had turned up to celebrate. I ended up parking half a block away and walking. Alva grumbled the whole way. All of her angst disappeared when we reached the doorway of the house, where my mother stood with outstretched arms.

"Come here, sweet girl!" Mama grabbed me and gave me the tightest hug. "Ooh, it feels so good to be back. I was starting to think we'd never see Fairfield again."

"Home sweet home." I wriggled out of Mama's embrace to give my father a hug. I couldn't help but notice he'd done something new with his hair. "Welcome."

"What in the world have you done to your hair, Herb?" Aunt Alva asked.

I stepped back to give him a scrutinizing look. "Yeah, what's up with that? You've done something different."

"What? Hmm?" His cheeks flushed red. And they weren't the only thing that was red.

"Pop? You dyed your hair?"

"Not dye. I used some of that Sun-In stuff. It's supposed to lighten your hair."

"I guess you're not supposed to use it on gray hair. I don't know." Mama waved her hand in the direction of my father's new 'do and groaned. "This is all the result of the man's pride. He has hair the color of sweet potatoes."

"I can think of worse things." He gave me a knowing look. "Don't judge my hair, woman. Besides, it'll grow."

Pop headed into Queenie's house, rambling about his hair. Alva followed on his heels, carrying on about how much she loved sweet potatoes. I'd just started to follow them into the house when Mama took me by the arm.

"Before you go in, have you talked to Queenie lately?" Mama asked.

"Not since last weekend. How come?"

"You haven't heard the news then."

"News?" For whatever reason, the words "She's pregnant?" slipped out.

Mama laughed. "No, but you're on the right track. Paul's great-granddaughter Corrie has come to live with them. She's five."

"What? Queenie and Pap-Paul are babysitting a five-year-old? For how long?"

"Not babysitting. They've taken her in. Period. No end date. She's inside right now, in one of the guest rooms. So you and Alva will have to share a space. Is that okay?"

"Of course, but I don't understand."

"I guess the little girl's mother is in some sort of rehab and the dad hasn't been involved in her life. So she needs a place to stay."

"But why her great-grandfather? Why not her grandparents? Seems strange that they'd skip a generation."

"Paul's daughter—Corrie's grandmother—has MS. She's in rough shape right now and doesn't feel like she could handle it. But she lives close by, in Teague, so she can see the girl as often as she likes."

I felt bad about the grandmother's struggles, but I also wondered if my own grandmother, who'd been battling knee problems and other health issues, was up to the task. Time would tell.

I carried my suitcase into the house and greeted the others, who'd clustered around the kitchen table, which was loaded with goodies. Through the crowd I caught a glimpse of a gorgeous little girl. The blonde reminded me a lot of myself at that age. A face filled with freckles. Tiny wisps of buttercup-yellow hair framing her face, the rest pulled back in a loose ponytail. Fair skin that begged for time outdoors. Only one difference: I'd always been tough as nails, athletic and strong. This little one looked thin. Frail, even. And where I'd always been bubbly and outgoing, she seemed shy and withdrawn. Not that I could tell much at first glance, but still . . .

"Corrie, I'd like you to meet your . . ." Queenie's eyes narrowed. "Hmm. What would she be to you, Katie?"

"Let's just say we're cousins." I put out my hand and she shook it, then pulled away just as quickly.

"Corrie's staying in the room Alva usually uses, Katie Sue." Queenie's brow wrinkled. "We're thinking Alva should bunk with you in your room."

"We have a fold-out sofa in the fifth wheel." My father gave me a look. "You should come party with us. Mama and I are a laugh a minute."

"Um, no thanks, Pop. I'd rather have a real bed, thanks."

"Your loss." He reached for a piece of cheese and a couple of crackers from one of the trays on the table. "But if you change your mind, we'll be in the driveway."

"One more reason why I'll share with Alva. Don't want to sleep in the driveway."

He sauntered out of the room with the goofiest look on his face. I glanced at my mother, who looked a little . . . odd.

"So, how's it going, Mama? Really?"

"Our travels, you mean?" She crossed her arms and then glanced to her right and left, probably checking to make sure Pop wasn't listening in. "It's okay."

"Just okay?"

"Look." She took me by the arm and pulled me to the side of the room. "I love your father. You know that, right?"

"Well, I would hope so."

"I love him."

"Sounds like you're trying to convince yourself."

"No. No convincing necessary. But honey, to put two people in such a small space, day after day after day after day . . . well, it's just not natural."

"Are you saying he's getting on your nerves?" I asked.

"Would it be awful if I said yes?" Mama slapped herself on the forehead. "He chews *so* loudly."

"He's always chewed loudly."

"You should hear it in the trailer. It's exaggerated. And he gargles for three minutes every morning. Three minutes. He sets a timer. We don't have room for a timer in that little bathroom. And who gargles for three minutes, anyway?"

"At least he has kissably fresh breath," I countered.

"That's the worst part." Mama tugged me farther away from the crowd and spoke in a hoarse whisper. "He's gotten . . . frisky."

Ew. I could've lived my whole life without hearing that. "Maybe just the empty nest thing?" I suggested.

"Well, yeah, but he's wearing me out. I'm trying to get him interested in scrapbooking. Cards. Cooking. Anything. But he keeps giving me that look."

"That look?"

"Yeah. You know the one. He keeps giving me that look. Do I look like a twenty-something? I'm an old woman. We're not on our honeymoon, after all."

"Well, maybe to Pop this is like a honeymoon. You know? He feels young again. Free."

"Which would explain why a few days ago he asked me to go skinny-dipping in the pond at the RV park in the middle of the night."

Oh, gross.

"Don't say it, Katie. I can tell from the look on your face what you're thinking. I'm thinking it too. But I'm tired of thinking up new ways to say I have a headache. I've taken to pretending I'm asleep when I'm really not."

I couldn't help myself. My laughter rang out across the room. Several of the others turned to look at me, including Queenie.

"Go ahead and laugh." Mama waggled her finger in my face. "Your day is coming. One day your kids will be grown and Brady will be chasing you around the RV park with that 'come hither' look in his eyes, and you'll be so worn out you won't know if you're coming or going. When that happens, you'll remember we had this little chat." She paused. "Only, by then I probably won't be around anymore."

"There are far bigger problems in the world, Mama, than having a husband who adores you."

"Sure. Side with your grandmother."

"Oh? You told Queenie all of this?"

"I did. And she said the same thing. I told her to get back with me when Pap-Paul takes to chasing her around the living room when no one's looking."

"Okay, I've heard enough." I put my hand up in the air to stop her. "I'd say I'll be praying about this, but I'm not sure how I'd word the prayer. So you're on your own there, Mama."

"Sure. Abandon me in my hour of need." She plopped down on a bar stool at the kitchen counter. "It's okay. Really. First my children grow up and move away. Next they forget about me in my hour of distress."

"What's this hour of distress you're talking about?" Pop's voice rang out from behind me. "I thought I'd cuddled all the distress right out of you, woman." He slipped his arms around her from behind and nibbled on her ear.

Gross.

"It's just you and me now, honey-babe. All the distress is behind us now that we're free and easy." He pinched my mother on the backside and then slapped her bottom.

My mother's face turned a rather violent shade of pink. "See what I mean? This is my life now."

"And what a life it is, eh?" A chuckle rose up from the back of his throat. "We're living in paradise. I'm the Adam to your Eve, woman."

Okay then. Enough already. Time to run for the hills. I grabbed my suitcase and headed into the guest room, the same room I'd stayed in as a teenager whenever I'd spent the night. The same room I now claimed as my own every time I came for a visit. A lovely sensation came over me as I took in the multiplicity of pillows on the bed, the quilt rack in the corner, the small dressing table.

That same wonderful sensation stayed with me as I walked back out into the living room to join the others. I felt the usual coming-home-to-Fairfield feelings settle over me. Maybe it had something to do with the wood paneling. Perhaps it had something to do with the large oil painting of Jesus on the living room wall. Maybe it had more to do with the rose-colored floral curtains and sunshine streaming through the slits between the panels. I couldn't quite explain it. But being here, in this house, felt comfortable.

Comfortable.

That's just how I felt at Alva's place too. Comfortable. Oh, not with the grape-colored décor in the guest room, maybe. And not with the Herculon sofa in the living room. But the house itself reminded me of Queenie's home. Strange how my grandmother and my aunt had so much in common, what with them not speaking for nearly fifty years and all. Still, no one could deny the obvious. They both had the same taste in most everything.

I glanced at the breakfast table and thought about the many times I'd shared family meals there. How many times we'd played Skip-Bo and other card games there. The arguments that had ensued when, as a little girl, I'd been told that I wasn't old enough to sit at the big table with the grown-ups. Yes, my whole life—my whole history—was firmly wound around that table. This house. These people. This town.

And though I loved Dallas, though I didn't regret my decision to move there, a little piece of my heart would always remain here . . . in Fairfield.

15

When God-Fearin' Women Get the Blues

I'm an introvert . . . I love being by myself, love being outdoors, love taking a long walk with my dogs and looking at the trees, flowers, the sky.

Audrey Hepburn

After a bit of conversation with the family, I settled onto the sofa next to Corrie, who looked completely lost and overwhelmed. Though I tried to make small talk, I couldn't get much out of her, so I shifted my attention to Mama, who seemed more than happy to visit.

"What does it feel like to be home again, Mama?" I asked.

"It's the strangest thing." She sighed. "Now that we've passed the house off to your brother and his bride, we're strangers in our own country. So it's not quite the same. I mean, a piece of my heart will always be here—and I'm sure we'll come home for good once the grandbabies start coming—but I feel so out of sorts without a house to return to."

"Maybe Pop'll build you a new one someday. You think?"

"Who knows. I just know we can't go back to the one you were raised in. Jasper's having the time of his life there, from what I've heard. Crystal told me he's renovating the kitchen. Now, I'm not saying he shouldn't—it's his house now—but it'll be so strange to see it looking different."

"Not adjusting to change well?" I asked.

"It's funny." Her expression grew more serious. "I rarely think about it when we're on the road, but when we're home again, I get a bittersweet feeling."

"Trust me, that's a feeling I know well." I gave a little shrug.

"At least I talked the old flirt into bringing me back for the wedding. He even fought me on that. Said it was duck hunting season in Arkansas."

"Pretty sure he was just pulling your leg, but I'm glad you're here. How long are you guys staying?"

"Oh, probably a couple of weeks, then we're headed east. Your father has decided we've spent enough time out west. We're going to Eureka Springs. Then Hot Springs. Then, I don't have a clue. Thank goodness we can keep in touch by phone, right? And that book face site."

"Facebook. And speaking of which, did you realize those photos you posted of the Grand Canyon were upside down?"

"Yes." She sighed. "It's a sign of my life right now. I can't figure out how to adjust them either. Your grandmother told me she had to stand on her head to look at them. She's a laugh a minute."

"Well, I'm glad you're enjoying your retirement. But please don't travel too far. My wedding's in three months and I'm going to need you." I paused, suddenly terrified at the rapidly approaching date. "Speaking of which, you're coming to the engagement party next Friday night at Eduardo's place, right?"

"Honey, I wouldn't miss it for the world." Mama's eyes filled with tears. "You might think I'm more distant lately because your father has me out and about, but nothing could be further from the truth. My heart is with my kids." A lone tear trickled down her right cheek. "You're all growing up, and that's the point, I guess. Before long the grandkids will start coming. Then you can bet your bottom dollar Pop and I will be back full-time. I wouldn't miss those babies for the world."

"Babies?" Crystal slipped into the spot beside me. "Who's havin' *bay*-bies?"

"No one. Yet." Mama patted her on the arm. "But don't make me wait too long, honey. I'm already shopping for baby things."

"Oh, you know we'll have a houseful." Crystal giggled. "I just *luv* me some *bay*-bies!" She turned her attention to Corrie, who still looked a bit lost in the crowd of older people. Crystal fussed over the youngster and finally got her to smile.

"She's going to make a great mama, isn't she?" I said as I observed their interactions.

"Indeed. And as I said, I hope she and Jasper don't wait too long to have a baby. I'm not getting any younger."

"Wait." My brother's voice sounded from behind me. He joined us, a look of panic on his face. "Who's having a baby?"

"Crystal," I told him.

"Not sure what you've heard." He put his hand up. "But let's stop that rumor right there."

"No, I meant eventually." Mama rolled her eyes. "I'm ready to become a grandmother."

"Well, let me get married first, Mama." Jasper's cheeks turned red. "That all right with you?"

"Yes, of course." She left us and headed toward the crowd of people in the breakfast room.

"Welcome to your new life." I patted my brother on the arm. "Wedding planning will soon be over and she'll be planning your baby showers."

"Ugh." He groaned. "Let's change the subject. Where's Brady?"

"He had some sort of meeting with Stan today, but he'll be here tonight for the rehearsal. I know he's looking forward to being a groomsman. Thank you for including him."

"No problem. Just makes sense that the two of you would walk the aisle together." My brother nudged me with his elbow. "Won't be the last time, a'course."

"Right." Man, was it hot in here, or what? I suddenly felt a little faint.

I managed to get control of myself and drew in a deep breath. "Anyway, he's coming tonight. You have everything ready for the rehearsal dinner?"

"Yep. Arrive at the church at 6:00. Rehearsal ends at 6:45. Rehearsal dinner in the fellowship hall at 7:00. Catered by Lone Star Grill."

"I thought you guys were using that place from Corsicana?"

"They're catering tomorrow. The wedding's going to be a full-out Southern plantation event, Katie."

"So I've heard."

"The WOP-pers are happy. Took some work, but you know my bride—she found a way. She put them all to work decorating the community center for the reception. Queenie said they've turned the whole place into Tara. Even added a faux stairway for photos. Pretty grand, from what I hear."

"Well, there you go." I pondered my sister-in-law's ability to make everyone happy. If she could do it, so could I.

I didn't really have much time to think about my own wedding. The next couple of hours were spent helping Crystal with last-minute details. Lori-Lou and her crew arrived around 5:00. Brady pulled in at 5:30. I could tell he had something on his mind, but we didn't have time to talk, what with all of the chaos going on around us. We all gathered at the church at 6:00, where I played my role as a bridesmaid with grace and ease. Of course, having my sweetie at my side as we walked down the aisle made it all the better.

I couldn't help but admire Joni and Casey, who worked in tandem to coordinate the rehearsal. She stood with clipboard in hand, telling folks where to go and what to do. Casey ran the sound and buzzed up and down the aisles of the church, checking the microphones and the lights. Turned out they made a pretty good team. Who knew?

When the rehearsal ended, we gathered in the fellowship hall for food. Our options? Chicken-fried chicken and chicken-fried steak—true Southern fare. The bride- and groom-to-be thanked the wedding party and offered small gifts. I had to laugh when I opened my gift box and saw the water globe of Tara. I turned the little key and listened as the theme to *Gone with the Wind* played.

Brady and I never did have a chance to talk. He ended up back at his hotel and I headed over to Queenie's place, where I tumbled into bed, exhausted. When I awoke the following morning, the smell of bacon greeted me. Yum. I ate a quick breakfast, then headed straight up to the church to meet Crystal and my fellow bridesmaids—Dahlia and Twiggy—to get ready for the 10:00 a.m. ceremony.

I found Crystal in an emotional state. It took a bit of doing, but we finally got her calmed down. Dahlia, cool as a cucumber, helped her into the ruffled, hooped gown, and I gasped when I saw the finished product.

"Oh. My. Stars." I stared at my future sister-in-law, my jaw hanging. "This is what Eduardo and Dahlia have been working on for you?"

She turned to face me, and I took in the fabulous gown with its off-the-shoulder ruffled neckline and hooped skirt.

"Do you like it?" Her Southern drawl seemed even more exaggerated with this magnificent gown. "It's a replica of the gown that Scarlett wore in the barbecue scene of *Gone with the Wind*. Do you recognize it?"

"Well, it's very familiar, and very Southern." I stepped a bit closer to see firsthand. Dahlia tied the dark green bow, which served to accentuate Crystal's tiny waistline.

"You're looking at nearly twenty yards of fabric," Dahlia said as she fussed with the train.

"Twenty?" I shook my head and tried to picture the cost. How had Crystal managed this? She and Jasper barely eked out a living at the hardware store.

"I know you're never going to believe me," Crystal said. "But Eduardo had this fabric in his stash at his house. Did you know he has a whole room filled with vintage fabrics? This entire gown is silk organza and taffeta."

"I guess he left off that room when we got the tour of the house. Don't recall any silk or taffeta, unless you count the curtains in his personal theater." I chuckled.

"It's true." Crystal used her palms to smooth out a wrinkle in the skirt. "He donated the fabric, Katie. Donated it. Can you believe that? And he donated his time to help Dahlia design and construct the gown too."

"Whoa." This just confirmed my love for Eduardo. He was a peach of a guy.

Peach. Ha-ha. I was Fairfield's Peach Queen. He was a peach of a guy. Funny.

"You don't see as many hoop skirts in modern wedding gowns," Dahlia said. "And for good reason. The hand-stitched hem is nine inches deep. And would you like to guess the circumference of the hoop?"

I shook my head. "Wouldn't even know where to start. Five feet? Six?"

"A hundred ninety inches. That's over five yards, not five feet. If you laid it out end to end, it would be wider than your office. But the hem of the skirt is a lot wider than the hoop. Want to guess?"

"Ten yards?" I tried.

"Wow, you're good!" She gave me an admiring look. "How did you know?"

"Totally guessing."

"Believe it or not, the bodice took the most time. It's boned, all the way around."

"Uncomfortable?" I asked Crystal.

"Not too bad. I'm wearing a corset underneath."

"Boy howdy, is Jasper gonna have a doozy of a time getting all of this off you," Alva chimed in from the doorway.

"Alva!" Crystal gave a nervous laugh, looking more than a little embarrassed.

"No, she's right." Dahlia twisted the bow a bit tighter. "That bodice is loaded with hooks and eyes. And they're all concealed, so he's going to have a doozy of a time, all right, especially when it comes to locating the ones that connect the bodice to the skirt."

"My goodness." Was it getting warm in here, or what? Hopefully this awkward conversation would not be repeated on my wedding day.

"My favorite part is all the ruffles at the neckline." Crystal fingered the gorgeous, full ruffles and sighed.

"Circles of fabric," Dahlia explained. "Twenty-two circles, to be exact. Oh, and the whole thing is finished off with this luscious green velvet sash."

"Also boned." Crystal let out a little squeak as Dahlia tied it too tight. "But totally worth it to look like Scarlett."

"And from what I hear, Madge helped Jasper find the perfect tux. He's dressed like Rhett Butler?"

"But of course." Crystal giggled. "I wouldn't have it any other way."

"Well, this I have to see. If he goes through with it, I mean."

"Oh, he'll go through with it," Crystal said. "I can assure you he'll go through with it. If he wants to make it to the honeymoon."

Dahlia stood back and examined the bride in all her glory. "Scarlett herself would be proud! It's brilliant, if I do say so myself."

"It's huge." Twiggy's eyes widened. "Hope you fit down the aisle."

"Oh, it is, isn't it?" Crystal fussed with the skirt, swishing right and left. "But I'll fit. Joni measured the space ahead of time."

"Speaking of Joni, where is she?" I glanced at the clock on the wall. "Haven't seen her for a while."

"She's checkin' in with the decoratin' team at the community center." Crystal pouted. "Wouldn't even let me see one picture, can you believe that?"

"Good for her. I'm sure it's going to be amazing, Crystal. Everything you've dreamed of."

"Yes, this is *all* just like I pictured!" She reached over to give me a hug but couldn't manage it with her huge skirt. "Oops! How am I gonna kiss the groom?"

"My question is, how are you and the groom supposed to stand close to each other for the actual ceremony at all?" Twiggy shook her head. "Guess I'll just have to wait and see."

16

For These Times

Nothing is impossible, the word itself says "I'm possible"!

Audrey Hepburn

By 9:45 Crystal and Jasper's wedding guests had arrived. By 9:55 we were standing in the foyer of the church—Crystal looking a bit pale and the bridesmaids looking very . . . Southern.

Minutes later, with my arm linked through Brady's, I sashayed up the aisle in my soft green gown, a smile plastered on my face. Underneath the form-fitting dress, beads of sweat trickled down my spine. I felt a little woozy, what with the heat doing such a number on me.

Good grief. If it was this hot in May, what would our August wedding be like?

With Brady's help I made it to the front and took my place as maid of honor, but the room was looking a little out of sorts. Every pew looked doubled. Or tripled, even. I blinked and things cleared right up. Well, enough for me to catch a glimpse of my brother, anyway. Standing there in that Rhett Butler–esque tuxedo, Jasper looked a little overwhelmed. Who could blame him?

I allowed my gaze to travel across the sanctuary. Crystal had done a magnificent job of decorating. Swags of tulle draped along the edges of the pews, forming a welcoming aisle. The gorgeous columns must've presented a challenge, as well as the tulle and twinkling lights that connected them all. My eye was drawn to the candelabras all decked out with roses. The unity candle. The bridesmaids, all in a row, wearing their summery mid-calf gowns. The groomsmen in their tuxedos.

Mama snapped photos on her new smartphone. I gave her a "stop that" look, but she ignored me and kept on snapping. As my gaze shifted away from my mother, I noticed all of my friends from the bridal shop—Madge, Nadia, Hibiscus, and Jane. Hi gave me a little wave, but Jane sat, arms folded, looking pretty glum. Nothing new there. In spite of our words of encouragement, the girl wore her singleness like a shroud these days.

From up above, the ceiling fan finally spun around enough times to cool me down a bit. The woozy feeling passed right as the back doors of the sanctuary opened and Crystal walked through on Pop's arm.

The entire congregation gasped in unison. I heard Prissy and Bessie May whisper—a little too loudly—something about the width of the skirt. I understood their concerns. Pop had to hold her literally at arm's length, which meant the two of them took up every square inch of the aisle's width as they made their way forward.

But make it they did. I shifted my gaze back to my brother, who stared at his bride with big, round eyes. Yep. That's how a groom was supposed to look at his bride, with passion and fire in his eyes, balanced with equal parts stunned silence over her beauty. Or maybe he was stumped by the yards and yards of fabric and the massive skirt.

As they neared the front of the room, Crystal gave a little giggle as my father bumped into her hoop skirt. I heard him whisper, "Sorry 'bout that," to which she responded, "No harm done, Pop."

In that moment, as she called him "Pop," reality set in. Crystal really was becoming a sister to me. For the first time in my life I'd have a sister-friend to laugh with, to share hopes and dreams with, to babysit for.

But first we had to get these two hitched. My brother took Crystal's hand, her skirt shifting slightly the other direction as they stepped into position side by side. Perfection. Pap-Paul greeted the congregation and kicked things off with a prayer.

The ceremony was beautifully scripted to have a Southern flair from start to finish. Even Pap-Paul pulled a few lines of his text from *Gone with the Wind*. Priceless. I could tell from the expression on Crystal's face that she was loving every minute of this, and wasn't that just how it should be? Every bride deserved her day, after all—and this one appeared to be having the time of her life.

The ceremony came off without a hitch. Well, unless you counted the part where my brother almost dropped Crystal's wedding ring. He caught it just in time and the guests all laughed. By the time the bride and groom had their first kiss as husband and wife, I'd somehow managed to get the "I'm going to pass out from the heat" thing under control. Maybe the AC had kicked in. Either way, I made it back down the aisle on Brady's arm with no woozy feelings—well, other than the ones that happened when he tipped me backwards for a big kiss in the church's foyer.

"It'll be us next, Katie," he whispered as he brought me upright. "You ready for that?"

"Ready to be married, yes. Ready with all the wedding plans? Hardly."

"I still say we could skip all that and go to Hawaii."

I caught a glimpse of Joni and Casey together and shook my head. "Nope. The Fisher clan would murder us and bury our bodies."

"What's all this talk of murder?" Joni asked as she walked our direction. "Not at any wedding I'm coordinating . . . though I did think those WOP-pers were going to murder Casey yesterday at the community center when he hung some of the set pieces incorrectly."

"Set pieces?" Brady looked perplexed.

"Oh, honey . . ." Joni waved her hand dramatically, and her voice took on a strong Southern flair. "Don't *tay*-ul me you haven't seen the community *cen*-tuh *yay*-ut? It's Tara, sprung to life!"

"We've heard about it," Brady said.

"But haven't seen it," I finished.

Twenty minutes later, we saw it firsthand. I stepped inside the ornate community center and gasped as my gaze shifted from one set piece to another. "Heavens to Tara!"

"Whoa." Brady's eyes widened. "I feel like we've stepped onto a movie set."

Bessie May approached, hands clasped together. "What do you think? Do you like it? We had the time of our lives working together." Her eyes misted with what could only be described as happy tears. "All of the ladies of the town, pulling together to make this happy for Crystal and Jasper."

"It's really . . . something." Brady turned his head to look at the staircase. "Wow."

Bessie May put her hand on my arm. "You know, Katie, there's much to be said for team-work. Once we laid down our desire to do things the way we'd always done them, we all came out winners. I might be in my golden years, but I'm never too old to learn. So much can be accomplished when we all come together."

I thought about the truth of those words. How many times had we pulled together at Cosmopolitan Bridal? We'd put together a terrific Black Friday sale, hadn't we? Through teamwork. And we'd weathered several storms and several temperamental brides. Again, teamwork.

"Bessie May, that's one of the things I love most about Fairfield." I felt a lump well up in my throat. "For as long as I can remember, this town has felt safe to me. I knew I could count on everyone and they knew they could count on me. It's hard to describe to people who live in the big city, but small towns just have that family feel to them. We're all brothers and sisters."

"Well, yes." She gave Prissy a sideways glance. "But don't you go calling Prissy my sister. She drives me out of my ever-lovin' mind half the time."

"Okay, okay." I laughed.

Bessie May headed over to the punch table, and I somehow got my giggles under control. My grandmother gave me a little wave and hobbled my way, her knee looking stiffer than usual.

"What was all that about?" she asked.

"Oh, just Bessie May telling me how the women worked together to make the community center look like Tara. It's amazing."

"To say the least," Brady echoed.

"Yes, Bessie May pulled from her stash of Civil War gowns up at the historical society, though it was like pulling teeth to get her to agree to it. And Prissy decided we needed to have curtains that looked just like the ones Scarlett used to make her gown. Not that she sewed her own gown, but you get the idea. And don't even get me started on the food. Crystal was right to choose that wonderful restaurant in Corsicana to cater. They came up with just the right goodies to fit the theme."

"I noticed the theme. It would be hard to miss." I giggled. "Crystal takes her Southern roots very seriously."

"As should any Southern belle." My grandmother flinched and shifted her position.

"You feeling okay, Queenie?"

"Just a little tired. The knee's hurting today. It's a little swollen. But mostly I'm just exhausted. Don't seem to have a lot of energy lately. Having a five-year-old in the house is a bit more than I'd anticipated."

"No doubt. How's that going?"

She shrugged. "She's an adorable little girl, just feisty. Summer's just starting, so I have three months to keep her entertained before school starts. Grateful for Crystal, though. She's really taken a liking to her."

"Well, I'm glad about that. She's so good with people of all ages."

"Indeed." My grandmother nodded and yawned. "Sorry. Better go sit down."

I'd just started to fret over her condition when Twiggy and Hibiscus approached, deeply rooted frowns on their faces.

"What's up?" I asked. "Someone die?"

"Not yet, but give me time." Twiggy rolled her eyes.

"Miss Doom-and-Gloom is at it again," Hi added.

"Doom-and-who?" I asked.

"I *heard* that, Hi." Jane joined us, her arms now tightly folded at her chest. "And get a grip, would you? I'm not that big of a downer, am I?"

To my right, Madge cleared her throat.

"What's going on?" I asked. "Jane? You okay?"

She turned to face me. "I'm about wedding'd out, that's all."

"And isn't this a fine place to make such a negative statement?" Hibiscus gestured to the over-the-top décor. "You had to come into a perfectly lovely wedding and ruin it with your Debbie Downer speech?"

"Just stating my point." Jane put her hands on her hips. "Everyone's engaged but me. So yeah, I'm sorry if I'm bringing you down. It's just a hard pill to swallow, especially on days like this, when everyone has their own special someone to spend the day with."

"For the record, I'm not engaged," Dahlia said. "Dewey and I are dating, but we're not engaged."

"Semantics." Jane waved her hand as if to

dismiss that idea. "It's just a matter of time. Point is, you have a guy in your life. You have possibilities. Me? I've got no possibilities. Well, none but a life of solitude and loneliness and peanut butter sandwiches. By myself. In my apartment. My apartment that I live in alone. Yes, last time I checked . . . no possibilities."

"Well, isn't this a lovely event." Madge pulled a wedding program out of her purse and fanned herself. "Just lovely."

"Possibilities?" I asked. "Define *possibilities*."

"I'm just saying that life isn't always like you read about in romance novels," Jane said. "Not every girl gets her happily ever after. There isn't a hunky guy waiting around the corner for all of us. Sometimes things don't work out. Sometimes people go to bed exhausted with being single and wondering if they'll ever have the kind of life they dream of."

"Well." Brady shook his head. "I guess that calls for a glass of punch. I'll be right back." He slinked away, glancing back at me and mouthing, "Sorry."

Coward.

I tried to think of something encouraging to say, but only managed a weak, "Everything happens in God's time. Just be patient."

"It's so easy for engaged or married people to give advice, isn't it?" Jane looked perturbed. And don't give me that spiel about how I just need to be closer to God in order to feel fulfilled. I've heard that before."

Even if it's true?

"Sometimes a girl just wants a guy to wrap her in his arms. Is that asking too much?"

"No." I felt the sting of tears in my eyes as I responded. "But Jane, God knows that's your desire."

"Then why doesn't he do something about it?" She gave me a hard glare. "There are a thousand ways he could bring the right guy into my world, but it hasn't happened."

"Yet." Madge spoke softly. "It hasn't happened *yet*. But I think it's fair to say I can speak to this with some degree of authority. I've had a lot of 'yets' in my journey."

Jane's jaw flinched, and for a moment it looked as if she might punch someone. "Well, I can't handle the waiting. So forgive me if I don't jump up and down and cheer when I think about how long you had to hang on before Mr. Right finally showed up at your door."

"Ouch." Madge's eyes narrowed to slits. For a minute I thought she might take Jane down. Instead, she waggled a finger in her direction. "I get it, girl. I do. But I'll tell you what—you go on being bitter like this and you'll attract no one. Well, no one but the flies, anyway." Madge turned on her heels and headed to the cake table.

Her words served to stop Jane in her tracks.

Still, talk about awkward. Thank goodness Casey's voice came over the loudspeaker just then, announcing the arrival of the bride and groom, who took to the floor for their first dance as man and wife—to the theme of *Gone with the Wind*, of course. Likely not my brother's choice of music, but he didn't seem to be focusing on the song, anyway. No, his eyes were firmly riveted to his new bride. Mine were too. I noticed she'd removed the hoop and pinned up the back of the skirt. Good move.

When their dance ended, Crystal greeted her guests, stopping to laugh and talk with everyone. Then Casey, still serving as deejay, encouraged the guests to get their food. The rest of the morning whirled by like a colorful Southern vortex whipping around the community center, sucking us all into its grasp. Even Jane seemed to settle down a bit.

When the meal ended, the bride and groom headed to the cupcake table, where they did a lovely job of smashing frosting into each other's noses. Lovely. Corrie, who seemed to have fallen for Crystal, hovered close—to the point where Queenie had to scold her a bit. Crystal didn't seem to care, though. She offered the youngster a cupcake and then gave her a little kiss on the cheek.

Casey's voice came over the loudspeaker once more, and he encouraged the guests to hit the dance floor. I had a feeling most would oblige.

Pap-Paul slipped his arm around my grand-mother's waist. "I think what this gal needs is a spin around the dance floor." He extended his hand. "Would you do me the honor, Scarlett?"

"Why, certainly, Rhett." Queenie giggled. "I mean, Ashley."

"Call me whatever you like."

She flinched again and reached down to pat her knee. "Just promise to catch me if I go down."

"I promise."

Brady drew near and pulled me close. "Would you like to dance, Katie?"

"Maybe. In a minute." I rested against him. "Right now I just want to take it all in."

"Getting ideas for our big day?" he asked.

"Um, no." Laughter rose up. "This isn't my sort of theme, sorry."

"Mine either, but it's clear the bride is loving it, and it's equally as clear that your brother is going along with it all. I think he'd do anything to make his bride happy."

I turned to face my groom-to-be, my heart full. "Promise me one thing, Brady."

"What's that?" He gazed at me with such tenderness that I literally felt my heart swell.

"Promise you won't just 'go along with' my plans. I want you to chime in every step of the way, so that you're fully represented too."

He put his hand up in the air as if taking an oath. "I promise. Anything else?"

"Yes. I'd like that dance now."

Brady took me by the hand and led me to the dance floor, where he gave a deep bow before starting the dance. I curtsied—it just felt right—and then settled into his arms. There, in that lovely place, I felt completely grounded. Rooted. Settled. What did it matter where I lived—Fairfield, Dallas, or the moon? With this guy at my side, I'd always be at home.

17
Back in the Saddle

It's that wonderful old-fashioned idea that others come first and you come second. This was the whole ethic by which I was brought up. Others matter more than you do, so "don't fuss, dear; get on with it."

Audrey Hepburn

On the Friday after Crystal and Jasper's big day, Brady picked me up for our engagement party. The minute he saw me in my black dress, he let out a whistle.

"Whoa. I'm marrying a beauty queen."

"Hardly." I gave him a kiss on the cheek. "But thank you for saying that."

"No, really. You look amazing."

I gave a little twirl and my skirt flared. "You really like it? You're not just saying that? I've had it for ages but didn't think I'd ever get to wear it."

"You look like a million bucks. Want me to call the photographer from *Texas Bride* for another cover shoot?"

"Um, no thank you."

"Well, speaking of photos, don't be surprised

if my mother tries to snag a few tonight for the society column of the *Dallas Morning News*. She mentioned it earlier."

"I can live with that. No doubt the sports page will want to cover the story too. Basketball players will love the pictures, I'm sure."

"Well, speaking of basketball . . ." He pursed his lips, the silence between us suddenly awkward. "Remind me to talk to you about that later. Now that my knee is better, Stan's trying to cut a new deal with the Mavericks."

"W-what?" My thoughts went off in several different directions at once. "Are you serious?"

"Nothing solid. And I haven't talked to my orthopedist about it—or anyone else, for that matter. But the knee feels so much better now and I'm almost back to full range of motion. Maybe God is giving me a second chance at something I love."

"Wow. Brady, that would be . . ." I let my words trail off because I didn't know what to say. Amazing? Terrifying? Wonderful? Risky? All of those words seemed to fit. If he went back to basketball, we would lose him at the bridal salon. And he might injure his knee again. But if he let this opportunity pass him by—if he really felt he could handle it but didn't go for it—he might never forgive himself.

Brady led the way to his truck and opened the passenger door. I tossed my purse inside and then climbed up into the seat. Seated up so high, I felt a little like a queen. Checking my appearance in the mirror, I realized my lipstick needed a touch-up, so I did that while he walked around the truck and got inside.

My mind kept shifting back to the basketball conversation, and my heart swelled with emotion. I could hardly stand the fact that he'd had to give up something he loved so much. If God opened a door for him to return to pro ball, who was I to squelch his dreams? Instead, I opted to shift the conversation. "I'm so relieved your mom sent me home from work early." I smacked my lips together and tossed my lipstick back in my purse.

"She thought you might enjoy having extra time to get ready. Speaking of which, did you realize Eduardo left the shop at noon?" He stuck the key in the ignition.

"Yes. He picked up Alva before heading to his house. Whatever they're doing, they're doing it together."

"Yep. Any idea what they have up their sleeves?" Brady asked. "You don't suppose he's turning his house into a movie set for us, like Crystal did with the community center, do you?"

"Surely not."

He started the truck and put it into gear. "You okay not knowing?" He glanced in the rearview mirror and backed the truck up.

"I am. The whole 'top secret' thing makes it extra special."

Knowing that Mama and Pop would be there made it special too. And Queenie and Pap-Paul. And my brothers. And Lori-Lou and Josh, who had hired a sitter for the kids.

"I hope Eduardo isn't feeling overwhelmed right about now." I glanced out the window, distracted by incoming rain clouds. Hopefully we wouldn't run into bad weather. I turned to Brady, my thoughts shifting back to Eduardo. "Do you think he's regretting offering his house for such a big event?"

"I don't know." Brady put on his turn signal and eased the truck into the right lane. "He was sweating when he left the shop today."

"Well, it *is* hot outside," I argued.

"True, true." Brady laughed and then changed the direction of the conversation to talk about a problem with one of our customers.

I'd never been the sort to expect pampering, especially not from family members, but this whole idea of holding an engagement party at Eduardo's house made me feel like a princess. I knew the moment we arrived that the evening would be spectacular. We were greeted at the front door by a gentleman in a tuxedo who offered to take my purse.

"You can trust him, honey," Aunt Alva said as she appeared behind the man. "No worries. He won't steal it."

The gentleman looked slightly offended by this, but regained his composure.

"Of course." I handed the man my purse and he took it to the front hall closet. I gave Alva a closer look, whistling as I saw her fancy gold dress. I'd seen my aunt in a variety of situations, but never as mistress of the manor. Wowza. She looked like a million bucks in her glittering gown. And the hair and makeup! Whoa.

"I had a little help getting ready." She leaned in to whisper, "Eduardo thought it would be fun to pamper me, so he hired a team. Apparently it takes a village to get your old auntie looking like a princess."

"Well, they did a fantastic job. You look amazing."

Her eyes sparkled with mischief. "If you think this is great, just wait till you see what he's cooked up for the party, Katie. I'm so glad you let him do this for you. He's had the time of his life. I don't believe he's been this excited since we told him he could make my lavender gown for your wedding."

"I'm so glad." From the looks of things, we were all about to have the time of our lives. I could hardly believe someone had gone to so much trouble for me and Brady.

Alva ushered us into the large living area, complete with exquisite—if not over-the-top— décor. I'd been here before and couldn't wait to see what our guests thought when they saw the place. If Liberace had a living room in heaven, it probably looked a little something like this. Shimmering white sofas with fringed gold pillows. Glass coffee tables loaded with art pieces from all over the world. And the pièce de résistance? A fabulously large grand piano— white—with gleaming gold candlesticks. Yep. I could almost hear a heavenly choir singing as they took it all in.

Eduardo swept into the room, dressed in white. Well, except for the teal ascot. His suit could have easily come straight off a movie set from the olden days.

"My darling!" He reached for my hand and kissed it. "You have arrived." With his index finger Eduardo made a twirling motion. "Turn, please. I must see this exquisite gown!"

I did a spin and he sighed. "My only regret about this dress is that I did not make it myself. Wherever did you find it?"

"At a little boutique in Fairfield. It's closed down now. They're turning it into a bakery. I bought the dress last year but haven't had a chance to wear it till now."

"I'm glad you've saved it until tonight. You look like a princess." He gave Brady a quick glance. "And you've brought your prince, I see. He looks the part in this new suit."

Brady tugged at his collar. "I think I'm more

comfortable in my basketball shorts, to be honest. But I'll do just about anything for this girl of mine."

When he spoke the word "basketball," my heart skipped to overdrive.

Stay calm, Katie. He's going to be just fine.

"You are our first guests," Eduardo said. "But the others should be here shortly."

"I do hope they're not too late." Alva's nose wrinkled. "The hors d'oeuvres will grow cold."

"They're meant to be served cold, my precious." Eduardo gave her a tender look. "And never you worry about that. The cook has been keeping an eye on the temperature, I assure you, and the servers are only now filling their platters with the delightful delectables."

For a minute I thought Alva might swoon at the idea of such fineries, but she appeared to take it in stride. Or maybe she was just distracted by the ringing doorbell.

Hibiscus and Jane arrived first. Hi let out a whistle as she looked around the expansive living room with its furnishings. "Eduardo! Why didn't you tell us?"

"Tell you what?" He feigned innocence as he followed her gaze around the room.

"That you live like a king." Hi shook her head. "This changes everything. I always thought you were a regular guy."

"A little over-the-top," Jane added. "But regular."

"Oh, he's regular, all right," Alva said. "But you can thank me for that. The fiber drink I told him about really helped."

Good grief.

Jane walked over to a scantily clad Greek statue in the corner of the room and stared at it. "Is this real?"

"I got it while in Athens many years ago," Eduardo said. "Carved by a local man with a hunched back. Poor dear soul. Have you ever seen anything like it?"

"Not in anyone's living room," she muttered.

"It's amazing, Eduardo," Hi said, a look of admiration on her face. "In fact, the whole house is."

Those words were repeated many times by our guests as they took in his excessive décor, especially my parents, who couldn't seem to relax in the ornate room. One by one they entered, most oohing and aahing right away. Madge arrived a bit later than the rest of the guests with Stan at her side.

At least, I thought it was Madge.

My jaw dropped as she entered the room wearing the most gorgeous green sparkly dress I'd ever seen. For the first time, I noticed the woman had a waistline. And curvy hips. Who knew?

"Wow." I couldn't manage anything else. Wow. I'd seen Madge in a variety of situations—at work creating window displays, setting up for our

Black Friday sale wearing her T-shirt and slacks—
but I'd never seen anything like the woman
standing before me now. To say she'd transformed
into a butterfly seemed a bit of an understatement, but I couldn't think of any other way to
describe the metamorphosis.

"Who is that woman?" my father asked. "She
looks familiar."

"That's Madge, Pop. From the shop."

"Madge?" My father squinted and shook his
head. "I really need to get my eyes checked. These
old glasses of mine are giving me fits."

"Well, my vision is twenty-twenty and I see
just fine. But I'm so distracted by all of this
finery." Mama pointed to a gold-framed mirror
on the wall that was nearly the height of the room
itself. "Who lives like this?" she whispered.

"Eduardo." I laughed. "And possibly Aunt
Alva—someday."

"Not sure I could get used to it." Mama turned
to her right and gasped when she saw the statue
of the near-naked woman. "My goodness."

"Oh, you missed the story. Eduardo got this one
in Athens," Alva explained. "He said he wasn't
drawn to it at first, but he felt compelled to
purchase it to provide funds for the artist's family
after hearing of his medical issues. Isn't that just
like Eduardo? Always thinking of others."

Yes, always thinking of others, like me. And
Brady.

Brady.

I'd lost him in this huge house.

No, I found him standing next to Stan, who couldn't seem to take his eyes off Madge, who visited with Nadia on the opposite side of the room. Interesting. I overheard Brady and Stan saying something about basketball. Hopefully they wouldn't interrupt tonight's festivities with shoptalk, even if it had something to do with Brady's career. Tonight was all about us, after all.

I moved toward Beau and gestured to the room. "What do you think, Beau?"

"Pretty sure Twiggy took one look at this and wished she lived here. Which means I'm just going to have to work even harder to give her a life like this."

"Pooh on all that." Twiggy drew near and slipped her arm through his. "I wouldn't care if we lived in an apartment with secondhand furniture, as long as we were together."

"Now this one's a keeper." Stan gave a curt nod. "Better snag her quick, Beau."

"Yes, listen to Stan, honey. Snag me quick." Twiggy gave my brother a gentle kiss on the cheek.

When all of our guests had arrived, Eduardo clapped his hands together. "Welcome, friends and guests. We are here to honor two people we love—Katie and Brady—with a lovely party. I have asked my chef to prepare some delicious foods. Servers await you in the dining room to lead you through the buffet line. Feel free to sit wherever you are comfortable—at any of the tables, or here in the living room. We want you to feel at home."

As Brady and I took our place at the front of the buffet line, I noticed the gorgeous silverware and delicate china plates. I couldn't even imagine how much money had gone into the serving ware alone.

Brady picked up a plate and it almost slipped out of his hand. I lost my breath for a second until I knew he had a firm grip on it. The servers filled our plates with some of the most divine food I'd ever seen—some sort of shrimp appetizers, followed by asparagus, risotto, and something the server called beef Wellington.

We ate our fill and then nibbled on Eduardo's homemade tres leches cake.

"The recipe was my mother's," he explained. "She would be honored that I served it to such wonderful guests." His eyes flooded with tears. "And you are all like family to me. Now that you know where I live, feel free to come and see me anytime. As I've said so many times, *mi casa es su casa*."

"I *wish* this was my casa," Twiggy said, then laughed.

"Oh, trust me, Eduardo really means it when

he says '*mi casa es su casa*.'" Aunt Alva's face turned pink, and she fanned herself with her napkin. "He really, really means it."

"From the bottom of my heart." Eduardo pulled her into his arms and kissed her hair.

"Wait. What are you two *not* saying?" I asked. "You're up to something."

"Oh, just saying that the totally fabulous house is about to be my new home. Once we tie the knot, I mean." She turned to Eduardo and tapped his arm. "Do you think we could change the wallpaper in the entryway, sweetums? All of that gold is dizzying. Affects my vertigo."

"But of course." He kissed her on the cheek. "I want you to be happy in your new home, my darling."

"I think I must've missed something," Pop said. "What are we talking about?"

Mama's eyes narrowed to slits. "I think perhaps they're trying to tell us something. Are you two engaged at last? Is that it?"

"Surely not." Queenie clucked her tongue. "She's my sister. She would've told me."

Alva and Eduardo remained locked in each other's arms. I continued to stare at the two of them. From the looks of things, they were play-acting, nothing more.

Right?

Then I caught a glimpse of the rock on Alva's ring finger, and my heart sailed to my throat.

"Oh. My. Goodness! You two really *are* engaged, aren't you!"

Alva squealed with obvious delight, then held her finger out to show off the brilliantly cut diamond masterpiece. "I thought you'd never notice. Do you realize how many times I've flashed this hand right under your nose tonight? And you never even noticed a thing!"

"Just call me Uncle Eduardo!" Eduardo opened his arms wide for a hug. "Get over here, girl," he said. "Congratulate us."

All of my co-workers and family members started talking at once. I took several quick steps toward the happy couple and Eduardo swept me into his arms for a tight hug.

Dahlia reached for my aunt's left hand and gazed at the ring, words of excitement spilling forth.

I gasped when I saw the diamond in its white gold setting. It looked like something from the 1950s. A luscious marquis diamond in the center, surrounded by exquisite dark red stones. Garnets, maybe?

"Wow, Alva!" Hibiscus squealed. "I've never seen anything like it."

"And you never will," Eduardo said. "I've had this ring since the early sixties. It's a one-of-a-kind, designed by Joseff of Hollywood. I bought it at a fund-raiser from Doris."

"Doris . . . Day?" Aunt Alva looked startled by this revelation. "This was Doris Day's ring?" Her hand began to tremble.

Eduardo reached for Alva's hand and gave it a squeeze, likely an attempt to quiet her nerves. "Well, I can't attest to the fact that she owned it, but I purchased it at a fund-raiser held by Doris. She was raising money for our local animal shelter. Even back then she always cared more about animals than stuff. But I'm glad you like the setting. I always thought it was exquisite. Still do, in fact."

"And just the right size for my finger." Alva held up her hand for all to see the gorgeous gems. "Which just goes to show you that Doris must have had really fat fingers."

"Posh. That ring is a size six," Eduardo said. "Not large at all."

"What fun! I feel kind of the same way I did when I found out that Cheryl Tiegs and I could both wear the same size panty hose." Alva giggled. "Such a revelation."

"Cheryl Tiegs?" Dahlia looked perplexed. "Who's that?"

"She's . . . oh, never mind." Alva laughed. "Wrong generation."

"Tell us everything, Alva. Don't leave out a thing." Twiggy pulled up a chair and insisted my aunt take a seat.

"Yes, how did he propose?" Dahlia asked. "Ooh, hang on a second. I want to grab Dewey so he can take notes."

I somehow doubted my brother would be taking

any notes from the slick, suave Eduardo, but I kept my mouth shut as Dahlia headed across the room to grab him.

Alva's voice grew animated as she spoke. "Eduardo came to fetch me a little after noon. I knew we had a lot of work to do for the party, so I never suspected a thing. He took me to the most glorious French restaurant—someplace I'd never heard of before with a name I couldn't pronounce. And right there, with half of the diners looking on, this sweet man pulled out a ring and got down on one knee."

"Did you hear that, Dewey?" Dahlia jabbed my brother in the ribs. "He got down on one knee."

"I heard." My brother took a bite of his tres leches cake and shrugged.

Eduardo swept my aunt into his arms. "Anything for this wonderful woman. I would kneel on a bed of hot coals just to get her to say 'I do.'"

"Well, for pity's sake, I hope it doesn't come to that. I felt bad enough having you down on the carpet at all. I would've said yes even if you'd hopscotched across the room toward me instead. All that mattered was hearing the words." My aunt's eyes flooded with tears. "I'd dreamed of them for weeks but to hear them firsthand? Oh, it was like magic, I tell you." She turned to my co-workers, who appeared to cling to her every word. "Ladies, there's nothing finer than a fella telling you that he wants to spend his whole life with you." Alva's nose wrinkled. "Of course, when you're in your eighties, you have to wonder about the interpretation of those words, but I'll take whatever time I can get with this amazing man."

"And I with you." Eduardo took her hand and kissed the back of it. "And don't count on a long engagement, folks. I don't know how much time I have left on this planet, but I want to spend every moment of it with this wonderful woman. So keep your calendars open and your hearts ready."

All of the ladies in the room swooned. Well, all but Jane, who rolled her eyes. And maybe Madge. She looked a little put off as she stared at Stan, who watched all of this from a distance.

Everyone continued to congratulate the future bride and groom, until Eduardo reminded them of the real reason for the evening's festivities. "I do apologize for drawing attention away from our guests of honor," he said. "But I simply could not resist proposing today, knowing we would all be together tonight. I pray Katie and Brady will forgive the intrusion."

"No intrusion at all." I gave him a warm hug. "This is the best night ever."

The night continued to get better and better as we opened some unexpected gifts, including our honeymoon reservations from Nadia. As the night grew to its rightful close, Brady loaded up our gifts and we said our goodbyes to our host and hostess and the few lingering guests.

"Brady, since you're taking Katie back to our place, can I hitch a ride?" Alva asked. Just as quickly she put her hand over her mouth, then pulled it away. "Oops. Guess it won't be our place for long. I'll have to put that old house of mine on the market, won't I?" Her broad smile faded a bit. I felt mine fading too.

"Should be easy to sell something with that much charm, sweet girl." Eduardo gave her a longer-than-usual smooch, and we headed out to the truck.

Alva took the backseat and I sat in front with Brady, who seemed lost in his thoughts.

"Not going to sleep, are you?" Alva asked.

"No way." He chuckled. "Just thinking about what a cool night it was and what great friends and family members we have. God's been mighty good to us."

"For sure," I said. "I'll be honest, that was probably the most extravagant party I've ever attended—and all for us. I can't get over the fact that Eduardo pulled it off. Is there anything the man can't do?"

"From what I hear, he's not very good at sports." Brady laughed. "But with an artistic flair like his, who cares?"

Sports.

Just that one word reminded me that Brady and I still needed to talk about his basketball plans. Later, of course, without my aunt listening in.

"Were you disappointed that we chose your special night to announce our engagement?" Alva asked. "You can be honest. It's just us now."

"Not disappointed at all. Tonight was all about love. Seeing that ring on your finger was the icing on the cake for me, Aunt Alva. And I really loved what Eduardo said about how he feels he's part of the family."

"Won't be long before we all really are." Alva yawned. Then I yawned. Then Brady yawned.

"Don't fall asleep on me now," my aunt said to Brady. "I'm in my eighties and I've never had a honeymoon before. If you drive off the road and kill me, I'll miss it completely. So keep your eyes wide open, if you please."

Brady laughed out loud at that one. I did too. As I settled back against the seat, as I thought through the truth of what Alva had just said, I realized something rather extraordinary: we were both about to get married. That meant we had not one but two weddings to plan! I had a feeling hers might be a little different from mine, but no doubt both would give us memories we wouldn't soon forget.

18

I'm Gonna Love You Through It

I was born with an enormous need for affection, and a terrible need to give it.

Audrey Hepburn

May eased its way into June, and before long the wedding shop was filled with more customers than we could handle—most preparing for June weddings. By the time we reached the first week in July, I was ready to collapse.

Not that I had time to rest. With wedding plans looming, I needed to stay focused. And I needed to encourage Brady, who—after many hours of prayer and conversation—had decided to try his hand once more at a new season with the Mavericks. Of course, this meant a lot of physical therapy. And hours on the court, testing his limits. This took him away from Cosmopolitan Bridal much of the time, but no one dared complain, not with his passion for basketball reigniting.

We somehow managed without him at the shop, but it sure did make for lonely days. On the first Tuesday in July, Alva asked if she could ride with me to the bridal salon.

"Itching to spend time with your fiancé?" I asked.

"Something like that." She gave me a girlish smile. "I'll take all the time I can get with him."

This only made me long for Brady's company even more. When we arrived at the store a short while later and I saw his truck in the parking lot, my heart almost burst into song.

"Brady's here today." I turned off the car and stared at his empty vehicle.

"Nothing too strange about that, right?" Alva asked.

"Oh, he usually spends the mornings at the gym or on the court. We rarely see him until later in the day."

"Well, maybe he needs to be here for something special." Alva shrugged.

"Looks like he's not alone." I shifted my gaze around the parking lot. "I can't believe Hibiscus beat me here."

"Hmm?" Alva looked up from her cell phone. "What, honey?"

"Oh, just saying that Hi is here. And Jane." I pointed to her older-model sedan. "And Dahlia. And Twiggy. Just so strange. If I didn't know any better, I'd say I was late, not early."

"Maybe they're doing inventory or something," my aunt said.

"Inventory." I considered that. Maybe. But wouldn't I have known about it? Nadia would've asked for my help, for sure.

Before I could think twice about it, Brady walked out of the store and headed right for us. At that very moment a text came through from Lori-Lou, asking if I wanted to go to the pediatrician's office with her on Thursday. Who had time for that? Didn't she know I had work to do?

I responded to Lori-Lou's text with "Let's talk later" and then noticed Nadia pulling into the parking spot beside me. She climbed out of her car, looking as glorious as usual in a lightweight suit and perfectly coiffed hair. Really? Who looked like that on a random Tuesday morning? If I worked all day, I couldn't look as put together as my future mother-in-law.

Brady approached my car just as his mother got out of hers.

Alva shoved her phone into her oversized purse. "Sorry, y'all, but I've got to go to the little girls' room. You folks take your time. Don't rush on my account."

"Okay. See you in a bit."

I turned to Nadia, giving her a wave, and then focused on Brady. He pulled me into a warm embrace and planted a kiss on my cheek. "Good morning, you."

"Well, good morning to you too. I can't believe you're here. Don't you have physical therapy or something?"

"They rescheduled for later in the afternoon, so I decided to swing by. That all right?"

"Of course." I glanced at his dress shirt and slacks and gave a little whistle. "This is twice now I've seen you dolled up. What's the occasion?"

"Oh, I have an event later today. I'll tell you all about it when we get inside."

"That's my boy," Nadia said. "Lookin' like a champ." This somehow led to a conversation about men's fashion, which—as always—led back to a lengthy discussion about wedding trends. Brady listened politely, but I had a feeling he wanted to bolt.

After a few minutes the front door of the shop opened and Madge stepped outside. She glanced our way and waved, then walked toward us. "Having a party out here?" she asked when she got within hearing range.

"Oh, just girl talk," Nadia said. Brady cleared his throat. "Okay, okay, just a talk with two of the people I love most in the world. Have I mentioned how blessed I feel?"

"You are blessed, my friend." Madge gave her a warm hug. "You've got the best son in town, the best incoming daughter-in-law, and the best business to boot. What more could a mama ask for?"

What indeed?

"Cosmopolitan Bridal is my home," Nadia said. "My baby. I guess that's what we empty nesters do—we fall in love with our work."

"If I had half your talent, I'd be in love with

dress design too." I sighed. "Even without the talent, I love this place. I have ever since the first time I laid eyes on it."

"I'm so happy you've fallen for the bridal shop like I have." Nadia's eyes filled with tears. "It's hard to explain the effect it has on me, but I fall in love with dress design all over again every time I walk through the front door."

"I still remember the very first time I walked through the doors of Cosmopolitan Bridal." As I spoke the words, I thought back on that amazing day. "I came to tell you that I couldn't possibly take the gown I'd won in the contest. But when I got here, I was so distracted—in a good way—by the shop, by the people who worked here . . ."

"And by my shocking good looks," Brady chimed in.

"Well, yes, that too." I giggled. "But honestly, I was so enamored with everything and everyone that I couldn't seem to think straight. This place has a magical effect on people, I think. It's not just a bridal shop, it's a . . . a . . ." I paused to choose my next words. "It's like entering a fairy-tale kingdom, one where dreams really do come true."

"Goodness. When you describe it like that, you almost make it sound like a trip to Disney World." Nadia looked rather pleased at this notion.

"Better! A kingdom for brides, where every

wish can be fulfilled. Where a roomful of designers and seamstresses will whip up a gown fit for a princess and her prince."

"I should hire you to do PR for the shop." Nadia gave me a wink. "I know, I know—that's already your job. But seriously, Katie, you're great at describing things. I think that's why I chose your essay to win the contest in the first place."

"Thank you. I just love writing about Cosmopolitan. I love describing it to brides. It's an ocean of white when you walk in the door. And the fabrics are so delicate, so pristine, that you're scared to touch them—and yet, you're so tempted to reach out and touch them because the shimmer and shine draw you in, like some sort of fairy-tale magnet. And don't even get me started on the beadwork. Sometimes I stare at the different beads and crystals, just trying to figure out how many hours it must've taken to hand-stitch them into place. I would never have the patience, but man, they're my favorite part. I could fill a whole room with them."

"That might be a bit much." Brady quirked a brow.

Nadia laughed. "Well, you're very dramatic in style, I must admit. But I've loved that since the first day, especially the parts about your life in Fairfield—the way you talked about growing up in such a quaint, lovely place. Being a cheer-leader. Being voted Ms. Peach whatever."

"Peach Queen." I squared my shoulders. "Quite the honor, if I do say so myself."

"Well, your essay was so well written I felt as if I'd up and moved to Fairfield myself. That's a real gift, to be able to use words to paint a picture for people."

I shrugged. "Never really thought about it."

"You should. Maybe you could write other things. Besides ads, I mean. Like . . . books. No, articles. You should write articles."

"I already do write articles about the shop for the local papers, you know. That reminds me, I've got another piece ready for the *Observer*."

"Awesome, but I meant more than that. Something bigger. What do you want to tell people, Katie?" She gave me an inquisitive look.

"I want to tell them that the bride needs encouragement, but she doesn't want to be plowed over. Every bride should get to have her own special day. It's hers, no one else's. Not to be selfish or anything, but no one really needs to tug her in one direction or the other. In the end, they're not going to be the ones with the special memories—she is. You know?"

"Every bride has her day. I like it." Nadia shifted her purse strap to her other shoulder. "What would you do with that? Maybe a column or something? Newspaper?"

"No." Brady snapped his fingers. "*Texas Bride* magazine, that's what. I say we talk to Jordan

Singer about getting you on at *Texas Bride* for a regular column from the point of view of the bride. You'd be perfect for that, Katie."

"Whoa, whoa. How did we jump from me writing PR stuff for the shop to writing for a statewide magazine? I never said I wanted that."

"Admit it, you'd love every second. You're so good at what you do, writing ads for the shop and doing articles for the local papers. But there's more in you, Katie. Much more. *Texas Bride* would be a great platform for you. You know brides better than almost anyone. You see them every day, and now you're going to be one."

I paused to think through his words. I did see a lot of brides. I listened too—to people like Bridget Pennington, who just wanted her big day to be the best it could possibly be. To a recent bride from San Antonio, who'd dealt with her crazy future in-laws. To Crystal, who defied the odds by pulling off a *Gone with the Wind* ceremony that no one would ever forget.

"When the bride has her day, she comes away content. It's simple, really, and you know what they say: 'Happy wife, happy life.'"

"Oh, is that what they say?" Brady slipped his arm around my waist. "Well then, I shall commit that to memory."

"I'll embroider it on a sampler for you so you don't forget." Madge gave him a playful wink. "Kidding, kidding. But I think you're right, Katie.

Think about the opposite—the bride whose dream wedding is stolen out from under her. We've seen plenty of those. They come away with so many regrets."

"Yep. Someone needs to give each bride courage to go for it. To dream big. There's a reason it's called a 'dream wedding,' after all. No one can take it from her. It's not theirs to take. It's hers. It's a day she's dreamed of since she was a little girl. She's planned for it for a lifetime. Her ideas matter. Her thoughts count." I found myself overcome with emotion at this point. And if I had my way, we'd get out of this heat and go inside to chat about the joys of being a bride.

"Every bride has her day." Brady nodded. "Sounds like a great title for an article. I'm contacting the magazine myself. And while I'm at it, why don't I ask Jordan if he wants to be our wedding photographer? He was there for the cover shoot. He was there for the proposal. Maybe he'll want to be there for the big day. You never know . . . we might just end up on the cover again."

"How funny would that be—contest-winning bride and basketball-playing groom ride off into the sunset at their quaint outdoor reception."

"Sounds good to me. Very good." Brady nodded. "I'm definitely calling him, if you're okay with it."

"Very okay with it." I thought back to all of the

years I'd spent dreaming of my wedding. The scrapbook I'd put together. The magazines I'd pored through. The venues I'd checked out online. All of this to ensure I'd have the best wedding day ever. And now we finally had a plan in place for the perfect day. I could hardly wait!

Brady glanced down at his phone.

"Everything okay?" I asked.

"Yeah. Just a, um . . . a . . ." I lost him as he typed something into his phone. "Sorry, what were you asking?"

"You just seem a little preoccupied. Please tell me you're not contacting Jordan already. And let's go inside out of this heat."

"Yep." Brady shoved his phone in his pocket.

A couple of seconds later, Dahlia popped her head out the front door. "What's up, people? You going to stay in the parking lot all day? We have a business to run."

"She has a point." I laughed and moved toward the door.

Brady slipped his arm through mine and appeared to be slowing me down on purpose. "So, you believe that every bride should have her day, right?"

"Yes."

"No matter which day of the week . . . or where."

"Right." I gave him a curious look. "What are you trying to get at?"

"If, say, someone you knew and loved decided to have her day in a random place at a random time, surrounded by the people she loved, you would agree that everyone else should be happy about it, even if the whole thing catches you completely off guard?"

"Of course." I gave him a suspicious look. "Why, Brady? What aren't you telling me? Are you still hung up on that 'let's elope in Hawaii' idea?"

"Over my dead body." Nadia touched up her lipstick.

"Okay, well, who are we talking about here?"

"Just remember your passionate speech a couple of minutes from now, okay?" he said.

"O-okay."

Brady opened the front door of the shop, and I gasped as I took in the interior. "Oh. My. Goodness." The racks of gowns had been separated, creating a wide aisle between them. I stared at several rows of chairs covered in gorgeous white satin covers, all facing the same direction. Seated in those chairs . . .

Whoa.

Mama. Pop. Queenie. Pap-Paul. My brothers. Their sweeties. And half the town of Fairfield, along with all of our local friends and relatives.

"What in the world is going on?" My pulse quickened. For a moment I thought Brady had done the unthinkable.

He squeezed my hand and leaned over to whisper in my ear, "Don't worry, it's not for us."

My heart slowed at once. Who, then?

"I believe your services are required in the changing room, Katie." He patted my shoulder.

"My services?"

"Yes, if you're going to serve as maid of honor, you'll want to look your best. Mama has the perfect dress for you, in a lovely shade of lavender."

"Lavender? I only know one person who likes lav—" I stopped mid-sentence and clamped a hand over my mouth. "Oh! No wonder she jumped and ran from the car! Are you telling me this was all planned ahead of time?"

"Well, for about a week, anyway. Eduardo was ready a few days after he proposed. I had to talk him into slowing down long enough to give the rest of us time to catch up."

Mama walked my way and wrapped me in a warm embrace. "Hello again, Katie Sue. Long time no see."

"I thought you guys were in Eureka Springs."

"Yep. Then we moved on to Hot Springs. But it seems like no matter how far we roam, we keep ending up back home again. I believe it must be some sort of sign."

"Sign, my eye." My father joined us, a look of exasperation on his face. "If everyone would stop getting married, I could enjoy my retirement."

"Well, wasn't that a thoughtful thing to say." Mama patted him on the arm. "That's why I married you, honey—your kindness and consideration for others."

He grumbled all the way back to his seat.

Mama glanced at me and laughed. "I thought your father was going to murder me in my sleep when I told him we had to drive back home, but I wouldn't miss this for the world."

"Neither would I." Queenie's voice sounded from her chair. "So let's get this show on the road."

"For pity's sake, yes." Lori-Lou wrangled her children while Josh held the baby. "Not sure how long I can keep this crew under control."

"But didn't you just text me?" I asked.

"Duh. I was trying to buy time for Aunt Alva so she could change. She wanted to surprise you."

"But . . . I'm the maid of honor?"

"And I'm the matron." Queenie pointed at her lavender gown. "Now, you get in that studio, honey, and put on your dress. We're not getting any younger, you know."

No, we certainly weren't. But if I didn't get my act together, Alva and Eduardo wouldn't have their big day. I gave my grandmother a nod and followed on her heels to the studio.

19

Love's the Only House

Success is like reaching an important birthday and finding you're exactly the same.

Audrey Hepburn

We located Alva in the studio, dressed in the most gorgeous bridal gown I'd ever seen. She looked like something straight out of a Greta Garbo movie.

"Alva!" I raced to her side and gave her a kiss on the cheek. "I can't believe you did all this without telling me."

"You put me through a doozy of a time, I tell ya. It's not easy keeping a secret from you. But I knew you were plenty stressed already with your own wedding plans. Most of all, I just wanted to surprise you, to put a smile on your face. Looks like I pulled it off."

"No kidding. And what a surprise! Makes me wonder what's next."

"We're not having any children, if that's what you mean. Now, tell me what you think of my dress. Eduardo made it. He's been working on it for ages now, long before he even slipped the ring on my finger. That silly man assumed I'd say yes, and he was right!"

"It's exquisite!" I let out a little squeal. "This is just too much."

The gown was a beautiful ivory satin with a luscious sheen. I'd never seen a design quite like it, and I thought I'd seen just about everything Nadia, Dahlia, and Eduardo had ever come up with. This gown had a distinct Grecian look to it: A sweetheart neckline with sheer fabric overlay. Tiny pleats. Darling little pearls at the high waist. Totally perfect for Auntie.

"What do you think of these sheer sleeves, Katie? Aren't they glorious?" Alva chuckled. "Just enough to cover the jiggle when I raise my arms." She lifted them to show me what she meant.

Queenie rolled her eyes. "Sister, trust me when I say that see-through fabric doesn't hide the jiggle. Not saying I don't like the sleeves, just saying we have to be realistic, especially at our age."

"Who says?" Aunt Alva stuck her tongue out at my grandmother. "Anyway, I love the dress. Eduardo designed it just for me. He wants me to look like Greta Garbo when I walk down the aisle."

"If I recall, our parents wouldn't let us see any Greta Garbo picture shows when we were young." Queenie gave her a knowing look. "Too risqué."

"I'm in my eighties, Queenie-Beanie, and getting married for the first time in my life. I'd say I've earned the right to be a little risqué!" Alva slapped herself on the thigh and laughed so hard I wondered if the folks out in the shop could hear her.

No. I could hear the music playing, piped in through the store's audio system. No doubt they couldn't hear us talking.

"My favorite part is the little hat. What do you think of it?" She pointed to the fitted hat with the beautiful crystal design on the side. "Look, Katie. It's a bird. You have to look close to see it, but the crystals form a lovely birdlike image. Eduardo says this hat is just like the one Greta Garbo wore in *The Temptress*." Auntie giggled. "Imagine that . . . your aunt a temptress." Her cheeks flamed pink, and Queenie gave her a smack on the backside.

"I'm tempted to swat you again if you don't let me finish fixing your hair. Now, hold still, Alva. And you, Katie Sue"—Queenie pointed at my slacks and blouse—"you need to change into your gown. Please and thank you."

Aunt Alva nodded, her eyes wide. "Yes, and hurry up, honey! I'm not getting any younger, you know. If you don't change into that gorgeous lavender dress that's waiting for you in the dressing room, I won't have a maid of honor."

"What am I, chopped liver?" Queenie fussed

with Alva's hair and then stepped back to give her a scrutinizing look. "You would think I'm not even here at all."

"Of course you're here, silly, and you're my matron of honor. You've been fussing at me ever since I arrived. But we need this sweet girl or the 'I dos' won't take place. Step on it, Katie Sue!"

"Yes ma'am." I saluted her and then sprinted to the dressing room, where I found the sweetest gown hanging up. I'd never been a fan of lavender, but this one had a swirly effect—sort of white and lavender all mixed together with teensy-tiny hints of soft green woven into the design. Eduardo must've had a hand in this one too, at least the color choice.

Moments later I heard a light tap on the door. "You need any help in there, Katie?" Dahlia asked. She popped her head inside and gasped when she saw me wearing the gown. "Oh, it's great! Even better than I'd hoped."

"Same here." I chuckled. "Not that I'd ever laid eyes on it until today."

"Let me help you with the zipper."

"Yes, please and thank you." I clamped a hand over my mouth and then laughed. "Oops. Sorry. Didn't mean to say that. I got it from—"

"Queenie." We spoke the name in unison.

"And Alva too," I added. "I've learned from the best."

"And so have I. Can you believe we pulled this

off? Alva didn't want you to know. The whole thing was supposed to be a big surprise."

"Well, it certainly was—er, is! I'm in shock, to be honest."

"Alva thought it would be fun. I didn't know myself until a couple of days ago. Just Eduardo, Brady, and Nadia knew. Oh, and Madge. She knows all things."

"I heard that." Madge's voice rang out from the other side of the door. "Right now what I know is this: Eduardo's getting tired of hanging out in Brady's office. That's where we've got him holed up until he hears Pachelbel's Canon playing."

"Start the music, then." I stepped back and gazed at my appearance.

"Oh no, this will never do." Dahlia left for a moment and returned with a hairbrush and barrettes with Austrian crystals. "We're pulling this hair up. And don't forget to touch up your lipstick."

I didn't argue the point. Instead, I let her fuss with my hair while I swiped on a fresh coat of lipstick. Off in the distance I heard the strains of Pachelbel's Canon fill the air.

"That's Eduardo's cue. Let's get Queenie and Alva and go out the back door. We'll have to go around the Mexican restaurant to the front parking lot to make a grand entrance."

"In this heat?" I asked.

"Yes." She nodded.

We joined up with Queenie and Alva and headed out the back door, then around the back of the restaurant. Just as we made our way into the front parking lot, a couple of cars pulled in and customers emerged.

"Sorry, folks, but we're closed until noon today," Dahlia called out.

"We are?" I asked.

"Well, sure. Don't need any interruptions," Dahlia said.

"If you come back at noon, you can have some wedding cake—on the house!" Alva hollered. "I'm gettin' hitched!"

"Congratulations!" a young woman in a red blouse and dark slacks called out. "This is so cool!" She pulled out a cell phone and started snapping pictures of my aunt, who posed in various positions.

"C'mon, Alva. Let's keep moving." Queenie patted her on the back. "We'll get plenty of photos later."

Dahlia inched the door open and popped her head inside, then gave us a nod. "Okay, 'Wedding March' is playing. I think it's time to roll."

Queenie went first, disappearing from view.

"Who's walking you down the aisle?" I whispered to Alva as we took a step toward the door.

"Who do you think, silly?" Alva looked at me with that lopsided grin of hers. "You are. I wouldn't have it any other way."

"Me?" Ah, it all made sense now. This maid of honor was doing double duty, apparently. "Well, in that case . . ." I gave her my arm and we walked up the makeshift aisle together. She gave everyone a queenly wave as she passed by, ever the dramatic one.

Perhaps not as dramatic as the groom, however. Now, I'd seen Eduardo done up before—the night we had dinner at his house, for instance, when he met us at the door dressed in old Hollywood attire. And I'd seen his slick, coiffed televangelist hair in various shades of gold and silver. But I'd never seen him in an elaborate gold and white tuxedo like he wore today. I could almost hear Liberace applauding from the grave. I nearly stopped in the middle of the aisle just to give a little whistle.

Aunt Alva beat me to the punch. "Lookee there, folks. If I don't have the handsomest fella in all of the Dallas–Fort Worth metroplex, I'll be hog-tied!" She slapped her thigh and laughed. The guests all chimed in, laughter filling the room.

Eduardo looked embarrassed but took a little bow.

For the first time I noticed Pap-Paul in his Presbyterian robes, ready to do the honors. He looked at me and offered an encouraging nod. "Who gives this woman to be married to this man?"

Every eye in the place landed on me. I had to

speak over the giggle that attempted to rise as I said, "I do!"

"Save your 'I dos' for another day, Katie Sue." Alva released her hold on my arm and marched up to take Eduardo's. "This is my day. You'll get your turn soon enough."

This got another laugh from the crowd. I wasn't quite sure where to go next—until Queenie gestured for me to stand behind her. As I took my position, I looked out over the crowd, unable to wipe the silly grin off my face. Was I dreaming all of this? Surely I'd wake up any minute and realize this was just one of Alva's silly radio show adventures.

Nope. This was the real deal. Several minutes later, after a lovely sermonette and the sharing of some bring-tears-to-the-eyes vows, my aunt became Alva Rebecca de la Consuela.

Off in the distance I heard Mama crying. Pop looked a little misty-eyed too. The one who really seemed to be an emotional mess, however, was Eduardo. I'd never seen him like this.

"I have waited for years to find the Juliet to my Romeo." He brushed the tears from his eyes with a swipe of his hand. "And you came waltzing in."

"Wearing my Mavericks T-shirt and slacks the first time we met, if memory serves me correctly," Alva said. "I can see why you were swept off your feet."

"Never sweep a fella in his golden years off his feet," Eduardo said as he slipped his arm around her waist. "Too dangerous."

Everyone laughed long and loud at this one.

Music continued to play overhead as Ophelia said, "I think it's time to have some cake." She pointed to a lovely two-tiered traditional cake on the counter near the register. "I carted this lovely little number all the way from Fairfield. Nearly lost it as I came through some construction on I-20, but we made it in one piece. Cake, anyone?"

"I would've driven through much worse to spend time with my friend on her special day." Bessie May's eyes filled with tears as she addressed the bride and groom. "I pray you both have many wonderful years together."

Before long my aunt was surrounded by all of the women in her age group—Queenie, Prissy, Ophelia, and Bessie May. They giggled like schoolgirls as they talked about her upcoming honeymoon. I couldn't help but smile as I watched them interact.

"Do you think that'll be us in forty or fifty years?" Lori-Lou asked.

I turned to face her and took the baby from her arms. "I hope so. I really do."

Nadia joined us, a relaxed smile on her face. She gestured to the older women. "So, is this what it's like in Fairfield? People gathered around you, loving you through the best—and worst—moments of your life?"

"Always," Lori-Lou and I said in unison and then laughed.

I felt the sting of tears in my eyes as I spoke to my future mother-in-law. "Oh, Nadia, you're just going to love Fairfield once you get to know it better. It's the sweetest little town. Everyone knows everyone, and anywhere you turn there's someone to help out if you need it."

"Sounds idyllic."

"It is. I can't remember a time when I didn't have three or four grown-ups patting me on the back and telling me how much they loved me or bragging about my efforts, whether it was at school or working at the hardware store. In some ways, Fairfield is a lot like Cosmopolitan Bridal. We're family. Lots of aunts and uncles and cousins and grandparents all gathered around, making every day an adventure. Some people are blessed to live in one world. I feel like I get to live in two at once."

"Two worlds?" She looked perplexed by this notion. "How so?"

"I'm just so lucky to have the luxury of knowing and loving people from two separate worlds—the world of Cosmopolitan Bridal and the world of Fairfield, where love rules the day and where people genuinely care. My cup is overflowing with loving, kindhearted people."

"Well, when you put it like that . . ." A bemused smile turned up the corners of Nadia's lips. "You make me want to move to Fairfield. It sounds so quaint."

"Oh, it is, but not in an outdated sort of way. They're up on the times, but they don't place a lot of stock in such things. In Fairfield, it's all about the people. They genuinely love one another. When Queenie was in the hospital, for example, half the town showed up with flowers and cards and well wishes. And when she went home, the ladies set up meals for her so she wouldn't have to cook. And a couple of the WOP-pers even came by to dust and vacuum her house for her."

"I don't know what a WOP-per is, but I need a couple of those in my life. My condo gets so dusty."

"WOP-pers. Women of Prayer." Lori-Lou gestured to Bessie May and the others. "Like they're doing now."

Sure enough, the ladies had gathered around Alva and Eduardo and were going to town, ushering up prayers for their future life together.

Nadia sighed. "It's just so sweet. That's how it should be everywhere. And we'll start right here. I heard Jane say that her car isn't working properly. I think I'll surprise her and take it for a tune-up and oil change."

"Nadia, that's a great idea. I know she would appreciate it."

"And I overheard her telling Hibiscus that she was worried about having enough money to pay her electric bill this month," Nadia added. "I don't want any of my employees worrying about things like that. Maybe it's time to give Jane a little raise, or even a bonus. She's been doing such a great job."

"There you go!" I wanted to pat my future mother-in-law on the back. "That's the small-town mentality. Reach out and love those who are closest to you. Then they'll take that love and spread it even further!" I glanced around and noticed Jane had gone missing. "Where is Jane, anyway?"

"I'm pretty sure I know." Nadia took me by the hand and led me to the studio, where we found Jane seated alone, working on a wedding gown.

Nadia walked toward her and put a hand on her shoulder. "Hey, you're missing the party."

"I know." Her eyes brimmed with tears. "Just needed to be alone."

"Sometimes it's better to be part of the family," Nadia said.

"Even if I don't feel like it?" Jane swiped at her eyes with the back of her hand.

"Especially then. That's when you need us most. And vice versa."

"I know what you all think. You think I feel sorry for myself."

"I never said that." I took a seat next to her and gazed into her tearstained eyes.

"I'm not complaining. I'm not. I have a good life. I have a great job and wonderful friends. And I know what you're going to say—I'm young. There are lots of years left to find the love of my life."

"That's not what I would say at all," Nadia said. "I lost my husband years ago, Jane, and I've never remarried. I work in the wedding business just like you, and I don't see the same potential for myself as I do for others. I think maybe I've just resigned myself to the fact that I'm not going to remarry."

My heart felt as heavy as lead when I saw the sadness in her eyes. In all the time I'd known Nadia, I'd never heard her say anything like this.

"But you know what?" Nadia's expression brightened. "I'm learning that happiness isn't found in my mate. If I can't be happy right here"—she pointed to her heart—"then I won't be happy with a husband. If I ever do find one, I mean."

Jane shrugged. "I think that's the pat answer all single people are given. Learn to love yourself before you can love others."

"You're a loving person, Jane," I said. "You already love others, so I don't think that's the key. The real answer is in knowing who you are in Christ. You're complete in him. There's no lack, no need. As long as you've given your life to him, there's no big, empty hole in your heart waiting to be filled."

"Then why does it feel like there is?"

"Feelings can be deceptive. But I promise you, if you're a daughter of the King, he's given you everything you need to be complete in him. And if a great guy comes along—one who's worthy of you—then that's just the icing on the cake."

"Mmm. Cake." Jane's eyes sparkled, the first sign of hope. "Have they cut it yet?"

"I believe they're just about to." I slid my chair back and stood up. "Now, come and join the rest of the family, okay?"

She sighed and rose. "All right. But only because there's cake involved."

We headed back to the front of the store. Alva and Eduardo cut the first piece and we all joined them moments later, eating larger-than-average slices of the yummy stuff. Beau and Twiggy stood next to me, talking about the events of the day, but I found myself distracted by Stan, who stood on the far side of the room, looking a bit ill.

"Is your boss okay?" I asked my brother.

Beau shrugged. "He's been acting weird lately."

"Something business related?" My heart rate skipped to double time. "Is there something going on with Brady that you're not telling me? The Mavericks don't want him back? Is that it?"

"Nothing to do with basketball, Katie. I have a sneaking suspicion there's more going on in Stan's head this morning than that."

I gave him a scrutinizing look, noticing for the first time how he watched Madge from a distance.

Yep. Stan was deeply troubled by something . . . but what?

Less than a minute later, Stan called the room to attention. Everyone stopped talking and looked his way. Dahlia lowered the music and we all gathered around him. I glanced at Beau and Twiggy, who stood side by side, eyes wide.

"Uh-oh," Twiggy said. "He's gonna do it, isn't he?"

"Mm-hmm." Beau nodded. "Can't believe he worked up the courage, but yep . . . looks like he's gonna do it."

"Do what?" I asked.

"Just hang on a sec, sis." Beau slung his arm over my shoulders. "I have a feeling you're about to find out firsthand."

20

Bring It on Home to Me

Remember, if you ever need a helping hand, it's at the end of your arm. As you get older, remember you have another hand: The first is to help yourself, the second is to help others.

Audrey Hepburn

Stan looked as if he might pass out, if such a thing could be judged from his pale face and shaky hands.

"You okay over there, Stan?" Brady called out. "Should we call 9-1-1?"

"No. Please don't. I'll be fine." He tugged at his shirt collar. "In a few minutes, anyway." His gaze shifted around the room until he focused on Madge, who stood behind the cash register, her usual place of refuge. "Could you come over here for a minute, Madge?"

"Sure." She looked terrified to be put on the spot, but who could blame her? Seconds later she stood in the middle of the room, hand tightly clutched in his. "What are we doing?"

"You're about to find out." Stan's words came out a bit shaky. He faced the crowd and cleared his throat. "Now, I know this is Eduardo and Alva's big day, and I don't want to steal anyone's thunder. But I couldn't think of a better time or place to do this, since we're all together."

Then the strangest thing happened. I'd seen Stan in a variety of situations—irritated, worried, sarcastic—but I'd never seen him with tears in his eyes before. He stood before us now, a man with eyes brimming and voice quivering.

"Most of you know me pretty well by now," he said. "In fact, I'd be willing to bet some of you know me even better than I know myself." He cast a hopeful glance at Madge, who offered a winsome smile. "The sports agent world is cutthroat and all about scoring the best possible deals—for our players and ourselves."

"You're the best, Stan," Brady said.

"Stan the Man!" several of us hollered at once.

Perhaps buoyed by our kind words, Stan grinned. "Now that you mention it, I've had a good run of it, and I'm mighty proud of the players I've represented. But there comes a time in every man's life—"

"Aw, get on with it, Stan." Madge tapped her foot. "Are you going to spend all day talking about sports?"

"No, woman, I'm not." Stan crossed his arms. "As a matter of fact, this little speech has nothing to do with sports whatsoever."

"Coulda fooled me!" Alva called out.

"This is something entirely different." Stan cleared his throat. "There comes a time in every man's life—well, nearly every man, anyway—when he has to admit that his work isn't enough. Oh, it'll keep him busy. It'll fill the hours. But if he's honest with himself . . ." He gazed at Madge with great tenderness. "If he's truly honest with himself, he has to admit that only the love of a good woman will fill the void in his heart."

"For pity's sake." Alva fanned herself with her napkin. "This is better than that radio show we listen to, Katie Sue. Much more romantic."

Indeed.

And the story grew more romantic still as Stan dropped to one knee and presented Madge with a ring.

"Yes!" Madge said. "Yes, yes, yes! For the love of all that's holy, yes! I'll marry you, Stan. I'll probably drive you out of your ever-lovin' mind, but if you love me as much as I think you do, you'll forgive me."

At this point—even before the gorgeous diamond was slipped onto her finger—the whole room came alive with cheers and applause. Dahlia, Twiggy, and Crystal let out squeals and rushed Madge, nearly knocking her out of Stan's arms.

I moved toward Brady, dumbfounded. "Did you know about this?" I whispered.

He chuckled. "You don't think Stan picked out

a ring that great without a little assistance, do you? And who do you think coached him on his big speech?" Brady paused. "Of course, he did deviate somewhat, but I blame that on nerves."

"Did Eduardo know?"

"Yep. And he heartily approved. Said he'd interrupted our engagement party with personal news, so it only made sense to return the favor to Stan."

"I can tell from the look on Madge's face that she was completely clueless."

"Which is how it should be. No groom wants his bride to know what's coming." Brady slipped his arm around my shoulders. "Remember how I proposed to you?"

"Duh. As if I could ever forget. Best day of my life."

"Okay then. Now hopefully Madge can say the same thing."

"I'm sure she will."

I watched as Stan and Madge walked over to my aunt and uncle. "Sorry to steal the attention, Alva," Stan said. "I hope you don't mind that I proposed right here and now."

"Are you kidding?" Alva clasped her hands together. "It's perfect!"

"Well, thank you for being so understanding." Stan gazed lovingly at Madge. "It's just that all of her friends are here, especially Nadia, her best friend. You folks at Cosmopolitan are Madge's family, and I just knew she'd want to share this moment with family."

"And you, Stan?" I flashed a warm smile.

"You folks are my family too, I guess." He shrugged. "At least, you are now. Whether you want me or not. I guess I'll just have to be the crazy old uncle everyone talks about during the holiday season."

"We'll only have great things to say about you, especially after a speech like the one you gave. You and Madge are going to be so happy together, Stan. Just promise you won't steal her away from the Dallas area."

"No way. My roots are planted deep here. I'm not going anywhere and neither is she. Tearing her away from the bridal shop would be impossible. You're stuck with us. Both of us."

"Happy to be stuck." Nadia's eyes brimmed with tears.

Just about the time I thought she might erupt in tears, Bessie May, Prissy, and Ophelia approached. Bessie May tapped Nadia on the arm. "Pardon me for interrupting, but you're that designer, aren't you?" She stuck out her hand to Nadia. "The one I've heard so much about?"

"Yes, I design vintage wedding gowns."

"I'm a bit of a designer myself." Bessie May squared her shoulders. "See this here outfit I'm wearing?"

Nadia's gaze shifted to the matching floral

cotton blouse and homemade slacks Bessie May had on. Her brow wrinkled. No doubt she was trying to come up with something kind to say, but what could be said about a style that went out in the eighties?

"I make my own patterns," Bessie May added. "So I guess it could be said that I'm a designer too, wouldn't you agree?"

"Of course."

"Bessie May, don't be ridiculous." Prissy slapped her on the arm. "If you were a designer you'd be making outfits for others. And no offense, but I don't know anyone else—even in a small town like Fairfield—who would wear the things you show up in."

"Well, I never!" Bessie May put her hands on her hips. "How dare you humiliate me, Prissy, and in front of a total stranger, no less."

"Oh, I'm no stranger," Nadia said. "I'm about to be family. Once Brady and Katie get married, I mean. And Prissy, I must disagree with what you've said to Bessie May here. I was sewing clothes for myself long before I sold my first gown to someone else. During those formative years I just had to keep reminding myself that my creativity—my patterns—were a special gift from God. He had called me to create, and if no one ever bought one of my dresses, I'd still be a designer."

"Humph." Prissy pursed her lips. "I stick to

what I said before. I don't think anyone would wear the crazy things she comes up with. I mean, I wouldn't."

"Ladies, ladies . . ." I slipped my arm through Prissy's. "Just a few minutes ago I told Nadia that we're all one big happy family in Fairfield. Right?"

"A poorly dressed family, apparently," Prissy said. "But while we're talking about things we disagree on, I might as well state my opinion on Ophelia's new hairdo."

Ophelia looked shocked. "What about my hairdo?"

"Friend, I have to speak it plain." Prissy wagged an arthritic finger in Ophelia's direction. "No one in their right mind would honestly believe that crazy shade of orange is your real color. You've got to go back to your natural shade of gray."

"That's the rudest thing you've ever said to me. You could learn a thing from our guest here." Ophelia pointed to Nadia, who flinched.

"Learn . . . from me?" my future mother-in-law asked.

"Sure. That platinum 'do you're sportin' ain't your natural color, right?" Ophelia gave her a knowing look. "I'm guessing underneath it all you're as gray as I am, but there you go, coloring it up with a shade that no one in our neck of the woods would've chosen."

Ohh noo.

Nadia paled. "Well, I, um . . ."

"I think it's a nice color." Bessie May gave her a thoughtful look, then reached out and touched it. "Not exactly real-looking—meaning, not a color God would've created—but nice all the same."

"I . . . well, I . . ." Nadia reached for a cookie and pressed it into her mouth.

"Ladies, let's fess up. We're all the same, whether we live in a city or a small town. We all color our roots and we all have our own taste in clothes." Ophelia slapped her thigh. "We don't all do things the same way, but what does it matter? Doesn't make us different. Just makes us sisters."

I had a feeling Nadia wanted to run as fast and far from this sisterhood as she could right about now. Instead, she reached for another cookie, snapped it in half, and gave one piece to Bessie May and the other to Prissy.

"If we're all sisters, then we all agree on one thing: chocolate is the cure for anything that ails you. And right now"—she glanced my way and sighed—"I have a hankerin' for some chocolate."

"I baked those cookies." Ophelia squared her shoulders, clearly proud of her work. "They're my own secret recipe."

"Don't let that stop you from trying them," Bessie May said. "We've all been eating them for years and none of us have kicked the bucket."

"Yet." Prissy quirked a brow and then took a nibble.

"Well, there's a glowing endorsement." Nadia reached for another cookie and stared at it. As soon as the other ladies began to squabble, she put the cookie back on the tray and glanced at me again, eyes wide.

"Told you they were just like family, Nadia. What else can I say? But just wait—when it comes to planning for my big day, they'll all come together in one accord. It's what they do."

"Mm-hmm." My future mother-in-law looked back and forth between Bessie May and Ophelia, who continued to bicker. "I guess I'll just have to take your word for it, Katie."

"Take her word for what, Mom?" Brady stepped behind me and slipped his arms around my waist.

"That folks in Fairfield all come together in one accord when it comes to the things that matter—like weddings."

"Oh, they do," Brady said. "I've witnessed it firsthand. So don't you worry about a thing. In just a few short weeks we'll all be gathered at the Baptist church in Fairfield with half the town looking on. We'll say our 'I dos' and then have the party of the century. Just you wait and see."

Out of the corner of my eye I caught a glimpse of Prissy arguing with Bessie May. Before long Ophelia joined in and things got a little heated. Queenie threw herself into the middle of it, and Pap-Paul ended up intervening to calm the waters.

Yep. Just like I'd said: one big happy family.

21

The Time Has Come

Paris is always a good idea.

Audrey Hepburn

For days we talked of little but Alva and Eduardo's wedding and Stan and Madge's engagement. In fact, everyone was so caught up in celebrating that they almost forgot about our wedding. Not that Alva and Eduardo were anywhere to be found. I had it on good authority—Queenie—that they'd boarded a flight to LA for a month-long stay at the Beverly Hills Hotel. No doubt Alva was swooning right about now, or possibly lounging at the swimming pool, gabbing with famous actors and actresses.

Then again, I didn't really want to think about what Aunt Alva was doing right about now. One thing I did need to think about, however, was my living arrangements. With Alva now Mrs. de la Consuela, she would be moving into Eduardo's house ASAP and listing her home with a realtor.

I didn't mind having the house to myself in the meantime. In fact, after all the chaos of the past few weeks, I rather enjoyed the solitude. At least the first couple of weeks. By the third week—

even with my workload growing exponentially—I found myself going a little stir-crazy.

When I headed to work the first Monday in August, Madge greeted me with a newspaper in her hand. "Guess what I've got!" She waved the paper in the air.

"The ad I put in the *Observer*?" I slipped my purse strap off my shoulder and caught it in my hand. "Was there a typo or something?"

"No, this is something else. Remember our Houston bride? Bridget Pennington?"

"Of course."

"There's a write-up in the society column of the *Houston Chronicle*. It's all about her wedding, which took place last Saturday."

"Oh, that's right."

"You take the *Houston Chronicle*?" Dahlia asked as she joined us. "All the way up here in Dallas?"

"I do when she mails us a copy and puts a sticky note on it that says 'Read this article.'" Madge laughed. "Want to hear it for yourself?"

"Let me get the others first," I said. "I'm sure they'll be interested."

Minutes later the ladies all clustered around the paper, which Twiggy snatched from Madge's hands. "'Local Heiress to Oil and Gas Firm Weds in Lovely Country Wedding.'" She looked up from the paper with a thoughtful smile. "That's on my bucket list, to be a local heiress."

Madge gave her a stern look. "Read the rest of the article and worry about your social status later."

Twiggy continued reading.

"Bridget Pennington, heiress to the Pennington Oil and Gas firm, married Evan Harris in a city-meets-country event in Magnolia on Saturday. Father of the bride, oil exec Bradley Pennington, escorted his daughter down a makeshift aisle flanked by beautifully adorned bales of hay. While others in their circle might have turned up their noses at such an event, I found the whole thing rather charming, especially the reception, which took place in a renovated barn, complete with chandelier and exquisite tablecloths and centerpieces.

My favorite part? The father-daughter dance. The senior Pennington hit the dance floor with his daughter to celebrate her nuptials. Then, in a grand, sweeping gesture, he passed her off to her husband for the sweetest Texas two-step this side of the Mississippi. All in all, I'd have to say Pennington Oil and Gas is safe in the hands of father and daughter, who pulled off a ceremony and reception that none of their friends will soon forget."

"Wow!" I clasped my hands together, thrilled with this news. "So happy for her. She did it!"

"Perfect." Dahlia grinned. "Makes all the work on that Martina McBride dress worth it. I'm thrilled for her."

"She had her day." I didn't mean to speak the words aloud, but there they were.

Nadia looked my way, curiosity in her eyes. "What, Katie?"

"She had her day. Every bride has to have her day. It's no one else's."

"Kind of sounds like it ended up being a great day for her dad too," Madge said.

"Yes, and that's the point, I suppose. When the bride's happy—when the wedding plans are within the scope of the dream—then others around her will sense her happiness and be happy too. Oh, maybe not every time. I'm sure there are grumpy relatives and friends who just don't want to play along, but when the bride has her day, everyone who loves her can share in her fun."

"That's such a sweet way of looking at it, Katie," Madge said. "And it makes me want to think outside the box for my wedding too."

"Mine too," Dahlia said. "When the time comes, I mean."

"And mine," Twiggy added. " 'Cause I feel sure Beau's going to propose . . . someday. I hope."

"Is that the end of the article?" Jane asked.

"There's one more line." Madge peered a bit

closer. "Something about the cake coming from some famous bakery—Crème de la Crème or something like that. Want to see a picture of it?" She held up the paper, and a photo of Bridget and Evan cutting the most glorious five-tiered shabby chic cake captivated me.

In that moment I wanted to throw a party. Well, not really a party, but I wanted to celebrate Bridget's big day. I wanted to say, "Good for you, girl! You did it! You had your day—just your way!"

I'd have to remember to send her a note offering my congratulations.

If she could make it through all of that chaos, all of that confusion, then surely I could manage to pull off a wedding in a town where we all loved one another unconditionally.

Right?

22

Where Would You Be?

If my world were to cave in tomorrow, I would look back on all the pleasures, excitements, and worthwhilenesses I have been lucky enough to have had.

Audrey Hepburn

I thought about Bridget as I worked later that afternoon. I tried to imagine what she'd felt like as she walked down the aisle, bales of hay on either side. I tried to envision her joy as she and her new husband took their photos in the sunset. What a glorious day it must've been. What a glorious day I would soon have! In less than two weeks I would marry my best friend, the love of my life.

Brady.

My heart swelled as I thought about him. Though I missed seeing him at the office, our times together were even more special now. I could read the excitement in his eyes as he talked about his workouts and picked up on the fact that his knee seemed to be holding up well. Yes, everything was—as Mary Poppins would say— practically perfect in every way. Our wedding, our lives, our joys . . . they were all coming together in a blissful crescendo.

As I prepared to leave work later that afternoon, my phone rang. I answered it, surprised to hear my mother's voice on the other end of the line.

"Katie?"

"Hey, Mama. Good to hear from you. What's p?"

"You're not going to believe it. You're just not. And the timing is so terrible too."

"Wait, believe what?" My pulse quickened. "Did something happen to Queenie?"

"No, honey. It's the WOP-pers."

Huh? "The WOP-pers? What about them?"

"You're not going to believe it, but they've disbanded. They're not praying together any-more."

"What? That's impossible." I took a seat behind my desk. "The WOP-pers have been a prayer team since before the beginning of time."

"I know, but not anymore. They had a huge falling out and have split into two groups. The one isn't speaking to the other."

"Are you sure?"

"Yes! I just talked to the sheriff, who heard it from the mayor, who heard it from Mr. Jacobs. He's coaching Little League now, did you know? Anyway, Coach Jacobs said that Mrs. Willingham—you remember her, Katie? She's the one with the prosthetic foot. Anyway, she told him that she ran into Bessie May at the gas station filling her SUV, and she asked for prayer for her son—Mrs. Willingham's son, not Bessie May's. I'm pretty sure Bessie May doesn't have a son. So when Mrs. Willingham asked the WOP-pers to pray for her son's ADD, Bessie May told her that the WOP-pers don't pray together anymore."

"I don't believe it. What in the world happened? Please tell me this doesn't have anything to do with Ophelia's hair being orange or Bessie May's fashion sense."

"Not that I know of. Why?"

"Oh, never mind. What happened, Mama?"

"From what I understand, it all started in the fellowship hall at the Methodist church. They were taking prayer requests, and Prissy mentioned that she was about to have hemorrhoid surgery."

"Ouch."

"Right? So she asked for prayer. I believe her words were something along the lines of 'I have pain in the . . . well, you know. We are talking about hemorrhoids here.' "

"O-okay." Where this was going, I could not guess.

"That's where things got complicated. Bessie May must've misunderstood her. Then again, she has needed a new hearing aid for ages. Everyone knows that. But Bessie May quoted back what Prissy said incorrectly. Instead of saying, 'You have pain in the . . . you know,' she blurted out,

'Yes, we know, Prissy. You really are a pain in the . . . you know.' "

"Just a misunderstanding."

"Yes, but the poop hit the fan, pardon the pun. Prissy got offended and said a few things she shouldn't have. Bessie May countered. Then Ophelia got involved."

"Oh dear."

"Yeah, and then Queenie tried to get everyone calmed down, but I guess it didn't work. So before anyone could even start praying, the whole group of 'em ended up on opposite sides of the room. Maybe not literally on opposite sides of the room, but you get my point. They never ushered up so much as one prayer. Prissy huffed off first, then Bessie May left, then the rest of 'em stormed off. All mad as hornets. Well, except Queenie, who swears she was so shocked she couldn't remember how to pray."

"Wow. Must've been really something to shock the prayer out of Queenie. She's the best prayer warrior I know."

"Now no one's praying. Except maybe Florence Wilson, who was stuck in the fellowship hall for nearly five hours until Bessie May remembered she'd driven her there. Poor thing, still recovering from hip surgery. She couldn't exactly walk home, and she doesn't own a cell phone. If the good reverend hadn't stopped by the church at the end of the day, she might still be sitting there."

"That's horrible. What a mess."

"Mess doesn't even begin to describe the chaos going on, and the men of the town are all caught up in it too. When he heard what happened, Prissy's husband got rankled and confronted Bessie May's husband at the Dairy Queen. So it's not just the WOP-pers who are split down the middle, it's their spouses too."

"This is terrible."

"More terrible than you know. The manager of the Dairy Queen called in the police. The whole place was turned into a police scene, and all because of Prissy's pain in the . . . well, you know."

"Heavens. I never pictured anything like this happening in Fairfield. Do you think they'll all kiss and make up?"

"I sure hope so, and fast. I mean, the timing for all of this really stinks. Your wedding is coming up a week from Saturday, after all."

"Right." So much for insisting we get married in my hometown where everyone loved everyone. And so much for working on a strategy to convince Nadia that the folks in Fairfield were loving and neighborly. If she caught wind of this, she'd probably call the Gaylord Hotel and book the grand ballroom.

Okay, maybe not. Maybe she didn't care as much about the town split as I did. But how could my own neighbors do this to me—and right before my wedding? Didn't they realize things were stressful enough already?

I ended the call with Mama in a hurry. Something to do with Pop chasing her around the RV park. But her words stayed with me as I shut down my computer and prepared to leave for the day. In fact, I could hardly think of anything else, which totally messed up my dinner plans with Brady.

When he arrived at my house to pick me up, I couldn't seem to focus on our event together. I could only think of Prissy. And Bessie May. And Ophelia. And the police. Had my hometown gone crazy?

Brady met me at the door with a broad smile on his face. He took one look at me and his brow wrinkled. "Katie? What's happened?"

"Don't ask. Ugh." I leaned against the doorjamb and tried to gather strength.

"Is everyone okay?"

"Physically, yes. But we have a fiasco on our hands."

"A fiasco?" Now he looked genuinely worried. "Something go wrong with the wedding planning?"

"Sort of. Only, not really." I groaned and then ushered him into my living room. "I didn't want to tell you, Brady, because it's just so . . . dumb."

"What's dumb?" He plopped down onto the Herculon sofa and gazed up at me.

"The WOP-pers have disbanded."

"No way." He shifted his position on the sofa. "Did someone die or something?"

"I know, right? I would've guessed that would be the only thing to ever stop them. But it's worse than that." I paced the room, my nerves kicking in.

"Worse than someone dying?"

"Not really, but it's bad. Very, very, very bad."

He patted the sofa, a signal for me to join him. "Start at the beginning. Tell me everything."

I groaned again as I took a seat on the itchy fabric. "Do I have to?"

"Yes." He reached for my hand. "In the beginning . . ."

I sighed. "In the beginning, Prissy had hemorrhoids."

Brady's eyes widened. "Not at all how I pictured the story kicking off, but you've hooked me with a great opening line. Now, for the rest of the story."

I told him, and within a minute or two he was laughing so hard he could barely talk. "Katie, that's priceless. It's a joke. It's got to be. Your mom is pulling your leg."

"She's not. The police are involved."

"The police? Why? Did they arrest Bessie May for disturbing the peace?"

"No, but the whole town is split down the

middle, and less than two weeks before our wedding. And to make things worse—"

"Worse than the town being split down the middle?"

"To make things worse, I went off on a spiel at Alva and Eduardo's wedding, telling your mom how sweet the town of Fairfield is. You know how skeptical she was about holding the wedding there."

Brady slipped his arm over my shoulders. "She wasn't skeptical about Fairfield. She just wanted me to have a great experience and thought the Gaylord would do the trick."

"Well, maybe we should've gone with her idea. But how could I have known, Brady? I never dreamed the whole town would fall apart."

"They haven't fallen apart, Katie. C'mon now. That's a little dramatic. Let's go to dinner and forget about all of this." He rose and gestured for me to join him. I couldn't. Not without telling him the rest.

"Queenie says she's forgotten how to pray."

"Whoa." He took a seat once more. "This is serious then."

"Yeah. You know if Queenie's troubled, it must be bad."

He looked my way, eyes narrowed. "So, let me get this straight. We have less than two weeks to fix the town, have our wedding rehearsal, and then celebrate the biggest day of our lives."

"Yes. Exactly."

"Without my mom finding out." He released a slow breath.

"Or anyone else from Cosmopolitan Bridal. I'd be devastated if the girls knew."

"You don't think Twiggy's told Dahlia? Surely she's already spreading the story around the shop."

"Maybe. I don't know."

"Did your mom mention anything about the church?"

"What do you mean?"

"I mean, you hear about churches splitting all the time. Do you think that will end up happening?"

"Surely not." I bit my lip. Then again, many of the ladies were members of the Baptist church. I'd have to ask Crystal about that one.

Great. If the whole town was split down the middle, maybe we'd have to split the church down the middle too. Wouldn't that be lovely. And while we were at it, we might as well split my heart down the middle, because that's what would happen if we didn't get this fixed—and quick!

23

Never Loved Before

I have to be alone very often. I'd be quite happy if I spent from Saturday night until Monday morning alone in my apartment. That's how I refuel.

Audrey Hepburn

The first weekend in August, Lori-Lou, Crystal, and a happily married Aunt Alva hosted my bridal shower. The original plan to use the community center folded because Prissy, who headed up the committee to rent the space out, wasn't speaking to Crystal, though Crystal couldn't seem to figure out why.

In the end, Queenie offered her home for the event, which turned out to be just the right amount of space, since half the ladies on the invitation list weren't speaking to the other half and hadn't RSVP'd. Not that I minded. I'd rather have a smaller crowd—all speaking to one another— than a larger one wreaking havoc. And I felt good about the fact that the girls from the bridal shop would all be at my side. That made up for the mess.

Sort of.

Still, it broke my heart to think about the divisions in the town, and all the more as I visited with Crystal before the shower kicked off. She looked visibly shaken by it all. Her hands trembled as she worked on the shower décor.

"You okay over there, honey?" Alva asked as she put the silverware in place.

Crystal sighed. "Not really. I don't even know what to tell y'all about the big brouhaha goin' on here in Fairfield. It's escalatin' to a ri-*dic*-ulous point." She put a lovely centerpiece in the middle of Queenie's dining room table and then leaned back to observe. "Do you like the china plates? Did you notice they're in a variety of pas-*tay*-uls, just like our dresses? I went on eBay and found 'em just for today."

"They're gorgeous, Crystal. I still can't believe you went to such effort for little ol' me."

"Yes, they're amazing." Hibiscus picked one up and ran her finger across the edge of it. "Beautiful."

"Only to find out after the fact that half the ladies aren't turnin' up because of their stupid pride." Her eyes flooded with tears. "I'm sorry, Katie. I hate to bring you down on your big day. Please forgive me for lettin' my emotions get the better of me." She swiped at her eyes.

"Nothing to forgive." I gave her a compassionate smile. "And technically my big day is next weekend. I had hoped to hear good news when I got to town this morning, but I guess not. Things are no better at all?"

"No good news, I'm afraid." My sister-in-law paled and almost looked ill. "I guess you know all about how this got started, with Prissy and Bessie May gettin' into it. Right? And how their husbands got involved."

"Right."

"I hate to tell you, but Mayor Luchenbacher found himself smack-dab in the middle of the mess. You know how his wife Nettie is. Always trying to prove a point. Anyway, she took sides with Prissy, and before you know it, the mayor did too. Which was fine, except the sheriff took sides with Bessie May, which put the mayor at odds with the sheriff. So the editor up at the paper—did I tell you that Mildred's husband Chuck is the editor now?—he decided to do a write-up slam-dunkin' the sheriff. So the sheriff's people came out swingin'. Before you knew it, there were half a dozen articles from locals singin' the praises of the sheriff and crucifying the mayor. Which, of course, has Nettie seein' red. No one, and I do mean *no one,* says a negative word against her husband. Not while she's livin' and breathin'."

"Oh my." Thank God Nadia wasn't hearing all of this. Hopefully things would simmer down by the time she arrived.

"Yes, 'oh my' is right."

"This is all so ridiculous and exciting at the same time!" Alva rubbed her hands together. "What a terrific plotline! I can hardly wait to see what happens next. Do you think there'll be a gunfight at the O.K. Corral between the sheriff and the mayor? Ooh, I'd pay money to see that."

"I sure hope not." I shivered just thinking about it.

"Don't be so quick to assume." Queenie's voice sounded behind us. "The sheriff is filing a lawsuit."

I turned to face her, praying I'd heard wrong. "I'm sorry, what?"

"The sheriff. He's filing a lawsuit against the mayor. Apparently there's some kind of old zoning issue that's been around for years, and it has something to do with Main Street. The whole street is divided down the middle with cones. The sheriff has let things slide till now. But with everyone up in arms, he's decided to take action against the mayor, who insists the sheriff is wrong. Can you believe all of this goes back to Bessie May misunderstanding Prissy's comments about her hemorrhoid surgery?" She sighed. "Do you ever feel like you're sliding down a slippery slope?"

"As a matter of fact, I do. My wedding reception is taking place on Main Street."

"You might be safe, as long as your reception is on the south lawn of the courthouse," Queenie said.

"It is. Whew." That was a close one.

"But keep in mind that the church sits kitty-corner on Main at Travis. It's half in one zone and half in another. The sanctuary falls to the mayor's side and the fellowship hall to the sheriff's. The original founders knew this but worked together to overcome the division. Back then, no one cared. Something about goodwill."

"Goodwill, huh?" I groaned. "What's happening to my little town? And why now?"

"I don't know. I've never seen anything like this, to be honest. I'm kind of scared to go outside because everyone's always up in arms."

Lovely. Just what I needed the week before my wedding. And to be perfectly honest, I was a little scared to stay indoors too—especially on Main Street.

Queenie sighed. "You remember Benny Walker, right? His dad ran the auto parts store before they tore it down and turned it into a gas station? Well, he got into it with the sheriff over the zoning thing. Next thing you know, the businesses are squabbling. Hotel owners are fighting with restaurant owners, people aren't frequenting the same stores anymore."

"Yes." Crystal groaned, still looking a bit pale. "And whatever you do, don't go onto any of their Facebook pages. You won't believe the things they're saying. Don't they realize that the internet is forever? You can't take that stuff back. Once it's out there, it's out there . . . forever. Let's just say the feudin' has definitely gone public."

"And all of this because of a misunderstanding?" I asked. "Are we really, really sure that's what started it all?"

"Yes." Queenie clucked her tongue. "And probably the dumbest misunderstanding in the history of misunderstandings."

"No kidding."

I didn't have time to think about it for long because Bessie May arrived, along with Ophelia and Mildred. Prissy was noticeably missing, as were the mayor's wife and several others. I tried not to let it bother me.

Queenie and Crystal greeted the guests and offered them snacks. Before long we were all gathered around the dining room table, plates filled with yummy finger foods. I would've expected the ladies to talk about my wedding— we were here for a shower, after all—but the topic turned to the goings-on in town.

Mildred looked particularly sad. She'd hardly said a word since arriving.

"Are you all right?" I asked, feeling a bit more like a psychologist than a bride-to-be at her own shower.

Her lips curled down in a frown. "It's just that nothing's the same since the WOP-pers stopped praying together. Nothing."

"Like what?"

"Well, for one thing, the peaches aren't as good this season. I tried making a cobbler last night and my husband told me it tasted like poison."

"You're blaming that on the lack of prayer?" Alva asked.

"What else could it be? I used the same recipe I've always used." She headed across the room to refill her plate.

"Her peach cobbler's always been nasty," Bessie May whispered in my ear. "But don't tell her, okay? More than likely her husband's just now worked up the courage to tell her."

"I have noticed that the Blizzards at Dairy Queen don't taste the same," Ophelia said.

Lori-Lou seemed more than a little perplexed by this. "Are you saying that's because of lack of prayer?"

"I think it's that old machine they're using, but if the WOP-pers were on the job they would've prayed in a new one by now. The real kicker is what's happening up at Brookshire Brothers. Would you believe they fired their chief baker? Carissa has worked there for thirty years. The manager up and fired her!"

"Why?"

"I have no idea. Something to do with fondant. But most of us believe it's because she was on one side of the feud and the manager was on the other. So he got rid of her."

"Bessie May, that's illegal. He can't do that."

"He already did." Her voice grew more animated as she continued. "Nobody cares anything about legal or illegal around here. They just do what they want. Like Bobby Rogers, the girls' softball coach. He kicked three girls off the team. Accused them of vandalism, but all they stole was some toilet paper so they could wrap another girl's house. Next thing you know, the police show up at their door and then they're off the team. I know what really happened there. Coach was on Prissy's side and the parents of those three girls were on mine. So there you have it. Split straight down the middle. This poor town."

"This poor *bride*." I groaned. "What am I going to do?"

Dahlia leaned my way to say, "Whatever you do, don't buy your groceries at Brookshire Brothers and don't toilet paper anyone's house. Those two things will land you on the wrong side of the law."

"And for pity's sake, don't drive down Main Street," Lori-Lou added. "That might just get you arrested."

"The real kicker is that half these folks are with the Chamber of Commerce." Ophelia clucked her tongue. "They've taken an oath to lead with integrity, respect, and passion. So much for that."

"Oh, I don't know . . ." Queenie filled her plate with little tea sandwiches. "I'd say they have a lot of passion."

"Misguided as it might be." Bessie May lit into another story, but Crystal took my arm and pulled me out of the room.

"I'm sorry, but I just had to get you out of there. This is your bridal shower, for pity's sake, not a meeting at city hall."

"Couldn't have guessed it by me." I glanced down at my plate and realized it was still empty. In all the chaos, I'd forgotten to get even one bite of food. Go figure.

"Tell you what." Crystal grabbed my plate. "You go to the living room. I'll meet you there with a full plate."

"Okay." I did just that. I found Lori-Lou and Queenie seated on the sofa. I settled onto the love seat across from them. "You guys hiding out too?"

"You betcha. Just can't take it anymore." Lori-Lou shivered. "Makes me glad I moved to the city."

"People get assaulted in the city," Queenie said and then took a bite of her sandwich.

"Yes, but not by their friends and neighbors." Lori-Lou settled back against the sofa cushions. "If you get my point."

"I for one am glad Mama hasn't made it back in town yet. This would break her heart. And Nadia . . ." Now I shivered. "She's set to arrive in a few minutes. Sure hope we can change the subject by then."

"I'll make sure they do, honey." Queenie gave me a knowing look.

"Yes, once we finish eating, we'll play a couple of games and then you can open your gifts," Lori-Lou said. "It'll be lots of fun."

Fun. Yes. We could all stand some fun.

Crystal arrived a moment later with my plate, which she handed to me, along with a fork and napkin. "There you go, Katie. Enjoy your bridal shower luncheon." She gave a strained smile as she took a seat next to me.

I nibbled on a carrot for a moment and then looked her way, realizing she wasn't having anything to eat or drink. "You doing okay over there? You look a little out of sorts."

"Who wouldn't be?" Her eyes filled with tears. "This is not how I pictured things goin' in my quaint little town."

"Me either."

I handed her a carrot and she bit into it.

"Tell me how you're doing—really," I said. "We've hardly had a chance to talk since you and Jasper got back from Atlanta. Things have been so crazy."

"Ugh. Tell me about it." She chomped on the carrot and then released the longest sigh ever. "I. Can't. Take. It. Anymore."

"That bad?" I asked.

"Worse! And it's gone on for weeks now. Let's just leave it at that. People have taken to timin' their visits to the store. Those who side with Prissy only shop in the mornin's now, and those who are sidin' with Bessie May only shop in the afternoon. It's a mess. And I can't keep up with the players—who's teamin' up with who."

"Whoa."

"Yes, exactly. I feel *so* bad for Jasper. He has to listen to everyone complain. I guess they think he's got a sympathetic ear, since he grew up here and all. But this whole fiasco's got me wishin' I still lived in Dallas."

This got Queenie's and Lori-Lou's attention right away.

"Oh, honey . . ." My grandmother paled. "Tell me it ain't so."

"Are you coming back?" Twiggy and Dahlia asked, their voices rippling in unison across the room.

"The thought has crossed my mind. This is just heartbreaking. And it's hurting our business. Sales are really down right now. Well, except for fencing—sales are way up on fence posts. People are shuttin' each other out. It's just awful, I tell you."

"I'm so sorry," I said. "Have you mentioned anything to Mama and Pop?"

"We haven't had the heart to tell them. Your mom calls every Sunday afternoon at four o'clock just to check in. I talked to her last Sunday and she sounded a bit suspicious. Someone must've told her something, though I couldn't be sure. But she knew enough to ask some rather pointed questions."

"How's Jasper handling all of this?"

"He says it'll blow over. He told me to pray. And I have been. It's just that I don't really know what to pray for, except peace. I certainly don't want to pray for one team or the other. You know? I think they're all wrong. They all need a swift kick in the backside."

"Whatever you do, don't say that anyone is a pain in the backside. That's what started all of this, you know."

"Oh, we know, all right." A reflective look settled over Queenie. "The sad thing is, no one even knows if Prissy ever recovered from her, um, well . . . health issues. Folks were so busy being mad, no one thought to ask if she's any better. I just find that so sad."

I did too.

Just about that time, Bessie May and Mildred got into a dispute over the chicken salad—something about almonds. Twiggy came into the living room to tell me that Jane was having some sort of meltdown in the kitchen. And Crystal—poor Crystal—bolted to the bathroom because her stomach revolted from the carrot.

Wasn't this just the perfect time for my future mother-in-law to show up at the front door with a smile as bright as sunshine on her face? Yes indeed, it surely was.

24

Always on My Mind

I've been lucky. Opportunities don't often come along. So, when they do, you have to grab them.

Audrey Hepburn

The following morning Nadia headed back to Dallas before sunup. Eduardo arrived a short time later to pick up Alva. They'd planned a little day trip to Paris, Texas, just a couple of hours away. This left me on my own to travel back to Dallas. Before we parted ways, though, we decided to have one last meal—an early breakfast at McDonald's. Pap-Paul couldn't join us, what with his church obligations, but Queenie decided to come along and then catch up with him for the second service. Imagine my surprise when Crystal and Jasper met us there with Corrie at their side.

"Did you have a wonderful time at the slumber party?" Queenie asked the youngster.

She nodded and dove into a lengthy story about how much fun she'd had at Crystal and Jasper's house.

"We had the time of our lives," Crystal said.

"Just what I needed to take my mind off things." Her stomach growled and she rubbed it. "Guess I'd better get some food or my tummy will be grumbling all the way through service."

"With that crazy rock-and-roll band, no one will hear it, anyway." Alva rolled her eyes.

We got into the serving lines, and I couldn't help but notice the looks of disdain between several of the customers. Great. The divisions continued, even under the golden arches?

I purchased a breakfast sandwich and took a seat at a table with my family. As I nibbled on my food, a little quarrel broke out at a nearby table between the girls' softball coach and one of the mothers. Lovely. It didn't take long for things to get heated.

"What a mess." Queenie dabbed her lips with her napkin.

"Yes. Talk about the worst timing in the history of all weddings," I said. "And it had to be mine."

"I'm sorry, Katie." My grandmother gave me a sympathetic look. "I really am. I hate this for you."

"Me too." No other words would come, so I took a big bite of my sandwich.

Crystal's gaze traveled the room. "There's got to be something we can do. How do we fix this?"

Queenie shook her head. "You know me, I'm a natural-born fixer. But this one's going to take supernatural intervention. I truly believe the only thing that could possibly bring this many divided people back together again is some sort of heavenly 'gotcha.' "

"Heavenly 'gotcha'?" Eduardo looked perplexed. "What do you mean?"

"I'm not sure, but something memorable."

"A natural disaster?" Alva suggested. "People always come together during a crisis."

"Are you saying we should pray in a hurricane so that the people will be bonded? That's just plain dumb." Queenie rolled her eyes, then took a little nibble of her sandwich.

"Well, not a hurricane, maybe, but something." Alva gave me an inquisitive look. "A tornado? Flash flood?"

"Sure. Like things aren't terrible enough already a week before Katie's wedding?" Queenie shook her head. "Sure. We'll pray in a flood."

She and Alva started to squabble. Eduardo put up his hand. "C'mon, you two. It isn't going to make things any better if you end up on opposite sides of the aisle."

My brother leaned back in his seat and gave me a tentative look. "It is true that people who oppose one another need something to unite them, and nothing unites like a crisis. That's always the way of it, from my experience. Not saying we should pray in a flood, but I've got to wonder if we can come up with something for the people to rally around. You know?"

I had to give it to Jasper. He had a point. People did come together during a crisis. But try as I may, I couldn't picture God wreaking havoc on the town just so that people would start talking again. Instead of praying for all of that, I would just pray for peace. For wisdom. For division to cease.

I made the drive back to Dallas with all of these things on my mind. The events of the weekend had worn me to a frazzle, and I felt like crying. Every time I thought about my hometown in such a state of chaos, I felt sick inside. And every time I remembered that my wedding was set to take place in that town in less than one week, I felt even more sick—heartsick, anyway.

With no one to witness my concerns, the tears flowed free. I thought about Bridget Pennington, how she'd stood up to her father and had the wedding of her dreams, how everything had come out fine in the end because she'd taken a stand for right. What would Bridget do in my situation? Dealing with a stubborn father was a sure sight easier than taking on a whole town, after all. Not that I wanted to stir up any more trouble. No, all I wanted at the moment was peace. Quiet. Sanctuary.

I swiped at my eyes with the back of my hand as I drove, and all the more as I realized the work awaiting me back home. I needed to start packing, and soon. Alva would be listing the house, and

I'd be hauling all of my stuff—what little there was of it, anyway—over to Brady's condo.

For some reason I just felt weighted down every time I thought about it. Then again, everything had me feeling heavy these days. I missed the good old days, the days of riding the Fourth of July float as Fairfield's Peach Queen. The days of cheerleading at high school games. The days of sitting in church, listening to our pastor's voice soothe my troubled soul.

That's what I needed right now—soothing. I turned on the radio to a Christian station, hoping for some worship music. Instead, I got a talk show. Politics. People divided.

Lovely.

I decided to turn it off and pray. I prayed all the way from I-45 to my house. Er, Alva's house. When I pulled my car into the driveway I noticed Brady's truck. Strange. He hadn't mentioned a thing about being here.

My sweet guy met me at my car door. He opened it and took one glance at my tearstained face, and a look of alarm came over him. "Are you okay?"

"Just . . . a rough weekend."

"Didn't you say the shower went okay?"

"Right, right. It was fine. Well, parts of it. Gifts are in the trunk, by the way. I hope you like toasters."

"O-okay. So, what's happening? The towns-people still brawling?"

"That would be an understatement. I just don't know what to do."

"For one thing, get out of the car and give me a kiss. Then let's talk about how great our life is going to be after we're married. In Dallas. Far from all the troubles back in Fairfield."

"Good plan." I tossed my keys into my purse, climbed out of the car, and stretched the stiffness out of my back as I stood. As Brady—my wonderful, precious Brady—pulled me into a cozy embrace, I felt my anxieties lift like feathers taking flight on a summer day.

"God always has a plan, Katie. Trust him. This is an interruption, but it's going to end well."

"I hope so. I think I'm just so exhausted that nothing is making much sense anymore. That doesn't help."

"True. You need to rest."

"Yes, but when? How? I have so much to do. Do you realize I haven't packed one box yet? Between my work schedule and wedding plans, I'm just . . ."

"Overtaxed."

"Yeah. I guess that's the right word. I'm weary. And feeling heavy, like I'm carrying around added weights. So many changes, so many decisions . . ."

"You're not regretting anything, are you?"

"You mean, getting married? No way." I flung my arms around his neck, and tears wriggled their way out of my eyes again. "That's the only thing that makes sense right now. Everything else is wonky, but when I'm with you I can breathe again."

"Well, that's good." He gave me several tender kisses, then gazed into my eyes with such compassion. "'Cause I'd hate to see you go without oxygen."

I sighed. "It won't be long before I'll be Mrs. Brady James and we'll be safely tucked away in our home, with all of the chaos behind us."

"Yep. Our new home. I can hardly believe we'll be sharing the same space—the same bed—in a week." He gave me a little wink. "I'm pretty excited about all of that."

"Me too." Still, a shiver ran down my spine as I thought of all the boxes yet to be packed.

"Let me get your suitcase, okay? I'll carry it in for you."

"Nah, I'll get it out of the backseat. It's the least of my worries. Thank goodness we don't have to unload the gifts until we get to the condo. Don't think I have it in me right now to drag all that stuff inside."

"All those toasters, you mean?" He chuckled.

"Yeah. We'll figure all that out later. Right now I just need to get my suitcase inside."

After grabbing my bag from me, Brady led the way to the front door. I'd just started to reach for my key when something caught my eye.

"What is this?" I pointed to a large bow on the front door.

He shrugged. "Looks like a bow. Do you think Alva put it there?"

I laughed and slipped the key into the lock. "Knowing Alva, yes. She probably got it on one of her wedding gifts and thought it was pretty. No doubt she thought it looked like a wreath or something."

"Yeah. Something like that. Or . . ." A suspicious look came over him.

"Or, what?" I asked.

"Or, maybe it's a little pre-wedding gift from someone who adores you."

"A gift?" My thoughts whirled.

"Yes." He shifted my suitcase from one hand to the other. "I hope you're okay with getting this one a little early. It only makes sense to do this now. You'll understand what I mean when you see what it is."

"Are you trying to confuse me on purpose?" I laughed.

"Yes. Just open the door."

And so I did. The minute I stepped into the living room, I knew something was very, very wrong. Either we'd been robbed, or—

I shot a glance his way, too overcome to speak as I took it all in.

25

You'll Get Through This

Happiest girls are the prettiest.

Audrey Hepburn

"Brady?" I gasped when I saw his gorgeous living room furniture in the very spot where Aunt Alva's Herculon sofa had once sat. "What is this? What's happened?"

"Just take a little stroll with me, okay?" He put the suitcase on the floor and reached for my hand. I set my purse and keys down and then latched my fingers through his and followed him across the living room.

"I'm so confused." In fact, I thought perhaps I'd wandered into some sort of alternate reality. Maybe I was dreaming all of this.

Brady's grin lit the room. "You told me once—no, you told me about ten different times—how much you love this house."

"I do. I've always loved it because it reminds me of Fairfield. Not Fairfield as I witnessed it this weekend, of course, but the Fairfield I grew up in—the one where people spoke to each other at the grocery store and brought meals to people when they were sick and cheered on each other's kids at baseball games. That Fairfield."

"Right. This home represents that for you."

"It does." The tears came again, though I wasn't sure why. It didn't make any sense to cry over a dumb house.

"I know you and Alva have different tastes in furniture, though. I've heard you say a dozen times how itchy her sofa was."

"Yeah. I definitely would've picked something more like . . ." I pointed to his living room set. "Well, more like this."

"Good. Glad you like it, because now you can have your cake and eat it too. Welcome to our new home, Katie."

"W-what?" For a moment I couldn't catch my breath. "Our . . . what?" Tears sprang to my eyes once again, only this time they were happy tears.

"I bought Alva's house for you," he said. "For *us*."

"Oh, Brady!" I threw my arms around his neck and gave him a kiss laced with passion and fire. "Are you serious?" I asked when I came up for air. "What about your condo? When did you do this? *How* did you do this? Is it really ours?"

"Whoa, slow down, slow down! I might be fast on the court, but my thoughts don't move as quickly as my feet." He gazed at me with such love in his eyes that I wanted to marry him right then and there.

"Okay, but tell me everything." My gaze shifted around the room, and I saw it, as if for the first time, as ours. His. Mine. Ours. Together.

"I've been talking to Alva and Eduardo ever since they got engaged. I knew that Alva would be moving into his house. I mean, who wouldn't—it's a bona fide mansion. At first it never even crossed my mind to buy hers, but I kept thinking of how you talked to me that one morning about the Formica table and how much it affected you. I didn't even know what Formica was, to be honest. But I knew one thing: I had to get you this house. I knew it meant something special to you."

"Brady, that's the sweetest thing ever. But what about your condo?"

"Stan's been looking for a new place ever since he proposed. Beau's still at his place, so it just made perfect sense. I sold him my place and Alva sold me hers." He paused. "Though, technically we haven't closed yet. I'll need your signatures on everything since it's going to be in both of our names."

"Wow! Just . . . wow! How can I ever thank you? Best gift ever!"

He placed a tender kiss on my cheek, his lips soft against my skin. "Thank you. But I think Alva's the one who gave you the sweetest gift ever. Follow me and you'll see what I mean." He led the way through the dining room, where I saw his gorgeous cherry dining set, and into the kitchen. The minute I clapped eyes on Alva's old Formica table, I wanted to burst into tears. I couldn't help myself. I sprinted to the table, ran my fingers across it, and started crying. No, weeping. Crying didn't seem to do it justice.

Brady slipped his arm around my waist. "Gee, if I'd known you had this kind of attachment to Formica, I would've planned this ages ago."

I spoke over the lump in my throat. "How could we have known even a few months ago that all of this would happen?"

"That you would fall in love with a table?"

"No, that we would meet and fall head over heels in love with each other. That Aunt Alva would turn out to be one of my best friends. That she and Queenie would reconcile after nearly a zillion years of not speaking. That I would end up working for your mom. That the very house that made me feel most at home in Dallas would end up being my house. *Our* house!"

The tears started again and he let me cry it out.

"Before you get too worked up," he said after I finally calmed down, "you might want to know that I've moved my king-size bed into the master bedroom. It was a tight squeeze, but I made it work. We can keep your current bedroom suite in the room where you've been staying, for when people come to visit."

"Of course."

"I'll be staying with Stan between now and Saturday, so no worries." He gave me a playful wink. "In case you were reading too much into what I just said."

"I know you better than that." I jabbed him with my elbow. "But does Stan have an extra bed?"

"Yes. We've got it all figured out, Katie, down to a tee. So follow me, please." He walked me into the master bedroom, and I gasped when I saw the bed in the center of the room with the large dresser off to the side. He'd done it. The room looked perfect.

"Wow." I pinched my eyes shut and tried to imagine what it would be like just a short time from now when we shared this room, shared this bed. I could almost see myself rolling over to catch a glimpse of Brady's wonderful face in the early morning sunlight drifting through the openings between the drapes. I pictured the two of us lying in that bed with a tiny bassinet beside it, baby cooing with delight. I imagined our little family all curled up together on a rainy night, weathering

the storm together. Oh, I could see it all now, and what I saw made my heart sing. Who cared if the people in Fairfield were divided? Brady and I would create one beautiful, unified, happy family.

"Welcome home, Katie."

Had Brady spoken those words aloud again, or was I hearing them in the deepest recesses of my heart? They resounded around the room and made me want to sing.

Home.

I pondered that word, let it sink into my spirit. Deep. All my life I'd heard the expression "Home is where the heart is." Now I got to witness that, not as a child in a home with her parents—or even her aunt—but as a wife, and hopefully a mother. One day. My heart was rooted here, not just because I liked the walls, the floors, the rooms, but because I had made memories here, and would continue to do so with the person I loved more than anyone else.

A flood of emotions captivated me.

"Oh, I love it! I love, love, love it. And I love you too!" I threw myself into his arms and gave him a kiss he wouldn't soon forget.

"I'll take that as a sign you're okay with all of this?" he asked.

"Okay? I'm in heaven!"

"Good. But we're not done yet, you know. Look around you. Lots of empty spaces need filling. Boring, undecorated walls. Remember, the artwork at my place was mostly basketball stuff."

"That's okay. We'll line the hallway with it."

He laughed. "I've got a remedy for my stuff, if you want to take a look at the third bedroom."

"Sure." I followed behind him to the room where he had recuperated after his knee surgery.

He swung the door wide, and I gasped when not one but two desks came into view.

"Welcome to our office. His and hers." He pointed to the basketball memorabilia that framed one half of the room. "Hope you can handle it. You're going to be seeing a lot more of it."

"I am, for sure? You negotiated your new contract?" When he nodded I flew into his arms again. "Oh, Brady, that's great. Congratulations."

"I'll be back on the court as soon as we get back from our honeymoon. You're officially going to be a pro basketball player's wife. Might not be the easiest gig of your life."

"I have a feeling it'll be easier than juggling cones on Main Street."

"I have no idea what that means, but okay." Brady grinned. "Anyway, we now have a house to live in, a couple of great jobs to pay the bills, and some really ugly drapes." He pointed to the purple curtains—Alva's favorite. "Pretty sure we can remedy that in a hurry. Want to go shopping?"

"Actually, we might not need as much stuff as you think. C'mon outside with me." I pulled him through the living room, out the front door, and into the driveway, where I reopened the back of my vehicle. "Check this out." I pulled out a gorgeous black and white comforter set in king-size. "Queenie and Pap-Paul got this for us. It was on our registry, remember?"

He ran his hand along the edge of the bag. "Oh,

that's right. Guess we can mark that one off the list."

"Yep. And guess what else they got us?" I dug through the bag and came out with the package in question. "Curtains! Remember picking them out?"

"Barely. I have slept since then. But they're going to be perfect for the master bedroom."

"No drapes to replace the purple ones. Yet." I gathered up an armload of stuff. "But that's okay. I love to shop."

"Yes, you do." He loaded up his arms with goodies and looked my way. "It's all going to be great, Katie. Every single minute. So promise me one thing."

"What's that?"

"Promise this will be the best week of your life. Put everything else out of your mind and just focus on the one thing that matters right now: us. I'm going to pray that God takes care of the details, including calming the waters in Fairfield. He loves us. He's not going to let us down. Do you believe that?"

I nodded, feeling invigorated by his words. "I do."

"Save your 'I dos' for Saturday evening." He grabbed the comforter and headed for the house.

As I watched him from behind, I suddenly felt invincible. With Brady's hand in mine, we were truly unstoppable. Suddenly I could hardly wait for Saturday night.

26

Where I Used to Have a Heart

As a child, I was taught that it was bad manners to bring attention to yourself, and to never, ever make a spectacle of yourself . . . All of which I've earned a living doing.

Audrey Hepburn

I spent every single minute of that week thinking about my wedding. Planning for it. Talking about it. Dreaming of it. By the time Thursday afternoon rolled around, I'd pretty much worn my co-workers out with all of my nervous chatter.

Brady came to pick me up from work at five, and we rallied the troops to give last-minute instructions. "You guys know what time to be in Fairfield tomorrow, right?" I asked. "Rehearsal's at 6:00."

"Yes." Dahlia patted me on the shoulder. "Don't fret, Katie. We'll be at Jasper and Crystal's place at 4:30, our dresses ready to go. I've even got a new hairdo for the occasion, not that you seemed to notice." She primped a bit to show off the shorter locks. "We'll see you tomorrow, right on time, I promise. And we'll have the time of our lives celebrating with you."

"Awesome. And you, Nadia?" I turned to face my mother-in-law-to-be. "Are you riding up with us?"

Brady looked at his mother. "You're more than welcome to, Mom. Katie and I will be leaving early tomorrow morning. Probably 8:00 or 8:30. We want to have plenty of time to visit with the family before the rehearsal and rehearsal dinner. Can you meet us at the house or should we swing by and get you?"

The strangest expression crossed her face— sort of a mix between excitement and fear. "Actually . . ." Her nose wrinkled as she looked at Brady. "I thought I might ride up with a friend, if you don't mind."

"One of the girls?" I asked.

"No." She shifted her gaze to one of the mannequins and fussed with the gown on it. "I, um . . ."

"Mom?" Brady faced her. "What aren't you saying?"

She released her hold on the gown and looked his way. "I don't want anyone to make too much of this. Please don't." She wiped her palms on her slacks. "But I've been talking to an old friend on Facebook."

"Friend, as in *male* friend?" Brady looked worried.

"Yes." She reached over and took Brady's hand.

"You've been so busy, I didn't want to say anything yet. Besides, we don't know that the relationship is really going anywhere. I mean, he drove up from Houston last week, and we went to a great French restaurant. He's quite the charmer, but really—"

"Whoa. Wait." Brady raked his hands through his hair. "Are you telling me you're *dating* someone?"

"Not dating, really. We're just getting to know one another again. It's been so long. We've had a lot of catching up to do."

"Someone from Houston?" His gaze narrowed. "An old friend?"

"Okay, okay." She released a slow breath. "It started innocently. Bridget and I spent a lot of time working on ideas for her gown, and one thing led to another . . ."

"Mom." Brady put his hands on his hips. "Are you telling me that you're dating Bradley Pennington, Bridget's father?"

"The man who wouldn't let his daughter have her own way at the wedding?" Twiggy clamped a hand over her mouth.

"Oh my." Hibiscus moved a bit closer, eyes wide. "This is getting good."

"Who do you think talked him down off the ladder?" Nadia released a nervous laugh. "Bridget didn't seem to be getting anywhere with him, so I, um . . . well, I made a call. He wasn't hard to find, you know. I mean, the man heads up an oil and gas firm, one of the largest in the state."

"And?" Brady's stare would've been enough to melt an ice cream bar, but Nadia didn't flinch.

"And the next thing you know, we're friends on Facebook. And the rest, well . . ." Her words drifted off and she shrugged.

"Now he's driving you to our wedding?"

"*Only* if you're okay with me bringing a date." She fanned herself with her hand. "Is it getting warm in here?"

"No!" we all answered in unison.

"Ah. Anyway, it turns out he has ties in Fairfield. Something to do with the oil and gas business. He goes up there all the time."

"Only, he's coming here first, to pick you up?" Brady asked. "Then it's not really a business weekend for him."

"Right. If you're okay with it."

An awkward silence rose up between mother and son. Madge broke it with a loud whoop. "Well now, isn't this just the best news ever!"

A resounding cheer went up from all in attendance. Well, all but Jane, who looked a bit blue. Oh boy. I could hardly wait to see what kind of grieving this would stir up. Would she try to ruin my wedding?

Oh, wait . . . half the town of Fairfield was doing that already.

I did my best to put all of the potential problems

out of my mind as Brady and I loaded my SUV with all of the things we'd need for the week-end. We left early in the morning Friday, and I realized, as we pulled out of the driveway of our home, that this would be the last time I'd see Dallas as a single gal. Next time we returned to this house, it would be together.

Forever.

A delicious chill ran down my spine as I thought about that. We had the sweetest conversation all the way to Fairfield, talking through the wedding plans, the honeymoon, and so much more. I was so grateful he never brought up the drama going on in my hometown. There would be plenty of time to deal with that later.

No, *avoid* that later. We wouldn't deal with it. We would continue to pray that God would find a way to bring everyone back together—hope-fully some way that didn't involve a hurricane or tornado. Or flood.

"We're headed to Queenie's?" Brady asked as we pulled off the interstate.

"Nope. Not this time. The whole family is meeting at our old house. Jasper and Crystal want to show us the renovations. It makes sense, because I'll need to unload my stuff there. And Crystal brought my gown over from Queenie's weeks ago, so it's waiting on me there."

"All right." He pulled onto Main Street. We drove past Sam's, beyond Dairy Queen, and through town. I sighed when I saw the orange cones still dividing the street, an ever-present reminder of my split-down-the-middle hometown.

"Don't let it get to you." Brady put his hand on my leg. "Stiff upper lip."

"Okay." I pinched my eyes shut to avoid the obvious . . . until we reached the corner where the courthouse came into view. "Look, Brady! Tomorrow night we'll have our reception right there!"

"Can't wait. It's going to be perfect, Katie."

He continued the drive to the house I'd grown up in. I couldn't wait to see Crystal and Jasper again. They were an old married couple now, one with a house and a business to run. My, how things had changed.

As we pulled into the driveway, I looked at my childhood home and a rush of memories overtook me. That oak tree? The one with the broken limbs? I'd fallen out of it as a kid and broken my own limb—my arm. And that front door? Those stains? They came from the night my friends egged our house. Mama never quite forgave them for that. Or me either, as if I had anything to do with it.

"You ready, babe?" Brady asked.

I nodded and he walked around to my side of the car to open my door. What a gentleman. He led the way to the front door, where we were greeted by Crystal, who squealed the moment she met us. "You're here! Let's get this party started!"

Jasper joined her minutes later, which raised the question, "Who's manning the hardware store?"

"We closed it for the day," Crystal said. "Business is down now, anyway." Her smile faded. "Anyway, today is all about you. Now c'mon in this house and let us show you around. Jasper's done so much work on the place, you'll hardly recognize it!"

"Hardly recognize it" was right. As we made our way from room to room, I was astounded by the changes.

"Wow." I gestured to the kitchen cabinets, brand spanking new and as modern as any in the city. "This is amazing."

"He's amazin'." Crystal slipped her arm around his waist and looked up at him with a shy smile. "That's my man."

Jasper's face turned red. "I tried not to change the essence of the house," he explained, "but Crystal had her own design ideas, especially in the kitchen. I think it turned out really well."

"I'm just so shocked, Jasper. I mean, I know you've always been good with woodworking, but I had no idea you were capable of this."

"She inspired me."

"I love lookin' through magazines for ideas." Crystal giggled. "And come into the livin' room, Katie. See what I've done." She took off sprinting and I could barely keep up with her. "Look right there." She pointed at a floral sofa. "I couldn't resist when I saw this lovely sofa on sale at the resale shop. Isn't it divine?"

Not exactly Mama's taste, but what did that matter now?

"Oh, and check out your room, Katie," she said. "We haven't changed it one little bit. It's just like you left it. One day it'll be a nursery, but for now it's all yours. We want you and your bridesmaids to feel at home."

"Ooh!" I gave Crystal a hug. "Thank you! It'll be so fun to spend the night in my old room."

"I know you won't all fit, but we've got the boys' old rooms and air mattresses too. We'll make it work."

"The guys are staying at Queenie's place?" Jasper asked. When Brady nodded he added, "That oughta be fun."

"Oh my." Crystal giggled. "Are y'all havin' a bachelor party?"

"Nah." Brady looked horrified by this notion. "Not the traditional kind, anyway. I think all the guys are going to hang out at Dairy Queen tonight, but other than that, they don't have a lot planned. That's not really my bag."

Crystal gave me a knowing look. "Well, we're going to have a lot of fun here with the girls, so I hope you're ready."

Less than an hour later, my parents pulled up in their fifth wheel. Mama came bounding into the house and threw her arms around my neck.

"Katie Sue! I can't wait to start celebrating!"

"Me either, Mama." I led the way into the living room.

"We would've been here sooner, but we stopped by the hardware store." Pop's nose wrinkled. "Surprised to see it closed, but I guess I understand."

"We peeked in through the windows and saw all the changes." Mama gave a little sigh.

"It's . . . different." Pop shrugged and took a seat on Crystal's new sofa without even noticing it. "Took a little getting used to, but I understand the logic behind the new layout, I suppose."

"Change can be a good thing," I said and then gestured around the living room. "So what do you think?"

"Yes, what do you think, Mama Fisher?" Crystal bit her lip. "Do you like what we've done with the house?" Before my mother could answer, Crystal took her by the arm. "Let me give you the grand tour." She led the way from room to room, singing Jasper's praises and carrying on about the décor.

Mama remained silent. I had a feeling this was a hard pill to swallow. When they landed back in the living room I glanced my mother's way.

"So? What do you think?"

"Yes, be honest." Crystal flashed a warm smile.

I couldn't help but think my sister-in-law would regret my mother's honesty, so I braced myself, preparing for an earful.

27

Sweet Dreams of You

Pick the day. Enjoy it—to the hilt. The day
as it comes. People as they come.

Audrey Hepburn

I have to confess, the house doesn't feel much
like home anymore." Mama's face contorted
and a little sigh wriggled out. "But it's lovely.
Absolutely lovely."

"Oh, thank you, Mama Fisher!" Crystal threw
her arms around my mother's neck. "That means
the world comin' from you. We want you to still
feel at home here."

"Home." My mother sighed again.

"What is it, Mama?" I asked.

"We . . ." She pointed to my dad and then back
to herself. "We're living in a different sort of
home now."

"One on wheels." Pop squared his shoulders.
"And we just keep rolling, wherever the Spirit
leads us."

"Apparently the Spirit likes to travel." Mama
leaned back against the sofa, her gaze traveling
to the fabric.

"Oh, and speaking of the Spirit, did I tell you we

went to one of those cowboy churches when we were in Arizona?" Pop's eyes lit up as he told the story with great animation. "We really liked it."

"Different from the Baptist church?" Brady asked.

"Well, it smells different, anyway." Mama wrinkled her nose. "It's filled with real cowboys who work with real cows and real horses. But I have to confess, we've met a lot of interesting folks."

"Yep." Pop nodded. "Met this fella named Bob at the cowboy church in Phoenix. Single guy, about my age. He took a likin' to us, and us to him."

Mama let out a humph.

"Widowed?" Brady asked.

"Nope. Divorced," Pop said.

Mama rolled her eyes. "If you ask me, he's just traveling around in his RV looking for a new wife."

"What makes you say that?" I asked.

"For one thing, he asked me to marry him." My mother quirked a brow. "I declined."

Pop looked flabbergasted by this news. "This would have been helpful information. You should've told me. Here I treated the guy like a friend, and all the while he was proposing to my wife?"

Mama adjusted her position on the floral sofa, running her hand along the fabric. "He's no friend. And just for the record, when his wife left him, he paid her back by taking a power saw to everything they owned and cutting it in half."

I gasped. "No way."

"Yep. It's true. He decimated a gorgeous cherry-wood dining set. Sawed it straight down the middle. Took half of everything out of the house—literally—and left half for her."

"That's crazy."

"Nearly as crazy as him proposing to me," Mama said. "The problem with a fella like that—other than the obvious—is that he leaves you with half a heart."

"Sounds painful." Pop scooted closer to her on the sofa and put his hand on her knee. "Aren't you glad you married me?"

"Well, of course. But speaking of everything being sawed in half, what's up with the cones on Main Street? I didn't notice any construction. I'm almost afraid to ask why they're there. Has something else happened?"

"Don't ask." I shook my head. "Better if you don't. Just know that we're holding the reception on the southernmost courthouse lawn as a result of it."

"So very strange."

"We've decided to make the best of this," Brady said. "Our goal this weekend is to get through every minute of it without dragging up any drama or even talking about it, if that's okay. I hope you all understand."

"Yes, please," I said. "I always pictured all of my friends and family gathered around me on my wedding day, everyone laughing and smiling. I never once pictured town properties with lines drawn down the middle and people arguing at every turn. So I'd be thrilled if people would just close their eyes to it and focus on our big day. It's going to be great."

"Yes," Mama said. "I promise not to speak a divisive word." She ran her hands along the floral fabric once again. "Just one question, though."

"Yes?" I asked.

"Is this Ophelia's old sofa? I could've sworn I've sat on this rather loud pattern before."

"Well, I . . ." Crystal stammered. "I had no idea. I just fell in love with it at the resale shop and bought it."

"Thought it looked familiar. She got this big floral number in the eighties, right about the time the country-blue look came in. The crazy pattern always drove me a little nuts, but I guess some people like that sort of thing."

Crystal's smile faded. So much for not being divisive.

We changed the direction of the conversation as we ate lunch together, then started unloading everything from the SUV. At 3:15 Alva and Eduardo arrived. Queenie, Pap-Paul, and Corrie got there a few minutes later. I couldn't help but notice how the youngster went straight for

Crystal, who swept her into her arms and carried on about how much she'd missed her.

At 4:00 Nadia showed up . . . with Bradley Pennington. The minute the well-dressed fellow walked into our family home, I knew we had a winner. I could see it all over Nadia's face as she gazed at him. I also saw those feelings reciprocated when he looked her way. Yep. This train was barreling down the tracks, whether Brady liked it or not.

Nadia made introductions and we settled onto the sofa for a chat. I did my best to keep the conversation light. When I asked about Bridget's wedding, a huge smile lit his face.

"Funny thing," he said. "I thought I knew what was best for my girl, but it turns out I was wrong."

"Takes a big man to admit when he's wrong," Alva said. "Good of you to say so."

"I couldn't quite picture the whole sitting-on-bales-of-hay thing," he said. "But I came around."

"Oh, you've been listening to that same radio program?" Alva slapped her knee. "I swear, they need new writers. Katie, you should go to work for them. You'd come up with something far better than that."

Mr. Pennington looked more than a little confused by this. I widened my eyes and shook my head, praying he'd take the hint. No point in stirring the waters even more.

"Well, I for one am thrilled that Bridget's wedding came off without a hitch." Nadia gave Bradley a warm smile. "We worked for a long time on that gorgeous Martina McBride gown, and I couldn't wait to hear how the day went."

"She looked beautiful." Bradley reached over and squeezed Nadia's hand. "You're so good at what you do."

Yep. She was good at what she did, all right, and she was doing it right now, whether she knew it or not. The flushed cheeks. The innocent smile. The sparkling eyes. She was showing him with every fiber of her being that she liked him—a lot.

Okay, so her son didn't like this—at all. I could tell from the furrowed brows that Brady was having a hard time with the whole "Mom's dating" thing. But he would get over it. Time would prove me right on that one. I hoped.

At 4:30 my grandmother's cell phone rang. She took the call, and her mouth dropped open. "Are you sure?" she asked after a moment. "When did it happen? Where?" This was followed by, "Is she all right?" and "Mm-hmm. Yes. I'll be right there, if I can get someone to drive me."

We all sat in complete silence waiting for an explanation as she ended the call.

"Queenie, what is it?" I asked at last. "What happened?"

My grandmother was pale as she pressed her

cell phone back into her purse. "It's Prissy Moyer. She's taken a bad fall and broken a hip. I'm guessing it's broken. Sounds pretty bad."

"Oh no."

"I hate to say it, but it happened on Main Street. She was backing her car up and hit a cone. When she got out of the car to fix it, she slipped and fell."

"That's horrible." Crystal rose and paced the room. "Just awful."

"Paul, could you take me up to the hospital?" Queenie gave him an imploring look. "I promise not to be too long, but I just need to see her. And Bessie May too."

"Bessie May?" I couldn't help but gasp. "What's she got to do with this?"

My grandmother slipped her purse strap over her right shoulder. "She was inside the bakery helping Ophelia with your wedding cake and witnessed the accident, so she called 9-1-1. She's at the hospital with Prissy right now."

"Whoa." We all spoke in unison.

"We can't let y'all go to the hospital alone," Mama said. "I'll come with you."

I glanced at the clock on the wall—4:40. We still had some time before the rehearsal, though I had to wonder what was keeping Dahlia, Twiggy, and the others. Hopefully they were just pulling into town now.

After a quick nod from Brady, who must've

read my thoughts, I tossed out the only words that made sense. "I want to come too."

"Katie, no." Mama shook her head. "You can't let anything interrupt your rehearsal and rehearsal dinner."

"I won't," I argued. "We'll still get to the church by six, and the folks at Sam's will have our room ready at seven. Everything will go as planned. I only want to swing by for a minute. I think it would be good to let people know that I'm there for everyone. You know?"

"Okay." My mother did not look convinced.

I tried to stay focused as Brady drove me to the hospital. We arrived just behind my grandparents and my mother and all rushed into the lobby of the emergency room. At once the overpowering scent of disinfectant washed over me. Ugh.

I stopped running. "I can't stand hospitals."

"You were born in one, honey," Mama said. "This one, in fact."

"Yes, but I don't like the smell. Or the long hallways. I always feel so closed in in hospitals." Just talking about it made me feel like I couldn't breathe. Ack.

"I'm going to clue you in on something, Katie," Brady said, giving my hand a squeeze. "No one likes hospitals, especially not on the day of their wedding rehearsal."

"Good point."

We asked at the information booth about

Prissy's room and were greeted with a firm, "You can't go in there. I've already told that to half the town."

"Can I at least wait in the hall outside her room?" Queenie pleaded. "Pretty please, with sugar on top. I need to pray."

"Well, I suppose that would be all right." The woman pushed a button and the door swung open. When we stepped through we saw the Baptist pastor, the mayor, the sheriff, and Bessie May standing just inside. Interesting, considering most of them weren't officially speaking to each other.

"Any word yet?" Queenie asked as she rushed their way.

"The hip is broken in two places," the sheriff said. "She's going to need surgery."

"Maybe more than one surgery." Mayor Luchenbacher ran his fingers through his thinning hair and shook his head. "This is all my fault."

"No, it's mine." The sheriff's face blanched. "I take the blame."

"You're both wrong." Bessie May released a sigh and leaned against the stark hospital wall. "It's totally my fault. And if these fool doctors will open the door and let me in her room, I'm the only one who can make it all right again."

The sheriff shook his head. "But you heard what the doctor said, Bessie May. No visitors until the meds kick in. She's in too much pain."

"Which is exactly why she needs me right now. She has no other family in town. I'm all she's got." Bessie May moved past the men and rapped on the door. "Let me in this room, Doc," she called out. "Prissy Moyer is one of my best friends in the world, and I'll be horse-whipped if you think I'm gonna stand out here in this hallway while she's in there all alone."

Alrighty then. Looked like we were about to have a come-to-Jesus meeting, right here in the Fairfield Hospital.

28
Wild Angels

The past, I think, has helped me appreciate the present—and I don't want to spoil any of it by fretting about the future.

Audrey Hepburn

The sheriff put his hand up just as Bessie May rapped on Prissy's door again. His jaw tensed visibly as he took a slow step forward, the toes of his boots almost coming to rest on the tips of her black orthopedic shoes.

"Now, Bessie May . . ." Warning flashed in his dark brown eyes. "We all know the potential for disaster if you go in that room. I can't let you in there—for your sake and hers." The man folded his arms and blocked the door with his broad physique.

Bessie May waved her hand as if to dismiss him. "Pooh on disaster. This whole thing was just a misunderstanding. I've been saying that all along. Every single person in this town is a pain in the . . . you know . . . but I love 'em anyway. And I love Prissy most of all. So you might as well step aside, Sheriff. I'm goin' in." She took a couple of steps away from him and I thought for a minute he might try to stop her. Instead, he reached for the door handle and pushed the door open. With a wave of his hand he ushered her inside.

I turned back to look at the mayor to get his take on all of this and noticed that several other townspeople had joined us, including the mayor's wife Nettie and her archenemy, Mildred. I also caught a glimpse of my co-workers, who must've just arrived. Dahlia looked the most out of place, but Twiggy seemed to find this entertaining. Hibiscus and Jane remained at the back of the crowd. I had a feeling hospitals made Jane a little queasy too, if one could judge from the pained expression on her face.

Okay, so this wasn't exactly what I'd planned for the evening of my wedding rehearsal, but at least Brady and I were together with people we loved, right? I gazed up at him, joy rushing over me as I realized the miracle we were witnessing right before our very eyes.

"Happy almost wedding," he whispered.

"Same to you," I whispered back.

A gentle kiss followed, which the crowd seemed to enjoy. Then we all hovered near the door and tried to listen in as Bessie May and Prissy spoke for the first time in weeks. Maybe it had a little something to do with the medication they'd given Prissy, but the words coming forth sounded loopy. Strained.

"Get out of here, you old . . . you old . . . fart."

Okay then.

"Over my dead body." Bessie May snorted. "You'll have to push me out, and you don't appear to be in any condition to do that."

"If I could get out of this bed, I'd . . . I'd . . ." Prissy's words faded away.

"You're not getting out of that bed. You're going to do exactly what the doctor says, you stubborn old woman. And you're going to let the rest of us—those who love you—help you until you're able to get back up on your feet."

I put my ear against the door and strained to hear the rest.

Bessie May cleared her throat and I thought I heard her crying. "We're gonna be here for you—all of us—until you're well enough to go home. Then we're comin' home with you, to help make sure you get your meals and your baths and such."

"You'll enter my house over my dead body."

"Let's hope it doesn't come to that," Bessie May countered, "but if it does, I say we should bury you in that teal dress you wore on Easter Sunday. It brings out the pretty blue color in your eyes. I've always thought you looked amazing in that dress."

You could've heard a pin drop after that.

"I've always thought I looked nice in teal too," Prissy responded at last, her words sounding a little more relaxed. "I should wear it more often, I suppose."

"I agree. And I like that purple dress too. The one with the built-in pearl necklace. It's always shown off your figure. I don't mind admitting I've been a little jealous of your girlish physique."

"Thank you. I walk two miles every day. Helps burn calories and keeps me in tip-top shape. If you don't count this busted hip." Prissy sighed and then released an exaggerated yawn. "What were we talking about?"

"Your purple dress."

"Right. I do love that one. Always have."

"Me too. Hey, remember the day we went on that shopping spree to Dallas? I had to talk you into buying both of those dresses. You wanted the purple but weren't sure about the teal?"

"I remember. You put me through fits, talking me into it. I didn't want to spend the money, so you . . ." Prissy's words drifted off. When she did speak, I could tell she was crying. "You. Paid. For. It."

"That's what friends do." Bessie May's voice trembled. "Especially when they see a dress that perfectly matches the color of their friend's eyes."

I eased the door open a few inches, just long enough to see Bessie May reach to take Prissy's hand. "Friends argue and fuss," Bessie May said. "And they boss each other around. And some-times—just sometimes—they are misunderstood.

They make mistakes. But then they forgive and move on. That's how friendship works."

We all leaned in close to hear Prissy's response. Instead, a loud snoring sound startled us.

"Well, there you go." Bessie May laughed. "I pour my heart out and she falls fast asleep. Good to know I have that effect on people."

She had an effect on people, all right. From out in the hallway, I watched as Nettie walked over to Mildred and threw her arms around her neck. Then, before we could count to three, the sheriff extended his hand in the mayor's direction. Before long half the town was gathered in the ER waiting room, weeping and hugging and begging for forgiveness.

Okay then. God hadn't used a hurricane. Or a tornado. He'd taken a rough situation—a woman in need—and woven hearts together out of love. Love trumped anger. No storms necessary. Not the literal sort, anyway.

A short time later I walked to Prissy's door once more to see if I could find Queenie. With the clock winding down—the time was now 5:45— we needed to head to the church. I reached the half-open doorway and listened for my grandmother's voice. Instead, I heard Prissy's.

"Katie Sue, is that you standing in the doorway?" she called out.

"Yes, Prissy, it's me."

"Come on in here. I can't exactly see you when

you're hiding behind the door, and this fool hip of mine has me stranded. Can't even wiggle an inch."

I took a couple of tentative steps inside. I couldn't help but notice Bessie May still sitting in a chair nearby. Looked like she'd dozed off.

Prissy clucked her tongue at me. "What are you doing here, girl? Aren't you supposed to be at your wedding rehearsal or something?"

"Well, yes. In fifteen minutes, anyway. My bridesmaids are already there, in fact. But things have been so . . ."

"Complicated."

"Yes. That's a good word."

"And now they're even more complicated. I've messed up everything."

"Oh, it's not your fault, Prissy. Please don't think a thing about it."

"Half the town is out in the waiting room. Am I right?" When I nodded, she sighed. "Then I'd say it's pretty much my fault you're missing your own wedding rehearsal. And my fault the whole town's been in a snit, folks not talking to one another. All because I've been too foolish to admit that I have a hearing loss. I could've sworn Bessie May called me a . . . well, a pain in the . . . you know. But she swore right then and there that I misunderstood her. And I've decided to take her at her word."

"That's great, Prissy."

Her eyes fluttered closed, and she spoke in a groggy voice. "She bought me . . . a lovely teal dress . . . once upon a time. Did I ever tell you about that?"

"No ma'am, but I'll take your word for it."

She appeared to doze off. Just as quickly her eyes popped open, startling me. "That's what I should've done when we first had our little tiff—taken her word for it—then none of this would've happened. The whole town's about ready to go up in flames, and I'm the only one who can fix it."

"Well then, let me lift your spirits. God's already fixing it as we speak."

"Now that they know we're friends again . . ." Bessie May's voice sounded from the chair. She rose and walked over to the edge of the bed, then rested her hand on Prissy's arm. "All will be right with the world."

"I sure hope so." Prissy fluffed her pillows and attempted to sit up, but could not. "Get that sheriff in here, will you? I need to have a little chat with him."

"I'm here, Prissy." The sheriff stepped into the room with Brady at his side. "Something you want to say?"

"Yes, Sheriff. I want to say that we need to learn to forgive and forget. Misunderstandings happen. People get offended and hurt. But when it all comes down to it, we're family. I'd hate to think . . ." She began to cry in earnest. "I'd hate to think I'd stand at the pearly gates with unforgiveness in my heart. And I'd hate even more to think that my last big feat on this earth was turning people against one another. So however you see this thing unraveling, let's get to it. Katie's got a wedding rehearsal to attend in fifteen minutes."

"Twelve," Brady said.

"But who's counting?" I added with a smile.

The sheriff looked our way. "I say you two go on up to the church and get the ball rolling. Once I talk to my wife, she'll help get this thing straightened out. You two don't fret, all right? I promise, everyone on the invitation list will be at that church tomorrow evening."

"Everyone?" Brady looked alarmed.

"Everyone but Prissy. I'm pretty sure she'll be right here."

"I'll be cheering you on, though," she said. "I'll be there in spirit. And don't let Ophelia talk you into letting her make the lemonade. I gave Bessie May my top-secret recipe."

Oh boy.

I gave Prissy a light kiss on the cheek, grabbed my fella's hand, and headed out, ready to get this show on the road. We arrived at the church at 6:00 straight up. Pap-Paul took his place at the front and Joni slipped into wedding planning mode. She talked the various couples down the aisle, one after the other. I watched in awe as she worked with clipboard in hand. Talk about a pro!

I'd just stepped into place to walk down the aisle when she stopped me. "You can't play the role of bride at your own rehearsal, Katie," Joni said as she shifted the clipboard to her other arm. "You'll have to sit this one out."

"Well, who then?"

She glanced around the room and pointed to Jane. "Would you mind doing the honors?"

Oh boy. Oh boy, oh boy, oh boy.

Without a word of complaint, Jane rose, took my father's arm, and walked the aisle toward my husband-to-be.

You could've heard a pin drop.

Well, until Bessie May came rushing in to inform us that Prissy was headed into surgery. Then we picked up where we left off, and I watched as Jane's face softened while Pap-Paul and the pastor worked as a team to perform the ceremony.

When they finished, Joni thanked her. "You're going to make a beautiful bride someday, Jane," she said.

"In God's timing." She gave a little shrug and glanced my way. "I guess it's starting to sink in."

Indeed. A lot of things were sinking in today. Love trumped all woes. It unified, it healed, and it offered hope.

And today, at least in the town of Fairfield, Texas . . . it didn't even require a hurricane.

29

We've Got Tonight

The best thing to hold onto in life is each other.

Audrey Hepburn

The morning of Saturday, August 13th, dawned bright and sunny, with ideal "gettin' hitched" weather. I yawned and stretched, comfy under the covers in the bed I'd slept in most of my life, in the room I'd decorated as a teen, in the home I'd known since childhood. For a moment I didn't move. I drank in the scene of the morning sunlight peeking in through the curtains and ushered up a prayer for the day ahead.

No, not just the day ahead, but the life ahead. I prayed for the service, of course, but my thoughts shifted quite naturally to the life Brady and I would share.

Until Crystal tapped on my bedroom door. "Wake up, sleepyhead." Her voice rang out from the partially opened door. "We have a wedding to get to."

In the bed next to me, Twiggy let out a groan. "Really? I think I only slept four hours. The baby cried most of the night. Did you hear her, Katie?

They're in the very next room and these walls are paper-thin."

I yawned and stretched. "Must be used to it. Never heard a sound."

"You're the only one who didn't," Crystal said. "Lori-Lou was up half the night with Izzy. She's colicky. But don't worry your pretty little head about that, Katie. Just come out into the breakfast room. The others are all awake and waitin' at the table for your wedding day breakfast, prepared by yours truly."

I threw on a robe, nudged a griping Twiggy out of bed, and headed to the breakfast room to greet my friends and loved ones.

Lori-Lou argued with her husband on the phone. "Josh, I know it's hard to take care of all four kids at once. Trust me, I know. But you promised you'd come get Izzy so I could have fun with the other bridesmaids."

A long pause followed.

"Today is all about Katie. I want to be one of the girls." Lori-Lou pointed to the others. As if Josh could see over the phone. "Like them."

Everyone stopped talking and waited to see what would happen next.

"Yes," Lori-Lou said. "You can take them to the park. Then Dairy Queen. Then back to Queenie's for a nap. All that matters is that I don't see any of you until the wedding. Got it?"

Another long pause.

"Five o'clock," she reminded him. "You're escorting me down the aisle, remember? . . . No, not with the kids. Katie and Brady have hired a babysitter during the service."

The pause was a bit shorter this time.

"Okay, love you. See you in a bit. I'll have Izzy ready." Lori-Lou ended the call, handed the baby to Crystal, and headed to her bedroom to pack up the diaper bag.

I settled in at the breakfast table, and Crystal looked my way. "I hate to kick off the day with any controversy, but . . ." Her words drifted off and she bounced the baby on her knee.

"Please don't tell me the townspeople are fighting again." I reached for a biscuit and put it on my plate.

"Sort of, but not over the same thing as before. Prissy's not in the middle of it. You are."

"Me?"

"Yes. Ophelia insists that you asked for chocolate ice cream at the ice cream stand, but Bessie May is arguing with her, saying it's supposed to be vanilla. Apparently they have several tubs of each. So which is it? Which one did you ask for?"

"Really?" I laughed. "Honestly, I never specified. Do me a favor, though. Don't tell them that. Just say that they're both right. I love chocolate and vanilla, and I'm sure the guests will enjoy having options."

"Ooh, speaking of options, let's talk about how we're wearin' our *hay*-ur." Crystal's eyes glistened with merriment. "We have a 10:00 appointment at the salon, right?"

"Yes."

This led to a lengthy conversation from all of my bridesmaids about their choices in updos. I listened in, realizing this would be the last argument I'd hear as a single woman.

I hoped.

Josh arrived a few minutes later to get the baby. Eduardo dropped off Alva at a quarter to ten. She grabbed a biscuit, slung her purse strap over her shoulder, and hollered, "Let's get this show on the road! I'm too old to stand around and collect dust."

Alrighty then.

We drove to Do or Dye, the local salon, where the stylists were waiting on us. I settled into a chair with my bridesmaids clustered around me like so many mother hens. For years I'd pictured my wedding day, and I'd always imagined the pre-ceremony time just like this: getting ready with those I loved.

My chipper young stylist—a gal named Nancy Jo—worked diligently on my hair, talking all the while about the miracle that had taken place in the town the night before. "I just couldn't believe it when I heard the news. Prissy and Bessie May are speaking again. This changes everything."

True, but right now I wanted to focus on my

bridesmaids, thank you very much. I glanced over at Twiggy and took in her elegant bob. Then Crystal, whose beautiful blonde locks looked amazing pulled up. Then Dahlia, who gave her stylist what for in not getting it right. Hibiscus and Jane looked on, snapping photos right and left. The one who really grabbed my attention, though, was Aunt Alva. Talk about gorgeous.

I'd also never seen so much teasing or smelled so much hair spray in my life.

When Aunt Alva started coughing, her stylist, Frenchie, apologized. "I'm so sorry, y'all, but it can't be helped. This is Texas, after all."

"What does that have to do with anything?" Jane asked.

"Well, in Texas everything's bigger, including the hair." Frenchie put her trigger finger on the bottle and let another round fly.

"Oh, honey, it's true." Crystal waved a hand in Jane's direction. "I've lived in the South all my life and never seen hair as big as in Texas."

"Keeps me in business," Frenchie said. "Gotta love that."

"The things we do for those we love." Alva chuckled and looked at the stylist's reflection in the mirror as she continued to work on her hair. "I just can't believe our Katie-girl is getting married!" A little pause followed her words. "I just got married myself! First time ever. I'm still in the honeymoon phase."

"First time ever?" Frenchie looked stunned by this.

"Yep. I'm a blushing bride," Auntie said. "And my oh my, were those folks right about the thrill of the honeymoon. Eduardo and I had the most remarkable four weeks at the Beverly Hills Hotel. Lovely. And you'll never believe who we met at the pool. Jennifer Aniston!"

"No way." Frenchie lit into a thousand questions about the actress. After a while Alva ran out of answers and started talking about her honeymoon once again.

I prayed she wouldn't share too much information. Thankfully, the conversation took a turn as Dahlia's stylist showed off her finished hairdo.

"You're gorgeous!" I squealed. "Perfect!"

In fact, all of my bridesmaids looked amazing. Hibiscus snagged several shots and then Nancy Jo finished my hair. We all gasped as we saw the magnificent updo with all its twists and turns. I observed the back of my head with a mirror in hand and almost couldn't speak.

"It's exactly like I always pictured it!" I wanted to burst into tears, but thought twice about it. No point in having poofy eyes on my big day.

Just as we wrapped up, Alva's cell phone rang. She took the call, her cheeks flaming pink. For a minute she didn't say anything. Probably listening to the person on the other end. Then she spoke loud enough for all to hear. "Oh, Eduardo, you sweet man. I miss you too." My aunt giggled. "Yes, I know this is our first time apart since the honeymoon." The color of her cheeks deepened. "For pity's sake, I hope your heart goes on beating. At our age the alternative is a daily possibility. But I promise to see you soon. We'll be at the church in no time." She glanced my way. "Isn't that right, Katie? Aren't we leaving soon?"

"Yes, we're headed to the church in a few minutes."

She ended the call and sighed. "Have I mentioned that I love that man?"

"Only a couple thousand times." Her stylist winked.

After Nancy Jo finished off my look by pressing my crystal tiara into the top of my new 'do, she brought out a champagne bottle. "I thought we'd all have a glass of bubbly to celebrate," she said.

The girls let out a squeal. All but Crystal, who fussed with her hair, her gaze firmly planted on her reflection in the mirror. "I, um, I . . . well, I can't have anything alcoholic."

"Oh, it's just the fake stuff—no alcohol." The stylist poured the glasses, which she then passed to each of us. I couldn't help but wonder about Crystal's quick response that she couldn't have the real thing. I'd never known her to drink, but I had a feeling there was more going on.

After toasts were made and more photos taken, I approached my sister-in-law. "Okay, what's up?"

"What do you mean?" She took a little sip from her glass and shifted her gaze away from me.

"You haven't been yourself lately. You disappeared in the middle of the rehearsal dinner last night, looking pale. And you were quick to respond that you have to be careful what you drink. Is there something you want to tell me?"

Crystal clamped a hand over her mouth. "Today is all about *you,* Katie, not me." Her cheeks flushed the prettiest shade of pink.

"Crystal! Are you saying what I think you're saying?"

"I didn't say a thing." She batted her eyelashes dramatically. "So there."

"Mm-hmm. You didn't have to." I slipped my arms around her neck and gave her a hug. "Oh, this is the best news ever. I'm going to be an aunt!"

"Today you're going to be a bride, and the most beautiful one Fairfield has ever seen. Got it?" She gave me a knowing look.

"Okay, okay, I won't breathe a word." I winked. "But just so you know, I'm going to throw the best baby shower ever. It'll be the first in the family."

"Hardly." She laughed. "Lori-Lou has sixteen children, right?"

"She has four, and yes, she's family, but she's not a sister. You are."

"Aw, thank you, Katie Sue." Crystal threw her arms around me and I heard her sniffle. "You have no idea how much it means to me to have you in my life. Sometimes I think we've known each other forever, like I've lived in Fairfield all my life."

"We have the rest of our lives to deepen the bond."

"Starting today, at the best wedding ever."

"Better than your own?" I asked.

"Well, different. You saw our ceremony. Nothing like what you've got planned. Your picnic on the courthouse lawn is going to be something folks around here talk about for years to come."

"Hopefully for the right reasons." I laughed. "And hopefully the guys have all the tables set up by now. I'm praying Bessie May and Ophelia figured out what to do with the tablecloths and centerpieces. And do you think Pop is really helping set up the ice cream stand like he said he would? Sometimes he gets distracted."

"Katie Sue, slow down!" Crystal put her hand up. "I can't keep up. But I can promise you this, with Joni and Casey at the helm, everything is going smoothly. It's all going to be perfect—just you wait and see."

"Okay then. You'd better get me to the church and into that gorgeous Loretta Lynn gown or I'll miss my own ceremony."

"I would never let that happen."

Crystal gathered the troops and we prepared to

head to the church, where we would eat a leisurely lunch, put on makeup, get dressed, and take some pre-wedding photos.

First things first, though.

"Let's drive by the courthouse on the way," I said. "I want to see what it looks like."

"No ma'am." Crystal's stern voice surprised me. "No can do."

"What? Why not?"

"Because, Katie Sue, half the town has been up at the courthouse square all morning working to put things together, and they want it to be a surprise for you and Brady. That's why. So we won't be going by on our way to the church. Joni made me promise, and I'm a girl who always keeps my promises."

"I see. Bummer."

"Oh, trust me, you'll love it." Crystal clasped her hands together and I could see the excitement in her eyes. "Jasper sent me a picture a few minutes ago, and I swooned. It's a Southern girl's dream, I promise. You won't be disappointed."

"Oh, I'm sure it's wonderful. I just wanted to make sure the florist showed up and Joni remembered to put the gerbera daisies in the mason jars before putting them into the picnic baskets. And I've been a little worried about the lemonade stand. And—"

"Katie, look at me." Crystal clucked her tongue. "It's. All. Taken. Care. Of. You have one job today. One. Get dolled up and head down the aisle to say your 'I dos.' "

"That's technically two jobs." A nervous giggle escaped. "Getting dolled up is a challenge all by itself."

"When you're as pretty as you? Hardly." Lori-Lou laughed. "Just wait till you've had four kids, like me. You won't even be able to fit into that wedding dress anymore."

Crystal drove my SUV, deliberately avoiding the courthouse area, though I did take note of several people clustered on the corner of Travis and Third.

We got to the church at one o'clock, enjoyed a wonderful luncheon prepared by Mama and a couple of her friends, and then went to the bride's room to get ready.

I felt like a princess as Joni and the others clustered around me to do my makeup. It felt nice to be dolled up. Almost reminded me of that infamous day when I'd modeled my wedding gown for the *Texas Bride* photo shoot. Things had truly come full circle, no doubt about it.

At 4:45 the moment arrived. The girls, all dressed in their lovely pastel dresses, helped me into my Loretta Lynn gown. In that instant I was reminded of the first day I'd put the gown on. The style suited me to a tee—ruffly and sweet, but not fussy. I'd loved it then, but even more now.

Nadia entered the room just as the girls zipped up the dress, and helped adjust the train.

"It's just like I pictured," she said. "The day I drew the sketches for this dress, I knew that one day a gorgeous young woman would win that contest, put this dress on, and walk down the aisle for her happily ever after." She reached over and gave me a hug. "Just never dreamed she'd be walking toward my boy."

"Brady." A wealth of emotions overtook me as I spoke his name. How I loved that amazing, godly man. How my life had changed as our relationship took twists and turns. How it would continue to change as I took his hand, his name, today.

And all because of this dress.

I stared at my reflection in the mirror and sighed. "Nadia, it's even more beautiful than the first day I tried it on. I love it so much. Thank you. A thousand times, thank you!" The tears started to flow, but Joni stopped them in a hurry.

"None of that!" she scolded. "You don't want us to have to redo your makeup, do you? Besides, it's time for the photo shoot. Jordan's already gotten shots of the guys. Now it's your turn."

"Jordan?" Lori-Lou gave me a curious look. "Who's Jordan?"

"The guy from *Texas Bride* who did the cover shot of me in this dress. He also took our proposal pictures."

"That's so cool." My cousin's face lit up. "Do

you think he'll use these pictures in the magazine too?"

"Maybe." I gave a little shrug. "I wouldn't be surprised."

In fact, nothing surprised me these days, including the news from Jordan that the editor of *Texas Bride* might be interested in some of my articles. Only time would tell, of course, but I could hardly wait to give it a shot.

We made our way into the sanctuary, where Pop saw me for the first time. His eyes filled with tears and he headed my way. "Katie Sue, you look . . ." He brushed away a tear and smiled.

"Beautiful." Mama's eyes glistened as she took my hand. "The most beautiful bride ever."

"Thank you both . . . for everything"

I wanted to embrace them but worried about the train. And the veil, which Nadia now slipped into place.

The next twenty minutes were spent taking photos. Then the other ladies headed back to the bridal room, leaving me alone with Joni and Jordan.

"What are we doing?" I asked.

"We're getting a couple of you and Brady before the ceremony," Joni said.

My heart quickened. "No way! He can't see me before the 'I dos.' It's tradition!"

"He won't." Joni patted my hand. "Trust me, okay? I saw this online. We just need an open door. You'll be on one side, he'll be on the other—

facing opposite directions, but holding hands through the opening. Does that make sense?"

"Nope. Not at all, but I trust you."

She led the way to the church foyer, making sure Brady was outside the church. Then she eased the gorgeous wooden door open—the same door I'd walked through thousands of times as a girl, as a teen, as a young woman.

From outside I heard Brady's voice, though I could not see him at all.

"Brady James, if you open your eyes I'm going to personally see to it that you don't get any cake at the reception," Joni said through the opening in the door.

"You guys bringing me here just to tempt me?" The sound of his voice worked its magic on me, soothing all worries and putting everything in its right place.

We stood back to back, the open door between us, as Jordan snapped photos. I heard Brady's voice, steady and sure, as he began to pray over our relationship, our wedding, our future life together. I did my best not to cry as he shared his heart with the Lord and asked for God's guidance and direction over us as a couple. When he finished praying, the clicking from the camera continued, but I didn't focus on that. Instead, only one thing held me in its grasp, a simple revelation. Right now, I took Brady's hand for a photograph. In less than an hour, I would take his hand as his wife.

30
Safe in the Arms of Love

If I'm honest I have to tell you I still read
fairy-tales and I like them best of all.

Audrey Hepburn

I'd pictured my wedding ceremony for years.
Okay, so I'd pictured it with a different
groom—my teenage heart being so foolishly
wound around Casey Lawson—but how could I
have known the Lord would have someone far
better in mind for me? As I stood in the foyer of
the Baptist church, awaiting that moment when
the doors to the sanctuary would swing open
and the first bridesmaid would begin her descent
down the aisle, I forced back tears. All of the
planning in the world couldn't have prepared me
for this awesome, holy moment.

"You okay over there, kid?" Pop squeezed my
arm. "There's no crying in the wedding biz."

"Puh-leeze." I sniffled. "This isn't baseball,
Pop. Weddings are all about crying."

"Oh." He cleared his throat. "That would
explain this unusual sensation that's plaguing me
right now—kind of a lump in the throat and
moisture in the eyes. Wish I had a tissue."

As if on cue, Joni appeared and handed my father a tissue. "You need one too, Katie?"

"I think I'm okay."

"More than okay." She gave me a wink. "But no crying, okay? You don't want to mess up your mascara."

From inside the sanctuary I heard the strains of my favorite worship song draw to a close. Time to get this show on the road.

"Okay, people," Joni whispered in a hoarse voice. "That's our cue." She reached for the handle to open the door leading to the sanctuary and looked back at the bridesmaids and groomsmen. "Okay, people, remember what I said. Twiggy and Beau, you guys take your time getting to the front, then you part ways. Girls on the left, guys on the right."

"Girls on the right, guys on the left. Got it." Beau gave her an impish smile and Twiggy jabbed him with her elbow.

"Don't ruin your sister's wedding." She glared at him.

His eyes twinkled with mischief. "Hey, can't a guy have a little fun?"

"Not at a wedding." Twiggy waggled her finger.

"Dang." He sighed and slipped his arm through Twiggy's. "Getting hitched is no fun at all. Might have to reconsider whether or not I'll go through with it myself."

This provoked another glare from Twiggy. Joni

pulled open the door and they entered the sanctuary. I stepped to the side, out of view, so that no one inside would see me just yet.

Joni's confident smile spurred me on. "Okay, they're halfway up. Dahlia and Dewey, you're next."

"Don't mind if I do." Dewey offered Dahlia his arm and they began their walk to the front of the church.

"Okay, Crystal and Jasper." Joni glanced down at her clipboard, then back up at them. "Your turn next."

I couldn't help but notice that Crystal looked a bit green around the gills.

"You okay over there?" Joni's expression conveyed her alarm. "You gonna make it?"

"Yes, I, well . . ." Crystal still looked nauseous.

"Here, sniff this." Joni pulled out a bottle of peppermint oil. "It'll calm the stomach."

A few seconds later, tummy issues under control, Crystal and Jasper booked it down the aisle.

"Guess we're next, huh?" Lori-Lou took her husband's arm. "This won't be the first time we've walked the aisle, will it, babe?"

"With four kids, I would certainly hope not." Alva waved her hand. "You two get a move on. It's almost show time for this old gal, and I don't want to miss my cue. I'm the matron of honor, you know."

"I thought I was the matron of honor," Lori-Lou said.

"Nope. That would be me." Alva put her arm in Eduardo's. "Now that I'm a married woman, I'm the matron of honor, not the maid. Just makes sense. Now get on down there so I can make my entrance."

Lori-Lou grunted and took off down the aisle, a bit faster than Joni had instructed.

"Finally." My aunt glanced my way. "This is it, girlie. The moment we've been waiting for. This hunky fella and I might just steal the show."

I watched as Alva and Eduardo sauntered— *Really? Since when does she move that quickly?*—down the aisle. I couldn't help the chuckle that rose up when she gave a queenly wave to the crowd as she passed by. It figured that Aunt Alva would turn this into a production. Not that I minded. Oh, no. Right now I just wanted to get to the front of the church and say my "I dos" to the man I loved more than life itself, the one I'd waited my whole life for.

Still, we had one more person to get down the aisle. Gilly looked adorable in her soft pink flower girl dress. Joni gestured for the youngster to take her turn down the aisle, and I watched from a distance as she rounded the corner into the sanctuary, petals flying.

Joni closed the doors and fussed with my gown. My father gripped my arm and gave me a

355

crooked smile. "Your aunt Alva's a real show-boat, isn't she? Looks like she turned your wedding into a red-carpet event . . . for herself. Must be all of that time she spent in LA. It did something to her brain."

"I don't mind." And I didn't. I was just so excited that my moment had finally arrived.

The music shifted from Pachelbel's Canon to the "Wedding March." Joni released her hold on my train, stood upright, and put her hand on my arm. "Okay. The big moment. Remember what I told you yesterday. Don't lock your knees, and keep your focus on Brady."

I nodded, but my mouth suddenly felt like cotton. Ick.

"You ready, kiddo?" Pop asked.

"Sure am."

Joni reached to open the door and I stepped into place. As the room came into full view, I saw—for the first time—every detail. For a moment it looked like an ocean of people, many of whom snapped pictures with their cell phones. With everyone standing, I could barely make out the wedding party at the front of the room. Only after taking a few steps down the aisle did I catch my first glimpse of Brady.

Brady.

My heart flew to my throat and my hands trembled with excitement as I saw that gorgeous hunk of a man in his perfectly tailored tuxedo standing next to the pastor. As I drew closer, I couldn't help but notice the tears in his eyes. Of course, I found it difficult to see clearly, what with mine being in the same condition.

"There's still time to back out, kid," Pop teased. "Just say the word and I'll turn this train around and head back to the station."

I gave a nervous chuckle after hearing his playful words. "Um, over my dead body."

Oops. I hadn't meant to speak those words aloud, but I must've, judging from the look of horror on my mother's face. She glared at me from the front row. Thank goodness the pastor chose that very moment to speak those words I'd been waiting for: "Who gives this woman to be married to this man?"

For a moment I didn't think Pop was going to say anything. In fact, the silence went on for an extended period of time until Brady finally cleared his throat and the wedding guests laughed.

My father rushed the words, "Her mother and I do," and then slipped my arm through Brady's. In that moment, as my sweetheart and I took our place in front of the pastor, my breathing steadied. All of my nerves, my anxieties, my plans, my concerns, faded away.

This. Is. It.

The moment I'd waited for all my life had arrived at last. I felt joy flooding over me like a river, consuming me and giving me the courage to stand before the masses and declare my undying love to this amazing man.

The pastor offered an opening prayer and then instructed the congregation to sit. In that moment, as they all took their seats, I felt a little bit like Cinderella at the ball. I could feel the eyes of every person on me. And Brady.

On us. The two becoming one.

The pastor shared from 1 Corinthians, then handed off the microphone to Pap-Paul, who had offered to lead us in the exchange of vows and the giving of the rings. He greeted us with tears in his eyes, and my emotions got the better of me. How good God had been to us over the past year! He'd brought new family members into the fold and proven himself faithful in a thousand ways. Best of all, he'd given me this amazing, godly man to share my life with.

When my grandfather instructed Brady to say his vows first, I turned and gazed into my sweetheart's moisture-filled eyes. I did my best to maintain my composure as he read from the page in his hand.

"Katie, from this day forward, we're a team. And I guess it's pretty obvious that I've always been a fan of teamwork."

A light chuckle went up from the congregation, especially from a couple of his basketball buddies.

Brady gave my hand a squeeze, and I could see the paper in his other hand shaking as he continued to read. "The Bible says that one person can put a thousand to flight, and two people, working as a team, can put ten thousand to flight. I've never been very good at math, but this one was easy: that's nine thousand more enemies put to flight, simply by taking your hand in mine."

At this point, his eyes really began to sparkle. "From this point on, we'll pretty much be invincible. I've always wanted to be invincible, ever since I put on my first superhero cape as a kid. I just didn't realize back then that a girl would have anything to do with it."

The congregation laughed. As I took in the look of joy in my sweetheart's eyes, I wanted to laugh too.

"You have no idea how glad I am that you ended up at Cosmopolitan Bridal on that amazing day. I truly count it the most important day of my life, because it's when I met you."

Shoot. The mascara was on its own now. I couldn't help the tears that flowed down my cheeks as he continued to read.

"It's not just a coincidence that you won that dress"—he pointed to my gorgeous Loretta Lynn gown—"which looks amazing on you, by the way."

I mouthed, "Thank you."

"More than anything, though, I'm glad you saw past my struggles and pain to see who we could become—together. I take you to be my wife, my best friend. God has brought us together, and no enemy can tear us apart. From this day forward, we are one. I love you, Katie, and I'll do my best to be a husband you can be proud of, and hopefully one day, a father to several other team players."

Several? Did he say several? We might need to talk about that one.

Not that I had time to think about it right now, of course. I listened as our guests chuckled and sighed. Then, without hesitation, Pap-Paul instructed me to share my vows.

I'd waited for this moment all my life—to speak these words to the man who would be my husband. I gazed into Brady's eyes, those same amazing eyes that had sparkled with delight the day he slipped the ring on my finger, and my heart was overwhelmed with love and gratitude. The words I'd rehearsed for days hit the tip of my tongue with ease.

"Before God and these witnesses, I take you, Brady James, to be my husband. In joy and in pain, in adversity and in celebration, I will love you. Who you are. Who you will be. Who we will become together. My love will never fade. No matter where God takes you in your journey, I will be the one with my hand in yours, walking beside you. Listening. Learning. Loving. Your joys will be my joys. Your sorrows, my sorrows. Your faith, my faith. My heart has waited a lifetime to say these words: I am yours and you are mine. Always. Forever. Together."

Brady squeezed my hands, and I noticed his trembling had stopped. From now on, just like he'd said, we really were invincible.

I heard my mother sniffling. Out of the corner of my eye I watched as Pop handed her a box of tissues. She pulled one out and dabbed her eyes.

Pap-Paul turned his attention to Brady, all smiles. "Now, Brady, put this ring on Katie's finger and repeat after me: 'With this ring, I thee wed.'"

Brady gave me a little wink as he slipped the ring on my finger. "With this ring, I thee wed."

Pap-Paul glanced down at his book and then back up again. "An ever-present reminder of our vows and a symbol of my love."

"An ever-present reminder of our vows and a symbol of my love." Brady's eyes filled with tears.

"I offer all that I am, and all that I have."

At this point, my sweet fella's voice broke. "I offer all that I am, and all that I have."

My grandfather lifted his hand. "In the name of the Father, the Son, and the Holy Spirit."

"In the name of the Father, the Son, and the Holy Spirit."

"Amen," they said in unison.

Pap-Paul's moist eyes caught me off guard as he turned my way. "Katie, do you have a ring for Brady?"

I nodded and looked at my matron of honor. Alva, who looked a little glazed over—possibly from standing so long—snapped to attention and fished around in her little handbag until she came out with Brady's ring. A chuckle went up from the crowd when she presented it to me. I turned to face Brady and held it up, ready to slip it on his finger.

We did the whole thing all over again, but this time I repeated the words as I placed the ring on Brady's left hand.

Okay, so I lost it a little bit too when we got to the "I offer all that I am" part, but I somehow made it through. Behind me, I heard more sniffles than before and could tell that Queenie and Nadia had joined Mama in crying. I couldn't really focus on that, however. I needed to keep my eye on the prize and my head in the game.

The pastor stepped back into place and instructed us to light the unity candle. I gripped Brady's hand and we made our way over to the candelabra, where our parents gathered around us to pray. In that moment, with my mother, father, and mother-in-law hovering nearby, I realized just how blessed we truly were. Our future children—we'd still have to talk about how many—would have the best grandparents in the state.

Afterward, we joined the pastor and my grandfather back at the center of the stage for the grand finale. I still couldn't believe the ceremony had flown by that quickly. The whole thing felt like it had happened in a blip. The pastor gave a few closing remarks, but I barely heard them. My heart couldn't wait one second more. By the time he turned to Brady and said, "You may now kiss your bride," it was too late. I'd already leapt into my husband's arms, planting a kiss on him that no one in the town of Fairfield would ever forget.

31
Independence Day

I believe that tomorrow is another day and
I believe in miracles.

Audrey Hepburn

Whe the service ended, we made our way
down the aisle, hand in hand. Husband and
wife. I wanted to sing, to dance, to throw a party!
Oh, wait. We *were* having a party, and in just a
few minutes. On the courthouse lawn.

Joni rushed our way when we reached the
foyer and threw her arms around my neck. "It
went great! You looked gorgeous." She stood
back and gave Brady an admiring look. "And you
look like a million bucks!"

"Thank you very much." Brady spoke to her,
but his eyes were riveted firmly on me. I felt a
warm, tingling sensation all over as he swept
me into his arms and dipped me backwards for a
long, passionate kiss. Unfortunately, with the
doors to the sanctuary still open, the entire
congregation could see. Applause broke out,
which only further invigorated my husband to
pull the dip-and-kiss a second time.

Husband. Wow!

I. Am. A. Married. Woman!

Alva and Eduardo were the first couple to join us in the lobby. They took one look at us and decided to do a little smooching too. Then came the others, couple by couple, all laughter and smiles. The congregation poured out of the sanctuary, and congratulations were offered, one after another. The person who surprised me most with her tears? Madge. Even Stan looked a little misty.

They didn't stay that way for long, though. Joni sent most of our friends to the courthouse lawn to make sure everything was ready to go. Then the wedding party headed back into the sanctuary for a few more photos. Jordan led the way, snapping dozens of them. And though we had fun taking pictures, I really, really wanted to get to the party.

With the courthouse only a couple of blocks away, we decided to walk. Or, rather, have a wedding parade. Jordan snapped one photo after another as we made our way out of the front of the church, down the side street toward Main, and onto the south lawn of the courthouse. I couldn't help but notice that the orange cones in the middle of the road had been taken away. I also noticed a police officer guiding traffic around the courthouse square for our protection. I'd have to thank the mayor and the sheriff later, for working together to keep our little party safe.

Er, make that big party. As my eyes traveled to

the expansive courthouse lawn, I was blown away. "Wow! Brady, look!" I pointed to the tables. Gorgeous linen cloths. Hand-painted picnic baskets. Gerbera daisies. "Beautiful."

"My favorite is the lemonade stand." He pointed and I saw Bessie May and Mildred working together to hand out drinks. I couldn't get over their aprons and caps. Adorable. Straight out of a turn-of-the-century photo.

"Ooh, ice cream." A faint glint of humor blazed in Eduardo's eyes. "Don't mind if I do."

"Not until we've eaten the real food," Mama said as she stepped beside me. "Oh, Katie, just wait till you see the kabobs! Beef, chicken, pork, shrimp . . . I'm telling you, the folks at Sam's outdid themselves. They loved your ideas so much that they've added kabobs to the menu."

"Really?"

"Yep. And just wait till you see the fruit. I won't give it away, but let's just say that Eduardo has been busy. Very, very busy."

"Eduardo?"

"Yes." Mama laughed. "Why doesn't it surprise me that he's great with fruit arrangements? He's amazing with dress design. The man is an artiste! Of course, he had a little help from the WOP-pers."

"God bless those WOP-pers." Brady reached over and gave my mother a hug. "And God bless you, Mom."

At this proclamation my mother erupted in tears. I didn't blame her. The whole thing made me feel a little emotional too.

Twiggy touched my arm. "Katie, don't you see?"

"See what?"

She pointed at the courthouse lawn, complete with foods, friends, and family. "It really is like a themed wedding. Outdoor picnic. All of the foods handy to grab and go. You should create a Pinterest board and put up pictures from your wedding. Other brides will want to do this too."

"Um, one thing at a time." Brady shook his head. "We've got to go on our honeymoon first."

Honeymoon.

Bali!

Pinterest would have to wait.

Casey, acting as deejay, announced our arrival. I still couldn't get over the irony of that. Once upon a time I'd thought I would marry that boy. Now he and Joni were living their happily ever after, and I was too.

The crowd cheered as Brady and I walked to the dance floor—*So that's what the guys were working on all morning!*—and had our first dance as man and wife. What a picture we must've made—the six feet five basketball player and the five feet two cheerleader. Despite our differences in height, however, we were perfectly matched.

There in Brady's arms, with the town of

Fairfield looking on, I finally managed to gather my wits about me. I let my thoughts shift back to the ceremony, to our vows, to that magnificent kiss.

And the kiss in the foyer.

Oh, and the kiss Brady was giving me right here, as the crowd cheered.

"Hello, Mrs. James," he whispered in my ear when he finished kissing me.

I giggled. "Is it true?"

"Yep." A tiny kiss on my ear followed, sending tingles down my spine. "And you know what else?"

"What?"

He gestured with his head. "Everyone's here, having a good time. No feuding. No one telling anyone what to do or how to do it. You got to have your day, Katie, just like you said."

I thought about the truth of his words. Yes, I'd had my day, and what a glorious one it had turned out to be!

I rested my head against his shoulder. Off in the distance I heard the click of the cameras, but I didn't pay any attention. Let them get all the photos they wanted.

The next several minutes were a delicious blur. We sat at the head table with our wedding party, looking out on all of the other picnic tables loaded with happy, cheerful wedding guests. All around us, the various food stations were ready to roll. Shish kabobs with bacon, beef, onions, mushrooms, peppers, and cherry tomatoes. Teriyaki chicken with pineapple. Sesame shrimp with rice vinegar and soy sauce. Buccaneer pork tenderloin with citrus sauce.

My gaze shifted to the fruits. I'd never seen so many skewered fruits, all on colorful display. And it didn't stop there. Vegetable trays made up to look like flowers. Easy-to-handle sandwiches, ready to grab and go. Just like I'd pictured it all: fun, easy foods that the guests could hang on to while they visited with people from table to table. And wasn't that the idea, both in a small town and beyond—to get to know one another? To spend time together? To enjoy fellowship around the table?

Finally the moment came to cut the cake. I took in the cake table, marveling at the glorious, traditional five-tiered cake Ophelia had constructed. In all of my imaginings, I'd never come up with anything as exquisite. Hand piping graced each layer, and pastel ribbons in a variety of colors circled the bottom of every buttercream layer. Yum.

I gave Ophelia an admiring look. "If I didn't know any better, I'd say you've been taking lessons at culinary school or something."

"YouTube videos." Ophelia handed me the cake cutter. "You can learn almost anything you need to know from YouTube. Bracing and stacking cakes. Fondant work. Piping. Anything. I'm addicted to YouTube."

"You're so good, you should start your own channel," I observed. "Especially since you've opened the bakery."

"Already have." She grinned. "And if y'all like the wedding cake, come a little closer. I want to show you both a little surprise." She led the way to another smaller table off to the side. I gasped when I stared down at the basketball-court cake, complete with fondant figures dressed in Mavericks colors.

"Wow." Brady looked completely flabbergasted as he leaned down to give it a closer look. "Wow."

Ophelia clapped her hands together. "So glad you like it! See now, I know you asked for a chocolate groom's cake, but you didn't really specify a design. I couldn't help but think of basketball every time I got ready to sketch out an idea. But I didn't want to hurt your feelings, Brady, you being off that second surgery a few months ago and all."

He squared his shoulders as he faced her. "Actually, since you mention it, my knee is healing so well that the doctor is going to let me play again. We haven't shared this news publicly, but I've been back on the court for a while now, just to see if the knee will hold. Looks like I'm good to go."

"Oh, honey!" Ophelia clasped her hands

together. "That's the best news ever. And that makes this cake prophetic, doesn't it!" She raised her voice for all of our guests to hear. "Did you hear that, folks? I have the gift of cake prophecy! Thank you, Jesus!" She lifted her hands to the heavens and let out a whoop.

Pap-Paul quirked a brow at that one but didn't say anything.

"Okay, time to cut the cake." I focused on the many tiers standing before me. "Does it matter which tier we cut into?"

Ophelia shook her head. "Not to me, but if you're a fan of the Italian cream cake, it's the one on top. Chocolate's just underneath. Then lemon raspberry. Then butter pecan. The bottom tier— the big one—is white cake with almond flavoring. That's my favorite, but I'm kind of a plain Jane."

"Hardly."

"True." She offered a playful wink. "I did sneak in some strawberry preserves. They taste so yummy with that white cake. Mmm."

That sounded amazing, but the idea of cutting into the bottom tier terrified me. What if the four tiers atop it cratered? Nope, I'd stick with the Italian cream cake, thank you very much. Though my hands trembled a little, I managed to cut a small piece of the top tier and then put it on the plate Prissy handed me.

"Cut it in half," she instructed. "You'll both need a piece to feed each other."

I sliced the piece of cake in half and then set the knife aside. All around me, the crowd chanted, "Do it! Do it! Do it!" as Brady and I each took a piece in hand. We linked arms, then aimed—well, at least I aimed—the cake toward the intended target.

Brady got me right in the nose. Some wise guy—probably my father—hollered, "Three-point shot!"

I somehow managed to smash his piece into his left eyebrow. He wiped the frosting from his brow with his index finger, stuck some in his mouth, and proclaimed it to be the best cake he'd ever eaten. This, of course, delighted Ophelia, who went to work cutting up slices for our guests.

Brady leaned in close and pointed at my top lip. "You have a little something . . . right . . . here." Then, with all of our guests chiming in with a rousing, "Go for it!" he gave me a kiss sweeter than all five tiers of wedding cake put together.

32
Blessed

How shall I sum up my life? I think I've been particularly lucky. Does that have something to do with faith also? I know my mother always used to say, "Good things aren't supposed to just fall in your lap. God is very generous, but he expects you to do your part first." So you have to make that effort. But at the end of a bad time or a huge effort, I've always had — how shall I say it? — the prize at the end. My whole life shows that.

Audrey Hepburn

After a couple of bites of the yummiest cake ever, I caught a glimpse of my parents standing just a few yards away, talking to the sheriff and his wife. I walked their way and Brady tagged along. I threw my arms around my father's neck, which startled him a bit. He almost dropped his cup of lemonade.

"Katie Sue, you caught me off guard."

"Sorry, Pop. I just wanted to say I don't know how I'll ever thank you enough for doing all of this for me."

"You're my only daughter, sweet pea." My father's eyes flooded with tears, and a tremor of emotion laced his words. "I would've given you the world if you'd asked for it."

I could tell from the emotion in his voice that he truly meant it, so I offered a trembling "Thank you," gratitude overwhelming me.

My father's nose wrinkled. "On the other hand, I was a little relieved when you went with this whole picnic-in-the-park idea. Saved me a bundle, especially on the rental fee. Did I tell you that Mayor Luchenbacher was in such a good frame of mind after last night's prayer meeting at the hospital that he didn't charge a penny for renting out the property? But if you happen to see a couple of people who weren't invited show up, we have to let them stay. This is public property, even tonight."

Lovely.

"Kidding, kidding." He laughed. "I double dog dare anyone to crash my daughter's wedding. I'd sic your brothers on them." He looked around. "Where are those brothers of yours, anyway?"

"Pretty sure Jasper is with Crystal at the lemonade stand. Did I tell you that she decorated it and even helped the WOP-pers come up with flavors? Oh, and I saw Dewey and Dahlia going back for more food. No idea where Beau and Twiggy landed."

"Twiggy's serving cake. Jane and that Hibiscus girl are helping." Mama pointed to the cake table. Sure enough, tiny little Twiggy and the other girls stood alongside Ophelia, slicing up pieces. The five-tiered wedding cake was already down to just two tiers. Crazy.

"Now, one thing you need to know," Mama said.

"Please tell me you're not going to give her the speech about the honeymoon." My father looked ill at the very idea. I felt a little ill myself.

"Don't be silly." My mother rolled her eyes, then turned back to face me. "I wanted to warn you that Alva came up with an idea. You know how people gave you so much advice about your wedding?"

"How could we forget?" Brady laughed.

"She's got a scrapbook." Mama pointed to the gift table on the far side of the lawn. "And people are writing down their marriage advice. She thought it'd be good to read later."

"Aw, that's kind of sweet," I said.

"Yes." Mama grinned and looped her arm through my father's. "Just don't be surprised. I hear the WOP-pers have come up with some real zingers."

"Oh dear." I laughed.

"I'll start with the advice, okay?" Pop appeared to be thinking, then looked straight at Brady. "Don't forget to put the toilet seat down."

"I see." Brady nodded. "That will do the trick, sir?"

"Well, it won't hurt." Pop slapped Brady on the back and laughed so hard that several others, including my aunt and uncle, joined us to find out what was happening.

"What's going on over here?" Alva rested her hands on her hips. "Someone having a party without us?"

"Just giving them marriage advice," Pop responded.

"Ooh, marriage advice." My aunt clasped her hands together. "I've been trying all night to come up with just the right thing."

"It's easy." Eduardo slipped his arm around my aunt's waist. "Tell her every day that she's the most beautiful woman you've ever known. And mean it."

"That won't be hard." Brady gave me a gentle kiss on the lips, then whispered, "It's true, you know."

My heart did that funny little pitter-pat thing as I realized he truly meant it.

"I have some advice," Stan called out. "Don't get married by a judge."

I'd just started to say, "But I'm already married," when he grinned and added, "Ask for a jury!" Then he slapped his thigh and busted out laughing. Until Madge slugged him on the arm.

"I always say a fella just ain't complete till he's found himself a bride," Casey's dad, Mr. Lawson, said. "Then, after he's married her, he's finished."

Okay then. We were off to a great start.

Mrs. Lawson gave me the sweetest smile. "I have some advice, honey. If you feel the need to change something, then change the color of the walls. Change the curtains. But don't try to change your hubby."

I'd almost responded with, "Great advice," when her husband gazed at her, eyes narrowed. "Really? After forty years of you trying to change everything about me, you say this now?"

She punched him on the arm too.

My grandmother drew near. I could tell her knee was troubling her. She leaned against Pap-Paul, who seemed happy to hold her in place.

"Don't listen to these folks, Katie Sue. If you want to know the secret to a long and happy life as a married couple, just live every day as if it's your last, but enjoy the wonder of being together as if it's your first."

"That's what your mom and I are doing." Pop took Mama in his arms and tipped her backwards, then planted a big smooch on her. When he lifted her back up again, she looked a little dizzy. She pinched her eyes shut as if to somehow block out the embarrassment. The crowd, however, loved it. In fact, the WOP-pers loved it so much that they called for an encore. Pop was happy to oblige.

"My advice," Pap-Paul said, "is to agree to disagree. You don't always have to be like-minded about everything."

"Unless your wife is right, of course," Queenie added. "Then you should agree with her."

"Should I be taking notes?" Brady asked. "This is getting a little overwhelming."

"Nope." Mama, still trying to get control of herself after Pop's passionate kiss, shook her head. "Scrapbook. Gift table. It's all written down."

"Oh, that's right. Whew." He laughed.

Time to switch gears. With our bellies full of food, cake, and lemonade, the party really went into full swing. The band kept the music going, all sweet love songs from days gone by, and opened the dance floor for our guests—after the father-daughter dance, which made me cry all over again.

Pop managed to put the smile back on my face by telling a funny joke. Otherwise I probably would've lost it altogether. When the dance ended, Brady led his mother to the floor. I watched as Nadia—my boss, my friend, my mother-in-law—shared the dance of her life with her son. Afterward, Bradley Pennington cut in. Brady didn't seem to mind passing his mother off to the handsome stranger.

Much.

My husband joined me for a couple of dances, then we slipped off to the side of the dance floor to catch our breath. I watched Nadia and Bradley as the music shifted to a slow song. They remained in each other's arms.

"You okay over there?" I asked Brady.

He grunted. "Yeah. Guess so."

"Looks like Queenie and Pap-Paul are having a good time. And Alva and Eduardo are the life of the party." I pointed to the dance floor, where my aunt danced with great dramatic flair.

"She's something else," Brady said.

"Hey, you're related to all of these people now, you know. Better be careful what you say!"

"True. I love 'em, Katie. I do." He slipped his arm around my shoulders and pulled me close.

I looked around the courthouse lawn, my heart wanting to burst into song as I reveled in the beauty of it all. Twinkling lights strung from pole to pole provided just the right glimmer for the area as the sun began its descent. My gaze shifted westward, where the brilliant red-gold sunset begged for my attention. I stopped, captivated, as I drank it in. Brady slid his arm around my waist, and we observed it together in silence.

Until Bessie May drew near with the mayor at her side. "All we need is a white horse."

"Beg your pardon?" I turned to face her. "White horse?"

"Well, sure." She wiped her hands on her apron. "In all of the old movies, the couple would ride off into the sunset on a white horse, and you just knew that everything was going to work out well for them. It was the very best way to say, 'And they all lived happily ever after.'"

"Wait . . . did Twiggy tell you to say that?" I asked.

"No, why?" Bessie May looked a bit perplexed by my question.

"I really like that idea," the mayor said. "A lot, in fact." His eyes narrowed and then he snapped his fingers. "Yep. Like it a lot."

Before we could say "What idea?" he took off across the lawn.

"What do you think he has up his sleeve?" Brady asked.

"No idea, but I'm a little terrified just thinking about it."

My concerns dissipated a few minutes later when several of the WOP-pers and their husbands, dressed in old-timey aprons and hats, served up ice cream to go along with the cake.

"Want some?" Brady asked, a twinkle in his eye.

"Just a little. I'm more thirsty. Raspberry lemonade sounds amazing."

We stopped at the lemonade stand first. It truly

took my breath away. Crystal and Jasper had done a magnificent job putting it together. They both now served the guests. I was surprised to see that Corrie had joined them, dressed in an adorable yellow and white apron and cap.

"What flavor would you like with your lemonade, ma'am?" the youngster asked me. "Raspberry? Blueberry? Strawberry? Peach?"

"I'll have raspberry, thank you," I said in my most courteous voice.

"You're more than welcome, ma'am. I'll be right back with your order." She gave the order to Crystal, who prepared my drink by adding pureed raspberries to a glass of homemade lemonade. She gave it a whirl in the blender with a bit of ice, then passed it off to Corrie, who handed it back to me. "There you go," the girl said with a twinkle in her eye. "No charge."

"Except for the thousands of dollars it cost me to pay for this shindig." Pop's voice rang out from behind me. "But don't you worry your pretty little head about that."

Mama jabbed him with her elbow. "Really? Did you have to go and say that?"

I couldn't help but laugh. I took a sip and felt refreshed immediately as I swallowed the cold, sweet liquid. "Mmm." I pointed to the lemonade stand decked out with fabulous yellow and white décor. "I can't believe you pulled this off, Crystal." I let out a whistle. "It's like every little kid's lemonade stand . . . on steroids."

"I learned from the best, Katie Sue. You taught me how to do window displays at the hardware store, did you not? I'm figuring out how to make things visually appealing. And Corrie is the best helper ever."

The youngster gave a cute little curtsy.

"I think they both did a mighty fine job," Mama said. "Don't you, honey?"

"Hmm?" Pop was too busy fixing himself a cup of lemonade to respond.

"I said—oh, never mind." Mama rolled her eyes. "This is what you have to look forward to, Katie Sue."

"Ooh!" Crystal pointed to the dance floor. "Oh. My. Goodness. Look at that, will you?"

"What?" I took another drink of my lemonade and glanced out onto the dance floor. I saw an unfamiliar young man walk over to Jane at the cake table and ask her to dance. She hesitated, then took his hand and they entered the floor together. "Brady, who is that?"

He shrugged and then swiped my glass of lemonade. "No idea." He took a big swig and handed the glass back to me.

"I'm surprised you don't remember him, Katie Sue," Mama said. "It's Prissy's grandson Robert. You kids used to call him Snobby Bobby because he hardly talked to anyone. He was really shy when he was a kid."

"And a little awkward," Pop added. "You know the type."

"No way. That's Snobby Bobby?" I stared in complete awe. He'd obviously outgrown the awkward stage. And the shyness.

"He came into town the minute he heard about his grandmother's surgery," Mama said. "But you know Prissy. She insisted he come to the wedding tonight to represent their family. Hope you don't mind."

"Of course not. That's great."

Brady looked back and forth between Bobby and Jane, who seemed to be enjoying herself on the dance floor. "So, let me get this straight. If Prissy hadn't backed over that cone, she wouldn't have broken her hip. If she hadn't broken her hip, Snobby Bobby wouldn't be dancing with Jane right now."

"That about sums it up." Mama gave him a curt nod. "The Lord works in mysterious ways."

"Wow. Just . . . wow." He put his arm over my shoulders.

"And if we hadn't gotten married tonight, they wouldn't be out on that dance floor right now, so I guess we played a role too," I said.

Brady laughed. "True. God sure knows how to take the rough things and smooth them out, doesn't he?"

"Yep." I leaned my head against his shoulder

and sighed. "This will be a night to remember, for sure."

"Since you said that . . ." Jasper wiped his hands on his apron and walked over to Crystal, who looked a bit unnerved. "We might just have some news to make the evening even more memorable. Now's as good a time as any."

"Guess so." Crystal's lips curled up in an impish smile.

"You're having a baby!" Mama let out a squeal, which got the attention of several ladies standing nearby. "That's it, right?"

I knew the truth, of course, but didn't say a word. I'd let Crystal and Jasper share their own good news.

"We *are* adding to our family," Crystal said. "But there might be a little more to the story than that."

Okay, this caught me off guard.

"A puppy?" Pop asked.

"No, a little bigger than that." Crystal pursed her lips together as if trying to keep from saying something.

"I knew it! I knew it! I knew it!" Mama took off across the courthouse lawn, doing a little jig.

I gave my sister-in-law a curious look, but she refused to share her news. She had something else up her sleeve. Hopefully she'd spill the beans—and quick!

33
Trip around the Sun

I'd never worry about age if I knew I could go on being loved and having the possibility to love.

Audrey Hepburn

You could've heard a pin drop when Crystal finally made her announcement.

"Jasper and I are adopting Corrie." Her eyes filled with tears right away, and she pulled the little girl close.

"W-what?" I looked back and forth between my brother and his bride. "Are you serious?"

"Yes." My brother's eyes flooded with tears too. "And just for the record, we're both thrilled."

"This is the best news ever!" I threw my arms around Crystal's neck.

She returned the hug and then turned her attention to my mother. "And by the way, Mama Fisher, you were right. I'm havin' a baby too!"

"Ooh, I knew it!" Mama threw her arms around Crystal. "This is amazing news! The best! My, but you two didn't waste any time, did you?" She looked my way. "See now, Katie Sue? Honeymoon babies are the best. How do you think we got Jasper? Hmm?"

Ew. Too much information, thank you.

Dewey and Dahlia showed up at that very moment. My brother looked . . . strange. Like he wasn't feeling well.

"You okay, son?" Mama asked.

"Too many shish kabobs?" Pop tried.

"I'm . . . fine." He stuck his hands in his pockets but still looked a bit ill.

"Dewey, what's up?" I asked.

"Well . . ." He shrugged as he looked me in the eye. "Katie, you know how everyone's giving you marital advice?"

"Sure."

"Well, I have some."

"Okay." I took Brady's hand and we faced him. "What is it?"

Dewey's eyes sparkled. "Never kill your older brother when he steals the show at your wedding reception."

"Huh?" That made no sense at all.

Seconds later, with hundreds of guests looking on, Dewey dropped to one knee and ushered\ up the most beautiful proposal to Dahlia that anyone could've imagined.

Oh. My. Goodness.

She said yes before he even got the last few words out. The ring that he pulled from his pocket was on her finger lickety-split. The crowd went crazy, clapping and cheering and carrying on with lemonade toasts.

"Wait, let me guess . . ." I turned to Brady, speaking above the din. "You knew about this one too. Just like Eduardo. And Stan."

"Yep."

I would've asked him more, but a strange commotion off Main Street distracted me.

I could hardly believe my eyes when the mayor arrived leading a white stallion. He looked completely winded and red in the face, as if he'd rushed all the way here. What in the world?

Mayor Luchenbacher drew close and pulled a handkerchief from his pocket, which he used to wipe his brow. "I had to work like the dickens to get here before the reception ended, but here you go." He passed the horse's lead off to me.

I held it, my gaze shifting to the gorgeous horse. None of this made sense. "What are we supposed to do with him, Mr. Luchenbacher?"

"Ride him, of course. I've got him all saddled and ready. You can ride and Brady can lead. It'll make a great photo. The three of you heading off into the sunset—you, Brady, and Sovereign."

"Sovereign?" Brady and I asked in unison.

"Yep, that's his name."

"Did Twiggy put you up to this?" I asked.

The mayor shoved his handkerchief into his pocket. Wrinkles formed between his brows as he asked, "Who's Twiggy?"

"Never mind." I couldn't help but laugh.

Our wedding guests turned their attention away from Dewey and Dahlia and toward the horse.

"I haven't ridden a horse since I was seventeen," I said. "And I'm in my wedding gown."

"Sovereign won't care what you're wearing." Brady nudged me with his arm. "And with a name like that, we *have* to do it. It's a sign, don't you think?"

"A sign I'm going to look like a goober in front of hundreds of people." I wiped the sweat off my forehead with the back of my hand. I faced my husband head-on, completely flabbergasted. "Are you really saying you want me to ride that horse?"

"It might make for a fun memory. And you can't deny that the people want it." He gestured to the crowd.

I turned back to discover that approximately 150 of our wedding guests had their cell phones out, as if anticipating a great photo op. Jordan was perched and ready, camera in hand. Oh brother.

A little sigh wriggled its way up as I thought through the particulars. How could I possibly manage this?

"Just go for it, Katie," Nadia called out. "You wouldn't be the first bride to ride a horse in a wedding gown, and you won't be the last. The dress will be just fine."

"We'll use the photos to advertise the Loretta Lynn gown," Madge hollered. "It'll be great."

"My daughter rode a horse at her wedding," Bradley Pennington said. "Of course, she was in a field, but I suppose that's irrelevant at this point."

"They're right," Mama said. "It's the perfect photo op. Go for it, honey."

"Whatever you do, do it quickly," the mayor said. "The sheriff's hot on my tail. Apparently there's some sort of zoning restriction. No horses on the courthouse lawn. So get a move on, okay?" He looked back as if expecting the sheriff to materialize at any moment.

"Climb aboard, Katie," Aunt Alva called out. "It'll be better than any plotline on that stupid radio show we listen to."

"Let's get this ball rolling before the sheriff tosses you in jail," Jasper called out. "He's on his way. I can see him through the crowd."

"For pity's sake." I looked at Brady and sighed. "Are we really doing this?"

"Looks that way." He gestured to the crowd. "But no pressure."

"Yeah, right. Easy for you to say. You're the one walking. I'm the one riding."

The mayor pulled a chair up next to the horse. I stepped onto it and gave my guests a wave. Approximately a hundred of them took flash photos. At one time. I found myself blinded by the light. Lovely.

"Okay, okay." I hiked my skirt a few inches and put one foot in the stirrup. The edge of my petticoat got caught, but I somehow managed to lift my weight—gown and all. I could hear the click of photos being taken and realized Jordan had stepped beside me. Wonderful. After a bit of unladylike scrambling, I finally managed to straddle the horse without showing off too much of my petticoat. The crowd let out a cheer. I could only imagine how ridiculous I looked.

Brady grabbed hold of Sovereign's lead, and the horse took a few steps toward the sidewalk. Off in the distance I heard the sheriff arguing with Mayor Luchenbacher. Hopefully their little squabble wouldn't split the town straight down the middle, like before.

Thinking about the split reminded me of Prissy. I ushered up a prayer for her.

Thinking of Prissy made me think of the WOP-pers and the role they'd played in my life. And thinking of the WOP-pers sent my thoughts whirling back to Queenie, the guiding light for our family. And thinking about Queenie reminded me of that infamous day at Cosmopolitan Bridal when I'd connected with Alva for the first time.

Thinking of Cosmopolitan Bridal reminded me of Nadia and Madge, how nervous I'd been to tell them the truth about not being engaged to Casey Lawson. Thinking of Casey reminded me that I needed to send Joni a thank-you card when we returned from Bali.

And thinking of Bali . . .

Well, it got me to thinking about only one person—the awesome fellow leading the horse across the courthouse lawn, beyond the lemonade and ice cream stands, and onto the Main Street sidewalk.

Brady. If all of those crazy things hadn't happened, I would never have met him. If even one thing had changed, we wouldn't be married today. Who could work things out with such remarkable precision, such a deft hand? Only One, and it was Him I thanked right now—for my new life with the best guy ever, for an amazing job doing what I loved, and for opportunities yet to come.

Sovereign's hooves clip-clopped past our family's hardware store, past Ophelia and Bessie May's new bakery, and toward the intersection of Main and Travis.

"Where are we going, Brady?" I called out.

He glanced up at me, his joyous smile disarming. "Into the sunset, of course. Duh."

The hum of voices sounded behind me. I turned to discover that all of our wedding guests were following us.

"If we're riding off into the sunset, we're taking a throng of people with us."

"Wouldn't have it any other way, Katie Sue. Wouldn't have it any other way."

"Please tell me you're not going to start calling me Katie Sue," I pleaded. "Say it ain't so."

"Only when we're in Fairfield, darlin'," he crooned, his Southern drawl completely put on.

"And when we're hanging out with the Mavericks players and their wives?" I asked.

"Then you're my bride, plain and simple."

Alrighty then. I'd be his plain and simple bride from Fairfield, the one who got roped into riding a horse down Main Street on her wedding day.

I glanced back at my family and friends and took note of the mayor still arguing with the sheriff, while Mama and Pop bickered about whether they should head back out in their fifth wheel or stay put in Fairfield now that they were about to become grandparents. Bessie May and Ophelia argued about who was going to take a meal to Prissy's house when she was released from the hospital, and Queenie and Pap-Paul fussed about the weather. Alva and Eduardo, oblivious to all the complaining, sashayed down the sidewalk, talking about how this moment reminded them of some old movie they'd seen.

They were right about that part, but I still had no idea where we were headed. If we continued west on Main, we'd land at Dairy Queen. Might be a little weird to come riding into the DQ parking lot on a horse. In my wedding gown. With a couple hundred people behind me. Hopefully Brady would turn back before then.

Brady.

My gaze shifted back to my husband, who led the horse with a gentle hand toward the most brilliant sunset I'd ever clapped eyes on. In that moment, as I gazed at him in awe, I had to agree completely with what he'd said earlier. In spite of the chaos, in spite of the wacky people tagging along behind us . . . with Brady James at my side, I wouldn't have it any other way.

Acknowledgments

To Eleanor Clark: Thank you for introducing me to your fair city of Fairfield. What a precious, quaint place—both in reality and in this story.

To Martina McBride: I'm not a country music fan, but I could listen to your amazing lyrics all day (and have). What fun to use your song titles as chapter titles in this book!

To my team at Revell: You've been wonderful to work with. What joy to find a group of like-minded people who have seen the value in my wacky, off-the-wall stories. We've had a great run and I'm truly grateful.

To Jessica English: How can I ever thank you? You've used your red ink pen a lot over the past eight years as we've walked this road together. I'm so grateful.

To Chip MacGregor: You called it, friend. I have to give you kudos for coming up with the story idea for this series. Well done.

To my Dream Team: I have you in mind with every word I write. Thank you for your kindness to me all these years.

To Jesus: You are the love of my life.

Award-winning author **Janice Thompson** enjoys tickling the funny bone. She got her start in the industry writing screenplays and musical comedies for the stage, and she has published over ninety books for the Christian market. She has played the role of mother of the bride four times now and particularly enjoys writing lighthearted, comedic, wedding-themed tales. Why? Because making readers laugh gives her great joy!

Janice formerly served as vice president of Christian Authors Network (CAN) and was named the 2008 Mentor of the Year for American Christian Fiction Writers (ACFW). She is active in her local writing group, where she regularly teaches on the craft of writing. In addition, she enjoys public speaking and mentoring young writers.

Janice is passionate about her faith and does all she can to share the joy of the Lord with others, which is why she particularly enjoys writing. Her tagline, "Love, Laughter, and Happy Ever Afters!" sums up her take on life.

She lives in Spring, Texas, where she leads a rich life with her family, a host of writing friends, and two mischievous dachshunds. She does her best to keep the Lord at the center of it all. You can find out more about Janice at:

www.janiceathompson.com
or
www.freelancewritingcourses.com.

Center Point Large Print
600 Brooks Road / PO Box 1
Thorndike, ME 04986-0001 USA

(207) 568-3717

US & Canada:
1 800 929-9108
www.centerpointlargeprint.com